Ann Girdharry was born and educated in the UK. A trained psychotherapist, she has worked for many years as a manager in the not-for-profit sector, for agencies working with: carers, vulnerable older people, survivors of abuse, and victims of racism and racial attacks. Today, she lives in Montpellier, France with her husband and two children.

You can find out more about Ann Girdharry by visiting her website – www.girdharry.com

Titles by this author

Good Girl Bad Girl
London Noir
The Beauty Killers

Deadly Motives (previously entitled Killer Motive)
Deadly Secrets

Good Girl Bad Girl

Ann Girdharry

First published August 2016.

Second edition published 2020.
ISBN 9780993560248

This book is dedicated to Mr and Mrs Walker,

for all the years,
of day-dreams and flowers

xx

Chapter One

Alesha could no longer feel her legs.

They hung, lifeless beneath the surface of the water. Tied above her head, her wrists were rubbed raw. No point in struggling, she had done that for days. All the panic and terror had long since run out of her and coursed down her legs.

The pool deepened and the water lapped her bellybutton.

A few moments before, her two torturers had climbed a ladder, and a faint light drifted down from their escape route. Alesha watched the metal rungs disappear one by one beneath the inky blue.

How many times had she endured it? Twice, she thought, or was it three times? Each immersion she was left with less of her self. They were paring her down layer by layer. Stripping away her endurance and her will to live.

Alesha shuddered as the water climbed her rib cage. It would only be a few moments before she drowned. Dread engulfed her. She tried not to think about the moments ahead, pushing away the thought of them resuscitating her, then closing in for the interrogation.

Lapping at the sides of the chamber, the water sounded like gentle waves at the seaside. Alesha pressed her eyes closed. She wouldn't crack. She'd never tell them. They would have to kill her first. It almost made her laugh, and yes, she'd wondered about that too, wondered if she was losing her mind. Thing is, if she was dead she wouldn't be able to give anything away. So perhaps she should stop fighting it. Wouldn't it be better to take one last breath as deep as she could and hope her heart gave out? Then the water would take away her secrets.

As the water rose, Alesha crawled deep inside her own mind and she saw her husband when they had first met. He smiled at her. And the water reached her throat.

Now she could see her daughter, Kal, running with her black hair streaming out behind. At first, Kal was a little girl laughing, and then she became a young woman. Alesha took a deep breath and sealed her lips. If Kal was coming, Alesha knew Kal would never reach her in time.

The water covered Alesha's nose and she felt the air expanding in her chest. Fight against it, she commanded herself, don't take a breath. Her body thrashed and jerked. They would turn the water off soon. Then they'd bring her back from the brink. Alesha blacked out.

Chapter Two

I swept the platter to the floor, sending bits of food in all directions.

You see, I have indigestion which always brings out my worst side. The sugary scent of the Indian desserts is making me sick.

What's the real problem? Good question. It's the recent news telling me I will have to wait a little longer. My full revenge is not yet here, but I can console myself it's coming closer. Picking off my enemies one by one is flawless enjoyment. Yes, step by step. Patience would bring its rewards.

In an instant I was back in India. I remembered the huge, old wardrobe, large enough for a small boy to crawl inside.

Every Saturday evening, I hid there, ready to watch the spectacle, breathing in mothballs and dust. The anticipation brought a flood of saliva. Did my father know I was there? I don't think so, though, at times, I imagined my father performed for me— writhed and panted for an audience.

But we never spoke of it.

This was the Saturday night which changed everything. A crescent moon night.

Silvery light glanced off the bed and in the middle of father's moans I saw a shadow step through the window. The shadow crept silently. It bent. A glint of metal against my father's throat and with one swift stroke, he slumped on the covers, his head almost severed.

Blood cascaded onto the floor in a dark stream. I saw it all and knew how father looked up and in a split second faced his own death. And I stayed hidden, hands over my mouth to stop myself screaming, wetting my trousers as I hunched at the bottom of the wardrobe, amongst my father's smart suits.

Chapter Three

The taxi meter clicked to a stop, and Kal stared at the two red numbers. Up front, the driver pulled on the handbrake and waited a couple of seconds before swivelling in his seat.

"This is it–Inner Park Crescent. You all right, lo...?" The word 'love' withered on his lips and the driver corrected himself. "This is the address you asked for. Inner Park Crescent."

Kal didn't like endearments from strangers because they always sounded patronising and she made no effort to hide her annoyance. She pushed forward a twenty-pound note and the driver accepted it, his eyes avoiding hers.

Sarah, her mother's best friend, was pacing to and fro on the corner, her steps restricted by her executive skirt. Kal slid over the seat and out of the car.

"Oh gosh, poor you, there's nothing to worry about, Sarah," Kal said.

She knew it was a lie. Her mother, Alesha, never lost contact. It was their safety code–always keep in touch. Kal forced a smile and leant to plant a kiss on Sarah's cheek.

The driver shut the boot with a clunk and Kal took her backpack and hefted it over one shoulder.

"I can't contact Alesha anywhere. I blame myself," Sarah rushed it out, "I really blame myself, I should've called you earlier."

Kal tucked her hair behind her ear. Being alone would have been better, then she wouldn't need to hide under layers of bravado. She paused for a moment, her fingertips detecting tiny particles of grit near her temple, a leftover from her week at the refugee camp in Kenya.

"Mum's always dashing off on assignment, there's no need to worry," Kal said. "There's got to be an explanation."

A small part of her clocked the scent of suburban London, which was the usual blend of damp tarmac and traffic fumes. Sarah skittered along beside her.

Inside her mother's apartment block, the lift took an age to arrive. Without Sarah, she'd have soaked up the adrenalin by sprinting the seven flights.

"I should never have left it so long," Sarah said.

Kal put her arm around Sarah's shoulders and gave a gentle squeeze.

The elevator gave a *ting* as the doors opened. It wasn't long before Kal was taking strides down the passageway and when she reached apartment 701, her arm froze mid-air, fingers gripping the new spare key.

"What is it?" Sarah asked.

"Nothing."

She stared at the smooth grey metal in front of her. Without mentioning anything to anyone, her mother had fitted a high-security door.

"Like I said, there's going to be an explanation for Mum not being here, you wait and see."

"At least there's no sign of a break in," Sarah said.

Sweat on her fingers made the key slip a little, but it turned smoothly, and the door swung open.

"Mum?" she called.

No reply.

The lounge door was ajar. Sparse daylight filtered through the blinds and the sofa and armchairs were shapes in the gloom. Kal walked over and yanked one by one on the cords, letting in the light.

No signs of a struggle, no disarray. Ignoring the rapid beat of her heart, she forced herself to scan the room quadrant by quadrant, clocking every detail, just as she had been taught by her father, David Khan.

In the first quadrant, Sarah stood in the doorway. A book lay on an armchair. The scatter cushions on the sofa were piled in the corner. On the end wall, the Chinese scroll hung straight, something her mother had the habit of adjusting to the perfect vertical.

Kal's gaze moved to the second quadrant where a bookcase separated the lounge from the dining area. Then, as her gaze swept to the table, a cold dread seeped into her gut.

"What's wrong?" Sarah's voice edged towards panic.

The sheet of paper was a distinctive blue and not completely flat because it had once been folded in three.

Though her legs didn't want to obey, Kal ordered herself to cross the room. The sound of her steps came sharp on the wooden boards, then muffled on the rug, then sharp again as she neared the letter. She knew the wording by heart.

"You are SCUM
Filthy VERMIN
SUFFER
Because all of you will DIE"

The threat was written in the same way it always was. Her grandmother had burned them. Her mother had laughed and ripped them to pieces, and Kal had joined in the pretence it meant nothing, all the while seeing the fear behind their eyes. That's why, when she'd received her first death threat several years ago, she'd not told them. Nor any time since.

"What the h-" Sarah fumbled in her bag.

"It's nothing, ignore it." Kal was just as convincing as her family had been.

But Sarah was taking out her mobile and she dialled before Kal could stop her.

"I want the police. It's an emergency."

"I'll check the rest of the apartment," Kal mumbled.

In the hallway, she leant against the wall. Black dots danced in front of her eyes and she squeezed her lids closed. She never crumbled, and definitely not in front of other people. *You know how to deal with this,* said her father's voice, *this is what you were trained for.* Kal took several deep breaths. The police would arrive soon and she had no intention of handing this over to some substandard detective.

She went quickly to her mother's bedroom where a scent of jasmine hung in the air. The sheets were rumpled and a lipstick case lay by the pillow. A bathrobe had been discarded in a heap. Kal peered under the bed. As she pulled open the closet door, the clothes hangers rattled, her mother's clothes swaying, revealing nothing except normality. The room didn't give much away except it told her Alesha left after a usual morning routine, and if she'd rushed off on one of her journalistic assignments it wasn't to the middle of nowhere.

Kal discovered nothing strange in the second bedroom nor in the bathroom, where she found uncapped shampoo and a towel flung over the back of a chair. No surprises. Everything in its place.

Check every detail, prompted the voice in her head. So Kal bent to examine the contents of the bin, ran her hand down the door and window frames to check for scratches or nail marks, scrutinised the floor for blood or ripped strands of hair.

In the kitchen, a used plate sat in the sink. Kal circled back to the lounge where she answered Sarah's anxious look with a shake of her head.

"There's nothing wrong. I don't see any explanation."

The only thing not in its place was the death-threat. Why hadn't it been destroyed? Why had Alesha left it on display? There was only one conclusion–her mother wanted it to be seen. For the millionth time that day, Kal checked her phone and found no new messages.

A light sweat covered her back. Sarah's instincts were correct. Where was Alesha? Something was very wrong.

Chapter Four

In Kal's assessment, the man at the door was sharp. In his early fifties, and with a greyness to his pale complexion, he seemed to have been permanently impregnated with the dirt of London. Kal noted his shrewd sweep of the apartment.

"We received an emergency call from this address with the report of a missing person. I'm Detective Inspector Spinks."

Kal stared at Detective Inspector Spinks.

In her mind's eye she could see the poker table and smell the sweat of the players.

Her father taught her how to read people.

'Notice how he scratches his eyebrow when he's talking? It means he's not telling the truth.' 'Watch carefully, do you see the way her eyes flick to the left as she lies?'

When she became good at it, he sat her at the poker table. She had to relay an analysis of each player—their breathing rate, their inconsistencies, the subtle ways each of them handled their emotions. When was a player bluffing a poor hand? When were they anticipating a kill? Who was the weakest person in the circle?

David Khan demanded she learn it all.

As Kal waited for the memory to subside, the inspector stared back at her, no doubt taking in her Indian complexion and dark eyes.

"Please tell me exactly what's happened."

Spinks didn't shake her hand, nor wave an identification card. Instead, he inclined his body and shifted his weight onto the balls of his feet, as if he was about to walk in. Clever, thought Kal, and she stepped aside. Detective Inspector Spinks had an air of quiet confidence and she pegged him to have the mental endurance of a marathon runner. He had the appearance of a runner too, slim and willowy, built for the long-haul.

"It's my friend, Alesha Medi, she's vanished," Sarah said.

"The call came from Sarah Wiseman, is that you?"

"Yes, Inspector,"

He turned to Kal. "And you are?"

"I'm Kal Medi, Alesha is my mother."

Spinks seemed unfazed by her bell-bottom trousers, teamed with a colourful, woven belt. One of the refugee women had made it and given it as a gift. Kal had taken shots of the woman's deft fingers as she told Kal the horrific story of how three of her five children had perished during their flight to the camp.

"Our files show the person reported missing, Alesha Medi, is a respected, investigative journalist. She's on our high-profile list."

Detective Inspector Spinks pronounced each word deliberately and it made him sound a bit old-fashioned. Kal felt sure it was a reflection of his mental process, meaning he'd give every detail in a case his careful consideration.

"Detective Inspector," Sarah said, "Alesha's in danger. There's something you must see."

Sarah ushered Spinks into the lounge and waved at the paper.

"When did you last hear from Alesha Medi?"

"She didn't turn up for a meeting two days ago," Sarah said. "It's totally out of character. She knows my schedule's packed and she'd never not show without an explanation.

I've been trying to contact her since. I've spoken to people at Alesha's newspaper, at Capital Towers where I work, everyone I could think of, and no one has seen or heard anything."

"And you, Ms Medi, when did you last have contact with your mother?"

"A week ago. I've been working in Kenya at a refugee camp. One of the humanitarian agencies had a satellite phone and Alesha called me and asked if I could team up with her on assignment. I said I couldn't fly back until today. I didn't realise there might be something wrong until I got Sarah's message at the airport."

"May I take a tour?"

"Of course."

Spinks began his inspection at the table and then moved to the bookcase and seating area.

"And what's your occupation Ms Medi?"

"I'm a freelance photojournalist."

Spinks threw her a look which asked for more. Probably he wanted to compare her to her well-known mother, and, as usual, Kal kept quiet. Her shots of the camp had ended up in a national women's magazine.

"Kal's a fierce humanitarian just like her mother. She defends people who have no one," Sarah said.

Kal said nothing. The magazine was going to sponsor two more doctors at the camp's health clinic. Readers had become involved. If she pushed to do a follow-up, she might even be able to make it three doctors and she was proud of her part in it. Long hours, giving it all she had, bleeding herself dry, it was worth it when funding came in and ordinary people were moved to give support. Putting her mother off for a few days had been a choice she had to make.

"Mum didn't tell me anything about her assignment and that's the last time we spoke."

She remembered the moment. In their crackled exchange, Kal had realised her mother's call was urgent and she'd gambled it could wait.

Spinks fired questions as he moved to Alesha's workstation and Kal trailed behind. She got the impression Spinks not only visually examined everything, he almost inhaled the details, absorbing everything. They'd got someone competent after all.

Spinks headed to the hallway and Kal shadowed him, inspecting each area, searching for a clue, an idea, a direction to go in.

"Did your mother tell you about the death-threat?"

"No."

"Had she been acting strangely? Did you believe she felt in danger?"

"Mum has a crazy lifestyle. She works in conflict zones and places with no access and zero security, and if you know about her work then you know her list of potential enemies is long—people and politics she's exposed, cover-ups she's hit the front page with. Thing is, six months ago she got a bullet in the leg and she's been in physiotherapy ever since, so she had to slow down."

Spinks paused at the doorway to the second bedroom. "What happened?"

"Mum got shot in Eastern Europe when she was investigating mass burial sites."

"When I heard of Alesha's recuperation, I asked her to work for me at Capital Towers," Sarah said. "I'm putting together a documentary investigating medical research on children."

They circled back to the lounge and Spinks fell silent. Kal started to get impatient and part of her wanted to tell him to cut to the chase.

"I'll speak with the neighbours and from both of you I need a list of people who might have seen Alesha Medi last–

close friends, colleagues. Now tell me, what do you make of this?"

He pointed at the letter.

There was no point in glossing it over. "We've received them before," Kal said.

"That can't be true!" Sarah covered her mouth with her hand.

"We kept them a family secret, I suppose it was out of respect for my grandmother."

"You've received threatening letters and no one reported them to the police?" Spinks said.

Though she doubted it was his intention, said like that, it made them sound stupid.

"Hate mail is an issue we take extremely seriously," Spinks said, "and as a high-profile, Asian reporter at a national newspaper, your mother would be an obvious target for racists."

"Why didn't Alesha tell me?" Sarah whispered.

"I'm sorry, Sarah. It all started with my grandmother. We get one once a year. Mum never wanted it known outside the family."

Kal put her hand on Sarah's arm. Sarah and Alesha had been best friends since before Kal was born, and yet Alesha had kept her in the dark all this time. How could Kal explain the need her family felt for secrecy? How they had closed in to protect themselves? Wasn't that the natural reaction of immigrant communities? Nannie had no confidence in the British police then and probably still didn't have. Going along with her grandmother's wishes had been something they had done to protect her grandmother's dreams of a new life.

"I'm sorry, Sarah. We kept it ourselves for Nannie's sake."

"Ms Medi, when you say you've received these threats before, are you sure? Think carefully."

Did he think she was an idiot? "Of course I'm certain. We're wasting time."

It came out sharp. Of course, Spinks wouldn't realise her high level of investigative skills, most likely rivalling his own.

"What I mean is, we've received exactly the same threat for as long as I can remember. The wording is identical and the type-face, and the paper is the same. The problem is, we never kept any because no one took them seriously."

Sarah had gone white. "All this time and Alesha didn't say a word?"

"Please don't take it to heart. I can't tell you anything more Inspector, except my grandmother once told me the threats had something to do with Granddad Sunni, only I've no idea what that means."

"If your mother didn't take the threats seriously then why is one left as a centrepiece?" asked Spinks.

It was a good question.

"And your grandmother, is she still…?"

"Still alive? Yes, she's in a nursing home in Wimbledon, about twenty minutes from here."

"I think you and I should visit her, and meanwhile, with your permission, I'll ask Forensics to sweep this apartment."

She searched for a trace which would betray what he was thinking–a mannerism, a nuance, a suggestion, but Spinks kept his face remarkably clear and she made a mental note to keep alert around him. Spinks was an unusually sharp detective. In contrast, Sarah appeared stricken.

Kal wrapped her arms around her mother's best friend.

"It's all right, please don't worry," she said.

Kal meant it, because she couldn't trust anyone including Detective Spinks. She would be handling this investigation herself.

Chapter Five

Kal's grandfather, Sunni Medi

Since his arrival in England, Sunni had worked his way up from the bottom of the pile. Starting out helping a cousin, he now ran his own fruit and vegetable stall. This week Sunni made record takings and he decided to celebrate. It was Friday, so why not treat his wife to a gift? His wife made all the food at home for the two of them and their young daughter, Alesha, and she often made Indian desserts, which Sunni loved, but his wife had developed a taste for British chocolate. Her favourite was wrapped in shiny purple foil. Raj stocked it at his corner shop. Yes, he would stop by and get some as a surprise.

Sunni was half-way home with a fat slab of chocolate in his pocket when he felt a terrible pain across his chest. It was so intense, he saw stars. Staggering to a bench, he couldn't catch his breath. Then the pains got stronger and started shooting down his left arm.

It all happened quickly. One minute he was upright and next he was on the ground. Two men stopped to help and by then Sunni could hardly speak. One of them ran to call an ambulance.

Sunni closed his eyes and right by his head, the pavement smelled of dog piss.

He knew he had been targeted by his enemy. The bastard had done it the sneaky way.

Sunni's conscience was clear. He had done the right thing. He had protected those children in India and it was all that mattered. Yet his suspicions had been right–he and his wife had tried to escape except the devil had followed them across the seas.

Sunni struggled to whisper a warning for his family but his heart could no longer beat. As death approached, his last thought was of his little daughter, Alesha, and how he would never see her grow up.

When the report came back to me detailing Sunni's death, I laughed so hard it made me cry. Did Sunni think he could escape to England? Did he think he could hide in a new life? No, oh no, that was never going to happen. That scum would suffer.

Sending the death threat was a stroke of genius on my part. When it arrived, Sunni boarded up the windows and I know his wife didn't leave the house for weeks. Their lives changed and became smaller and closed in–and so it should be. They deserved it and they'd get it–deserved to spend every moment looking over their shoulder, scared of the shadows, suffocating on their own fear.

You see, as I grew older money started to flow my way, until I was able to invest in a man with no name who could carry out my wishes without a trace.

My employee found Sunni. He followed Sunni and his wife. He told me they had a happy marriage. Had spawn.

I'd waited so long for revenge and I wanted to see the result first hand, only the man with no name refused, so events reached me second-hand. I was told how Sunni collapsed on his way home and how his wife didn't get there in time. The coroner would find evidence of a heart attack but, thanks to my man, no trace of the substances which brought it on.

I keep an archive–Sunni's body on the pavement, photographs of the boarded-up house, the crowd outside the crematorium, a press announcement of the death. It was only my first step in avenging my father's murder. Revenge tastes sweet and don't let anyone tell you otherwise.

Chapter Six

On the drive over to Wimbledon, Kal stared out the window.

"Do you have any explanation for your mother's disappearance?" Spinks asked.

They were speeding along a suburban road of red brick houses and windows hung with net curtains and rubbish bins standing in tiny front yards. She let the question hang.

"You've an unusual ability to manage difficult situations, Ms Medi, and I suppose that comes from your work?"

Her abilities came from her father's training, but that was her secret.

"Very observant. Yes, I've had plenty of experience as a photojournalist."

"I get the impression underneath it all you're alarmed and not because of the threat. So that brings me back to my question."

"The problem is, I don't have an explanation, otherwise, with all due respect, you wouldn't be here. Mum *always* keeps in touch. There has never been a time she hasn't told me where she is. Since my father died it's been the two of us and she always keeps the habit and so do I."

Spinks looked more shrewd side-on, probably due to his prominent nose. He'd make a great character shot of a hawkish detective.

"You're right though, I've never been convinced by the threats. I imagine it's just some nutter with a grudge against my grandfather. Whoever it is, they might be in their nineties by now."

"Being close to death can be a highly motivating factor, Ms Medi. Of course, we have details on record of your father, David Khan's, death. I understand he died some years ago. Did anyone inform the police of the threats at that time?"

"My father lost control of his motorbike and the coroner concluded there was no one to blame. I was twelve years old, so I don't know for certain, though I'm guessing no one mentioned the hate mail. The social climate of Britain has changed, Inspector. I'm sure you won't deny it wasn't so long ago no one in the police would've taken it seriously so you can't blame my grandmother for not seeking help and then, I suppose, Mum and I fell in with the same habit."

The wheels crunched on the gravel driveway of the nursing home and Spinks pulled in at a parking bay.

"Before you ask, Grandfather Sunni died of a heart attack. He had a heart condition, though of course, his loss still came as a great shock."

"I'm sure it did," Spinks said, "and please satisfy my curiosity." He turned to look at her. "I know you've returned from a refugee camp, but you seem to have got very little sleep for a long time. Is there a reason?"

DI Spinks had balls, she'd give him that–usually no one dared mention the dark rings under her eyes. Not a night went by when her father's training didn't interrupt her sleep with nightmares and flashbacks.

"Sleep has never been my strong point."

They walked to the front gate. It was sixteen years ago her father skidded out of control and died from the impact. Her grandfather had died five years before her father's accident, and Nannie had already moved to live with them. Now, Nannie lived here. Kal rang the buzzer. Most of the residents had dementia, so the home had a system to prevent people wandering out.

They found Kal's grandmother in her room sitting by the window. Nannie's once jet-black hair had long since turned white, and she wore a long, dark green dress with gold border design. It was one of Nannie's favourites and made of silk the same as one of Alesha's saris. Kal had learned to judge Nannie's level of confusion by her appearance. Today, it looked like Nannie would be better than usual.

"Kal darling, how lovely," Nannie said.

Excellent. On bad days, Nannie didn't recognise her or mixed her up with Alesha.

She gave her grandmother a kiss and placed a bar of chocolate on the side table. Wrapped in purple foil, it was Nannie's favourite.

"I see you brought a visitor," Nannie said.

"This is Detective Inspector Spinks. We received one of those letters this morning and he'd like to ask some questions."

"It's none of his business." Nannie turned to stare at the garden.

"He's trying to help," Kal said.

"When did you last see Alesha Medi, your daughter?" Spinks asked.

"Yesterday, and that's none of your business either," snapped Nannie. "I suggest you leave, Mr Spinks. Or shall I call the Matron and ask her to escort you from the premises?"

Nannie had always been feisty. According to Nannie, her husband, Sunni, said the hot-headed streak ran all the way down the female line. It meant Kal could never pussy-foot around her grandmother.

She put her hand on Nannie's arm, feeling the puckering where Nannie had been badly burned.

"Mum's gone missing and Inspector Spinks is trying to find her."

There was a moment's silence.

"Why didn't you say so!"

The dementia could be so difficult–never knowing what to say or do for the best. Adding complicated, real-time events to the mix could have made it even more complex, though not, apparently, today.

"You said you saw Alesha yesterday. Did she say anything you found unusual?" Spinks asked.

"Not that I remember," Nannie said.

Spinks dragged over a chair. "Did she say she would be going away?"

"No, she didn't mention her work, we had a nice chat and then she left."

"And what time was this?"

"It was late afternoon, just after they served afternoon tea."

Kal wanted to tell Spinks how Nannie could be unreliable about days and times, but no matter, they could check at the office, all visitors had to sign in and out.

"And the letters, Nannie? Didn't you once say they were connected to Granddad?"

Nannie pulled her shawl tighter around her shoulders. "Alesha, you know that's untrue. I forbid you to talk about them."

Her grandmother became agitated, her eyes scanning from side to side as if she searched the room for an intruder.

"Nannie, it's me, Kal."

But Nannie closed her eyes and began a low moaning, rocking backwards and forwards, hugging her arms across her chest.

The good moment had passed. Kal turned to Spinks. "This happens sometimes, I'm sorry."

"No need for an apology, I completely understand."

Nannie's handkerchief fell to the floor. As Kal picked it up, she noticed a picture postcard tucked between the cushion and the side of Nannie's chair. The card crackled as she pulled it out.

On the front was a field of bluebells, the flowers a purple-blue haze amongst trees. In the corner was a bench and a small house. She recognised it. It was the bluebell grove at the Royal Botanical Gardens at Kew. Kew Gardens wasn't far from Apartment 701 and it was one of Alesha's favourite places.

Aware how Spinks watched every move, Kal placed the handkerchief on her grandmother's lap and casually smoothed out the postcard. She turned it over. A single line was typed on the back–'Watch What You Say or They'll Be Calling You...' Her heart started beating faster.

"Anything?" asked Spinks, holding out his hand.

Her mouth felt dry. "It's an old postcard."

He stared at the single line. "Do you make anything of this?"

"Maybe it's a gift from one of the other residents?"

Spinks' eyes rested on her, so she added a tiny bit more information, not too much, only the smallest of expert touches to confuse the trail. Her father would have been proud of her.

"A lot of Nannie's friends have dementia. Perhaps all the news about terrorism is getting mixed up in their heads."

"Hmm."

Kal concentrated on keeping a relaxed posture and a soft, gentle expression–one that in her photojournalism always threw people off the scent. She waited until Spinks blinked and shifted his shoulders, showing his thoughts had moved on.

Since he was a good detective, part of him would question whether she lied, except that one line would only mean something to her.

Spinks was pushing the chair back where it had been. "My first priority is to question people who may have seen your mother last," Spinks said. "Be sure to call me immediately if anyone contacts you issuing demands or if any new information comes to light. Nothing can be ruled out at this stage."

Kal nodded.

"Good. Now, will you stay with your grandmother or can I offer you a lift?"

She looked down and toyed with the fringe of Nannie's shawl. "I'll stay for a while longer."

Kal watched Spinks exit the driveway. Then she kissed Nannie goodbye and raced for the bus because she knew exactly what she needed to do next. Wherever this was leading, she was going to follow it to the end. Alesha had left her a clue.

Chapter Seven

Kal sat on the top deck of the bus. Now she understood why her mother left the death threat on the table. It had been a silent warning– 'Watch out'.

Sitting at the back, she did a search on her mobile. The words on Nannie's postcard came from a song, and she knew exactly what it was for.

A while later, she got off at Wimbledon Parkside where the road stretched long and straight in both directions. On one side lay Wimbledon Common, an area of nature slap bang in the middle of south London and spanning some four hundred acres. On the other side of the road, smart houses and apartments lined the street. It was a short walk to apartment 701 and walking fast she'd make it in five.

Judging by the amount of traffic, it was coming up to the evening rush-hour. Assessing the flow, Kal jogged between two cars but half-way across the road her instincts snapped to alert.

Reaching the other side, she spun around, the pavement making a damp, slippery noise underneath her shoe. Was someone watching her? She scanned quickly.

There was a man with a dog, two joggers in bright gear heading towards her, a young woman with her hands in her pockets and an older man carrying shopping. Kal checked each one, searching their body language. All appeared harmless yet hadn't she had the distinct impression someone was observing her? Her skin prickled. Always trust your instincts, it was the number one rule. Yes, she was certain. A man or a woman she couldn't say which but a figure had been standing still and intent and facing in her direction. And now they had disappeared.

The bus she just got off carried on down Wimbledon Parkside, the roar of its engine heading into the distance. Kal swept the pedestrians a second time and came up with nothing, so she took a deep breath and continued in the direction of 701. A nervousness fluttered in her stomach. No one was immune to fear but you could learn how to control it, and if there was one thing her father had been, he'd been an excellent teacher.

Now Kal slowed her pace, and a couple of times swivelled to glance behind and catch someone in the act. All it earned her was strange looks from passers-by. One stroller-pushing mother even crossed the road to avoid her.

Kal knew someone was there. The question was, who and why? *Keep alert*, said the voice in her head, *continue, and let it play out in its own time.*

Kal stared straight ahead and kept on walking.

At 701, she discovered a team packing up. A blonde woman pulled off latex gloves.

"Good afternoon, I'm Head of the forensics team. As requested by Detective Inspector Spinks, we've been through the whole apartment. Imaging has verified there are no unexplained blood stains. We've taken samples from each room and DI Spinks will be the first informed should we isolate further information, for instance from this."

The woman held up the letter sealed in a plastic bag.

"Right," Kal replied.

"We'll leave you in peace. Oh, and the technical team will arrive later to impound the computer. I got a call to say they're overloaded, so I've protected the hardware. Please don't touch anything before they arrive."

"Of course not."

Three other team members filed out and Kal closed the door behind them. Jettisoning her shoes, she ran to the lounge and her mother's workstation. In one motion, she ripped aside the layers of plastic covering the equipment. She could imagine the blonde woman's reaction. Yes, well, in Kal's world, following the rules never got you anywhere.

Click, click. In a blaze of blue, the screen sprang to life and asked for Alesha's password. Using the line of the song from Nannie's postcard she typed in the name of the album and the year.

'Incorrect password'

Damn. She'd been so sure. The computer would give her two more chances before it locked down. Getting up, she adjusted the Chinese scroll, wondering which technician moved it and why they hadn't put it back properly.

Inventing new passwords started out as an after-school game when her mother typed up her journalistic articles in the evening. Alesha had been a fan of music from the nineteen-eighties and she let her daughter pick a song and an album each week, and then used it to create a new password. Of course, her mother didn't do that anymore.

The adrenalin rush was making it hard to concentrate and her hands were shaking.

"Of course, dumbo, get your act together," she said to herself, "It's the other way around. The year first then the name of the album."

Bingo. The computer flickered and up came Alesha's desktop. Kal's eyes fell on a small icon in the corner. At last, she was getting somewhere. The file was named, 'For Kal'.

Chapter Eight

The file contained sets of photographs.

Each set showed a different person and six were men and one was a woman. Kal recognised the woman straight away. It was Selena Vankova, the new Mayor of London.

In some of the shots, Selena hadn't been captured fully on-screen. In none was she looking directly at the camera. Kal's throat went dry because it meant these shots had been taken covertly. This was one of her mother's investigations.

One of the men seemed familiar. He wore a striped shirt and a flamboyant, red tie and strolled down a central London street. In the background, she recognised Oxford Circus underground entrance. At that junction, Oxford Street intersects Regent Street, where Sarah's company, Capital Towers, had its head office. Yes, that was it, he was the Chief Executive of Capital Towers and Sarah's boss. Kal found his name on-line–Alistair Kealy–an influential London mover and shaker.

Fifties, distinguished looking with greying hair, the Arabic man in the next set looked familiar too. Dressed in traditional-style, white robe, he sat outside a cafe and was drinking an espresso. Judging by the background, this was also taken in central London.

When Kal pulled up a search of top businessmen it made her break out into a sweat. He figured at the top of the list–Farouk Assad. Assad was an oil magnate who owned half the real estate in the capital. Had Alesha had been tracking the elite? That ring of top politicians and businessmen who had so much power and influence they could do what they liked? Or thought they could.

She found no names for the remaining three people and a trawl of her mother's files and emails drew a blank. By the time she pushed away the keyboard, sweat ran down her back. Her mother had her eye on the big fish. Why? What had Alesha discovered? One thing was for sure, Alesha left a trail of breadcrumbs for a reason.

Her mind returned to the phone call at the refugee camp. Those women and children had needed her and the scoop with the women's magazine had been a chance she couldn't turn down because two extra doctors would save a lot of lives. And yet.

Closing her eyes, Kal felt the tears. She should have dropped everything and come running. This was her fault. If she'd been with Alesha she would have been watching her back. If anything had happened to her mother...

Part of her wanted to go straight out and track Mayor Vankova, Kealy and Assad, but that was amateurish. She needed to be much more clever if she was going to find out why Alesha had been following them. They would all have protection and buffers. What she needed was to get up close and personal and wheedle her way in without them even knowing she had tried. Yes, she could do that. In fact, she'd be good at it.

Darkness had fallen. Forcing back the tears, she leant against the window, looking down seven storeys. A few headlights still swept Wimbledon Parkside because Londoners were always on the move. Just as Kal turned away, goosebumps prickled her arms. She stood perfectly still.

Opposite the apartment, yellow lighting shone from a bus stop. The stop was deserted. But when she first stood up, hadn't someone been standing to the side, out of the pool of light? Hadn't there been a shadowy impression of a figure standing alone? And now there was no one.

No bus had passed and both pavements were empty. In blackness, the Common stretched for miles the other side of the main road. Was her mind playing tricks? Certainly not. She stared at the pool of light. Someone could still be there, crouching in darkness at the edge of the Common. Watching. Waiting. Reaching to the side, she flipped the light switch, plunging the lounge into darkness.

Had they watched her mother? Should she go after them? Her palms itched to take action. Skilled in kung fu combat, she could hold her own. *No,* said the voice in her head, *wait until the watcher shows their hand.* Kal stepped back and let down the blinds with a clack.

She sat for a long time tucked into the corner of the sofa, thinking through her plans. On her way to the spare bedroom, Kal passed by the front door. After clocking it earlier, she'd given no reaction to Sarah and not reported it to Spinks. Made of steel, with three deadbolts, the security door had a perfect finish, but it wasn't its cold, metal touch which sent a shiver down Kal's back. Clearly, her mother had felt in danger.

Chapter Nine

Yasmin turned on the television and sat back in her armchair. These days she was spending more time alone and the winter evenings were long. She didn't resent it. Soon she'd go to bed and tuck up with a good book. She was glad her daughter, Alesha, was head over heels in love. Glad Alesha had found someone to spend the rest of her life with, as Yasmin had hoped to spend the whole of her life with her late husband, Sunni. It had been hard and lonely without him, she didn't deny it, but Yasmin was made of stern stuff and life went on.

The news programme seemed to continue for ages with nothing good to say about the world. Yasmin pulled a blanket over her legs and, within a few minutes, she started dozing off.

If she had been more alert, she would have heard the soft *whuff* of the flames igniting in the kitchen. She might have smelt the smoke as it seeped underneath the door and into the living room, slowly filling her home with fumes. In her slumber, Yasmin coughed. She struggled, trying to awaken. It was an instinct for survival, primal and sharp, which kicked her into consciousness.

The whole lounge was full of acrid smoke. Choking, she fell from her chair. The fall saved her because air a few centimetres above the carpet was less laden. Crawling towards the window, Yasmin fumbled for the latch. Then came an explosion which blew off the kitchen door. Flames poured in and she screamed as her clothes ignited.

Desperation gave her strength to force the window open and somehow pull herself through. She tumbled onto the ground outside.

Yasmin was badly burned, yet she survived.

Later, she pretended she had left oil heating on the stove. In those days, pan fires were common and the fire service didn't investigate further. She didn't mention the death threats to the authorities and neither did her daughter, Alesha.

Every day I stop in front of the photographs of Sunni's body. It's my shrine and I enjoy the way Sunni's face is contorted. My favourite shot shows saliva dribbling in his final moments.

But Sunni's death didn't bring stillness and closure because a picture of the weeping wife played on my mind. Sunni had been cared for. Loved. And, in time, I turned my attention to Yasmin, Sunni's widow.

When the right moment came, I made the call and again sent in the man who could get things done.

This time it didn't go exactly to plan. The house burned except the old woman, against all the odds, survived. Still, I consoled myself with the years she spent in pain control and surgeries and skin grafting treatments.

Punishing the scum family was fitting vengeance for my father's death. He was a wonderful man, inspired and magnificent. How dare a lowly servant like Sunni open his mouth in my father's presence! How dare he question my father's actions. How dare he even crawl out from the stone he was born under! My father was a god. Without a doubt it was Sunni who had informed on my father and caused the families to send an assassin.

I had the widow's agonies documented and her disgusting disfigurements made me laugh so hard my sides ached.

Chapter Ten

Kal could not sleep. In the early hours of the morning, she hunted in the kitchen and made toast, then, inhaling the scent of a peppermint tea, she hunched in the corner of the sofa. The last time she saw her mother, Alesha had been rushing off on assignment. Their last visit to Kew Gardens, or anywhere, had been too long ago. Alesha had called Kal to ask for help and Kal had put her off. She had left her mother alone. Was it now too late? *Don't think like that,* she told herself, *that's the way to madness.*

The city crawled to life, and traffic outside built from a few cars to full flow. Her muscles demanded their usual workout. Even on location, she fitted in at least one hour of exercise every morning. Today, she had no time. She must fabricate meetings as soon as possible with Kealy, Assad and Mayor Selena Vankova. She wanted to see them up close, hear the intonation of their voices, analyse their reactions and dig and duck and dive until she had the intel she needed.

Grabbing breakfast at a bagel stall, Kal headed out and took the underground to Oxford Circus.

At Capital Towers, Sarah met Kal and they hugged.

"Did you get any sleep?" Sarah asked.

"Not much, but enough," Kal lied.

Sarah looked like she was running on anxiety.

A young woman walked towards them and she muttered a 'Good Morning' to Sarah and after she'd passed by, she turned to give Kal a glance up and down.

"I think she admires your style," Sarah whispered.

Kal arched an eyebrow. Today, she'd chosen a dark blue, figure-hugging, velvet dress. Velvet was one of her favourites because it was stretchy and allowed full body movement, which was important for martial arts and self-defence. She'd piled her hair on top of her head. Dressing in her own style was one of Kal's habits. She also knew how appearances worked well as a technique for sneaking under people's guard. A dress and heels would be perfect for getting Kealy to reveal his innards like a split sack of beans.

It was a long corridor and several of the offices were already occupied.

"Detective Inspector Spinks interviewed me yesterday and I was exhausted by the time he was through. He's definitely experienced and I'm sure he'll come up with something," Sarah said.

Kal read the name plates on each door, expecting to spot Kealy's office. Perhaps it would be simplest to ask Sarah to introduce her? When they reached Sarah's office, Sarah motioned for Kal to take a seat.

"I guess you're here to find out about Alesha's project?"

What project? No, she was here to probe into Kealy.

She'd barely sat down when Sarah launched into an explanation with one sentence running into the next.

"When I heard Alesha had been shot, I was horrified. Since our student days together, she's followed a career in the field, well, you know I think taking risks like she does is a younger person's game, and we both understand that's not how Alesha sees it, she thinks she can continue forever, anyway, I needed someone with an investigative mind and someone not open to outside influences and I knew she was available, so I asked her to do some work for me. I suppose

I was hoping to tempt her away from her job at the newspaper, you know, permanently."

Sarah picked up the percolator jug and misjudged, sloshing hot liquid over the rim of her cup.

"Would you like some, Kal?"

"No thanks. Coffee makes me rabid." She watched Sarah dab violently at the splashes.

"I'm working on a documentary on medical research on children. There've been a couple of headline incidents–children in Argentina in clinical trials for a multinational where the families claimed they were coerced into taking part, Ethiopian boys used as subjects for medical tests where there were rumours of deaths and then after an investigation, the big name company came out clean. That kind of research is forbidden in Europe and the States, so companies set up laboratories and trials elsewhere."

Sarah made to drink her coffee, then changed her mind. "The company I asked Alesha to investigate is ScottBioTec. Two years ago they were a lack-lustre, biotechnology enterprise and now they're top of the league. Their robotic limb is way ahead of their competitors and what catapulted them to success? It was the strides they made on research carried out on street children in India."

"The land of my ancestors and one of Mum's favourite countries. So Mum was to research the documentary?"

"I wanted a three-hundred-and-sixty degree, meaning meet the children, interview families, interview medical personnel, see first-hand the conditions and how the research is handled and what it entails, and including meeting with those against ScottBioTec's methods. There are pressure groups both sides of the Atlantic and there's been plenty of lobbying to close down ScottBioTec's Indian operation."

"Okay."

"Here's where it gets interesting. A few weeks ago, the topic shot onto the hot list because the government announced it's setting up a Special Commission on Children's Rights and Research Ethics. There are big players in the league, not only ScottBioTec. Big players with big profits they want to protect. Of course, they want a positive outcome from the Commission."

"Meaning they don't want stricter standards imposed?"

"The private sector wants to keep control and they say they've adequate checks in place. And they don't want governments and international agreements which could jeopardise their freedom to do research and get results, and that's results with a capital R."

"Nothing new there then, and I can see why it would interest Mum."

Across the desk, Sarah was fussing with her pen. Kal knew she was holding something back. She shouldn't push. Applying pressure would only make Sarah clam up, better instead, to offer a little encouragement.

"I'm sure Mum appreciated it. The whole injury episode bothered her more than she wanted to admit. And I can tell you, if the offer had come from anyone except you, her pride would've got in the way of accepting."

Sarah stirred her coffee, the spoon jangling. Kal waited. Whatever wasn't right here, Sarah was about to tell her.

"I thought it was a smart move involving Alesha because I trust her. I asked her specifically because I was getting pressure to turn in a positive angle on the documentary. This is confidential, Kal, but the suggestion came from the top, from Kealy and, of course, it wasn't official. I was expected to emphasise the benefits for the children. I couldn't believe it. That's why I wanted someone absolutely independent working on the project for me."

"And I can see how Mum would be exactly the right person. Did Kealy threaten you?"

"He'd never be so foolish. Take it from me, he knows how to pile on pressure in hidden ways and I'm certain he's been influencing other members of my team. The weird thing is it simply isn't his style. Kealy got to the top protecting our independence and he's built Capital Towers on that principle. We're impartial and proud of it and Kealy's stridently defended that right. I can't see any reason on earth why he'd be prepared to put everything he's worked for at risk."

"You think Mum's disappearance could be related to the documentary, don't you?"

"I don't know if it's relevant, I'm only saying it could be. You said yourself someone's been sending those death threats for years, so why should Alesha go missing now?"

There came a rap at the door and a man stepped into the room, the electric blue of his tie adding panache to his entry.

Kealy.

"Apologies for interrupting," Kealy said, not appearing even slightly apologetic. "I'm Alistair Kealy and you must be Alesha's daughter." He shook her hand. "I hear the police are trying to trace your mother and I'm so sorry. Has there been any news?"

"Not yet. I'm glad to meet you Mr Kealy, I'd hoped to speak to you after seeing Sarah."

"Oh, why's that?" Kealy asked, moving further into the room.

His body movements reminded her of a ferret or other small predator. He was quick, light-footed, on the alert.

She kept it vague and added a touch of flattery. "Mum spoke of you. She admires your, er, stance on recent issues." Not that Alesha had mentioned Kealy even once.

"Ah-hah, well yes, quite," Kealy said, accepting the compliment with ease. "Your mother has an outstanding reputation. It's an honour to have her with us."

Kealy was confident and slick but his stance held a tightness. Despite his flair, the top rat's body language showed him to be ill at ease.

Kealy adjusted his tie. "I understand you have a budding career, Kal. It seems you'll be a name to watch."

"That's kind of you," Kal said.

She watched for any tell-tale signs of deception. Despite his hyper-vigilance, Kealy appeared genuine. Maybe he was always on edge.

He turned to Sarah, "Remind me, which part of the work was Alesha covering for us?"

And there it was. The quick flick of his eyes downwards and to the left as he asked the question, almost imperceptible and so telling because it signalled Kealy lied.

Sarah remained deadpan, masking her dislike of her boss.

"I asked Alesha to investigate ScottBioTec," Sarah said.

"Ah-hah, yes, and has Alesha given us any feedback?"

"I handed the dossier over to her. She had free rein and I wasn't expecting anything yet."

"Yes, yes, I see." Kealy gave little nods in unison to his words like a toy bobbing in the back window of a car. "Well, Ms Medi, if I can help in any way, don't hesitate to ask."

"Thank you."

Kal gave Kealy a smile.

Once the door was closed and he was out of ear-shot, Sarah leant across the desk.

"What do you make of that?"

Her father liked to set her challenges.

At one time, he had an interest in their local newsagent and sent her weekly to make her assessment. The man kept an old dog, who lay in a basket behind the counter. Kal took her time to pet the dog and spent weeks digging nearer and nearer to, well, an unshapeable 'something' about the newsagent. Something not right. Something bad. It was the echo of that wrongness which her father wanted her to understand. He'd wanted her to put that gut feeling into words, into a diagnosis—and so he kept sending her back and her suspicions had been slowly forming. But the police had beaten her to it and the dog turned out to be friendlier than its owner because the newsagent ended up behind bars for drug dealing. The worst being he'd done it to fund his addiction to illegal blood sports—cockfighting, badger baiting. How could a person who loved his pet, conceal such cruelty? How could he hide such a monstrous side? These were the questions her father wanted her to confront so she would understand the capacities of the criminal mind. It made her wonder, too, when her father had known the truth about the newsagent because part of her suspected he'd known right from the start.

Kal didn't like Kealy. Likely he'd come to Sarah's office to find out what they knew which meant he was involved in something. And her analysis told her he was acting like a man pushed into a corner.

The same as animals, people who feel trapped could react unpredictably and Kal would prefer Sarah to be out of harm's way. But she wasn't about to tell Sarah all of that.

"To be honest, I didn't read much into it. It was nice Kealy came to see me."

"I suppose it was…"

"As you said earlier, Detective Inspector Spinks is competent. We can trust him to track down Mum. If you ask me, it's only a matter of time. No need to overly stress."

"Are you sure? I mean…"

"You're such a worrier, Sarah. There's no need."

To move it on, Kal decided to adjust her hair. She started a rearrangement, pulling out loose strands and then spending a few minutes with hairpins held between her teeth. She waited until Sarah sat back and began taking little sips of coffee, before pushing the final pin back into place.

"You know, I passed by Wyndham Theatre on the way here and it reminded me of your nephew," Kal said. "Is he still blazing a name for himself on the Dublin stage?"

Sarah narrowed her eyes. "Oh no you don't, Kal, I know what you're trying to do talking about my family in Ireland. I'm not going anywhere until they find Alesha, it's out of the question, so don't try suggesting a vacation, and," she pointed an accusing finger, "it means you're suspicious of Kealy."

No flies on Sarah.

Kal gave no reply because she had a very bad feeling about all of it.

Chapter Eleven

A long, red line of buses crawled along Oxford Street, with double-deckers heading towards Marble Arch. Pedestrians overflowed both pavements. Oxford Street was the busiest shopping street in Europe with an iconic buzz all of its own.

Kal had done her research. ScottBioTec was worth millions and Richard Scott was the entrepreneur owner. Their artificial leg and arm units had functional finesse way ahead of the field. She read how they pioneered the use of a pea-sized array of micro-electrodes implanted in the brain which interacted with chip technology in the artificial limb. ScottBioTec would soon be launching a third generation, robotic limb and it was provoking a media frenzy. Time to pay a little visit.

"Dr Scott has agreed to see you," the receptionist said, tapping at his keyboard. He didn't bother hiding his surprise at how Dr Scott would see anyone on such short notice. Handing over a security tag, he pointed to the elevators.

Kal's own reflection stared back at her in the elevator mirror. She pressed glossy, dark red lips together and they stuck a micro-second longer than normal. Usually she avoided cosmetics, never quite seeing the point, except right now she wanted to make an impact and she had followed her instincts and let her hair down too, wearing it styled over one shoulder in the way her mother often did.

As Kal stepped out of the elevator, Richard Scott's personal assistant glanced up from her desk.

"Good morning, I'm Kal Medi."

"Welcome, Ms Medi, and goodness, I hope you don't mind me saying, but you look just like your mother."

The woman directed Kal towards a waiting area. Massive windows gave a panorama over the financial district. The famous, glass-covered Shard soared to the skies. In the distance lay the Houses of Parliament and Big Ben, and beyond, she could see the smooth, white curve of the London Eye, the capital's touristic Ferris wheel which attracted so many visitors. Winding a route through the buildings, the river Thames looked like beaten silver. Only huge wealth could buy such a magnificent view.

In the centre, underneath spotlights, an android hand clenched and unclenched. The metal structure of the hand was more like science fiction than reality.

It wasn't long before Scott came out to greet her.

"I'm very pleased to meet you and I only wish it had been in better circumstances," Scott said.

Richard Scott had a deep voice and the smooth tone of someone who had paid for voice coaching. He was handsome, with white, European features, and grey eyes.

"You must be going through a hellish time, my dear. Detective Inspector Spinks visited yesterday and explained everything."

Scott emphasised the last word and kept hold of her hand and Kal made a split-second decision on her strategy, ignoring his irritating endearment and keeping her hand limp in his. Yes, this man was used to being treated like a king. To gain maximum information, she must make herself convincingly weak.

"Dr Scott, I..."

"Please, call me Richard, and let's make ourselves comfortable, shall we?"

She followed him into his office and the leather of the sofa creaked as Kal draped one leg over the other.

"Can I get you a drink?"

"Thank you, a mineral water would be nice."

While Scott's back was turned, she studied him. A similar age to her mother, he was greying at the sideburns. Clearly, he worked out, and wore a tailored shirt which highlighted his physique. Most striking was how he oozed authority except not from an advantage of height, since he was of average height, no, Richard Scott was unusual, he radiated confidence from within. She presumed most women would be falling all over him.

Kal switched her scrutiny to the room. It was chic, housing a drinks bar, an enormous, sculptured bureau which held nothing but a tablet and a silver hard-drive, a plush couch and two armchairs and a coffee table which was a masterpiece of enamel embedded in glass. The other decoration was a bronze statue of a naked woman. The woman was in a kneeling position and had her head flung back, hair streaming down behind, breasts thrust forward. No desk-top clutter. Everything perfectly positioned. Every surface immaculate.

Scott turned away from the bar and his sapphire cufflinks glittered as he passed her a glass. Taking a seat beside her, he draped one arm along the back of the couch. Kal caught a blast of his cologne and had to stop herself from inching away.

"You must forgive me. It's been mega hectic. We've a launch coming up and I've been so up to my neck I missed my usual date with Alesha, otherwise I'd have realised she was missing and notified the police myself."

Kal shot him a quizzical look.

Scott cleared his throat. "I see your mother hasn't told you, well... she and I have been seeing each other for a while.

We decided to keep it quiet until Alesha completed her contract with Capital Towers."

Alesha usually went for men much more genuine than Scott. For once, Kal couldn't think of a single thing to say.

Scott swirled his drink, then raised the glass to his lips, not rushed, not hurried and no sign of dishonesty though he displayed little emotion. Well, she thought, he drops a bombshell and then he sits it out. He'd make a great poker player. But why do I feel like I'm sitting in front of a fake?

"I've hired a private agency and it's the best in the business. You can rest assured they'll find her. I care about your mother very much." The ice tinkled in his glass. "I've taken you by surprise, haven't I? It was so strange meeting Alesha because business always came first and your mother made me realise what an idiot I was–I suppose it's because I'd never been in love until Alesha. Your mother told me the only time she'd been in love before was with your fa…"

Kal almost dropped her glass because she'd assumed he was talking about a fling not *love*. Why would Alesha have kept falling in love to herself? And why with this man? It didn't fit.

Scott gave her a charming smile. "I'm sorry, I'm going too fast. I didn't mean to upset you."

"It's not your fault. Everything's been happening at once." Whatever he was playing at, her best bet was to go along with it.

"Is there anything I can do? Alesha talked about you often, she's so proud of you."

"It's crazy. She's disappeared without a trace, without a word. She'd never do that; I know she wouldn't."

"Please, I'm here to help, and I apologise I can't spend more time with you today, you see we're about to release our third-generation product. I squeezed you in at the last minute and I've back to back appointments all day and half the evening. But hey, I've got a very special idea. Your mother was going to accompany me to my Charity Gala. Perhaps you'd agree to come in her place? It's an evening event and maybe we could get to know each other a little better? I'd like to offer you as much support as I can."

What an odious idea. Why did nothing about this man attract her? He had looks, he had wealth and charm and her mother was, supposedly, interested in him. That combination should have been powerful. It should have had an impact on her and all it did was make her skin crawl.

She left it a few seconds before replying. "What a lovely idea."

Scott's smile displayed perfect teeth.

"Excellent. My secretary will give you details."

Already, Scott rose to show her to the door. "I'm sorry, I'm keeping my media team waiting. They're ravenous out there about the new hybrid limb and we launch in two weeks. I'm afraid I shall have to go."

Kal walked with Scott and on the way her heel caught in the deep pile of the carpet. He put out his hand to steady her.

"Are you all right?"

Staring at his buffed complexion, the hairs on the back of her neck stood on end.

"I'm sorry, I don't know what happened, I must have lost my balance." Pushing her voice, she made it crack because the less strong he believed her to be, the better. "Everything's going wrong."

She dabbed at her eyes and in a few paces she was back in the waiting area, purposely slowing her footsteps and adding a little wobble as she skirted the display stand, until she sensed Scott no longer watched her.

Chapter Twelve

The bus was full of children in school uniform, their bags and chatter filling the aisles. It had been Kal's own route home from school years ago and she knew all the alleyways and side roads, which was why she'd chosen it to confront the person following her.

Earlier, she called by the nursing home and found Nannie lost in her own world, unable to recognise Kal and in no state to recall details about Grandfather Sunni.

Was the world stacking events against her?

To make it worse, someone had been tailing Kal ever since the love affair bombshell in Richard Scott's office.

Taking a few deep breaths, she cleared her mind, just like waiting on the bench for her turn in a kung fu tournament. She was three times regional Champion and while martial arts couldn't save you from a gunshot and it might not save you from a knife, combat was one of her strengths.

It was a typical spring day with the sky overcast. She got off the bus and turned down an alley. On both sides, high-rise, social housing reached skywards, the buildings silent and grey.

Kal kept her eyes forward and focused her attention on the zone behind her. Had her pursuer picked up the trail again? Yes, she was sure of it. She could sense it with that sixth sense you can enhance when you're alert and quiet. This was risky only she was sure she could take them by surprise and it was time to find out more. Who was it? And why were they following her? Why had they been watching her mother's apartment?

She cut out everything save the stalker, the grey of the buildings and the sound of her own footsteps. Her body tingled. She felt her clothing touching her arms and the brush of material against her legs. She still wore the velvet dress and heels and that wouldn't be a problem, on the contrary, it would give her pursuer a false sense of security.

The path stretched empty ahead. It ran around the back of one of the housing estates and was a gloomy short cut taken only by those brash enough, or stupid enough, to walk it. This was a volatile part of town.

Her pursuer followed as if led on a string. The *tack* of Kal's shoes sounded steady as she passed a line of bins and the stink of refuse filled the air. She strained for the slightest sound behind her, flexing her knees, balancing her arms lightly away for her sides. It was narrow and dim here and would be an ideal spot for her tracker to make their move.

Kal felt them padding closer and closer and she resisted the urge to turn around. The velvet dress felt soft against her calves and her heart pounded.

A small *click* sounded. Perhaps a shoe catching a stone. Or the flick of a knife.

Kal turned slightly. Out of the corner of her eye, she could see a solitary figure approaching. A man. She flexed her toes, ready to kick off her shoes.

Her pursuer walked lightly, well-balanced, and likely he wasn't an amateur because his footfalls were too sure. The man approached until he was twenty metres away, then fifteen.

A sweat broke out on her palms as she anticipated over-powering him, pinning him to the ground and grinding out information. *Come on now, come closer.* Kal reached into her pocket and dropped her keys. They fell with a *plink* and as she bent to get them, she saw him pick up his pace, recognising his chance.

In an instant he was on her. Kal anticipated the impact and twisted as she fell. They were both on the ground and grappling as he tried to pin her down. The man's movements told her this wasn't going to be blood and guts because he had no weapon. Which meant he wasn't there to hurt her beyond what was necessary.

"You bastard," she shouted. "Get the hell off me."

She was flat on her back with him on top of her, but, out of his sight, she reached her legs up to his neck and clamped on a scissor hold. It was a classic move yet he'd not expected it, nor could he get out of it. Kal squeezed her knees together, then she got a one-handed, Dim-Mak hold on his neck. Dim Mak was the ancient art of using pressure points to immobilise or inflict serious injury, even death and it had been one of her father's specialities. Now she was in control. The look of surprise on her attacker's face was priceless. One flip and she was the one on top.

"Got your attention now, haven't I? Why the hell are you following me!"

She forced harder into the pressure point and his eyes bulged. It must have been agony yet he tried to spit at her.

'Where's my mother you bastard."

If she used any more force he'd black out and then she'd get nothing. So instead, she lifted his head and smashed it against the ground. It made a horrible sound.

'Answer me."

Again, he spat. "You don't know what you're taking on. This is a warning. Back off."

Her anger was close to exploding and she struggled to get it under control. "I don't give a fuck about your warnings," she snarled. "Where the hell is my mother. If you don't tell me…"

She was a hair's breadth away from smacking his head down so hard it would crack his skull open. Then a shout rang out.

"Hey! Get the fuck away from her!"

From the far end of the alley, two youths came sprinting. Shit.

"And here's a message from me," she said, "you can tell your puppet-master to go to hell."

She loosened her grip and he flung a wild punch and sprinted off. When the two teenagers arrived, she was on the ground.

"Miss, are you all right? Do you need an ambulance?" One of the young men was early twenties with an array of nose piercings.

She wiped a trickle of blood from her lip. "I'm okay. At least he didn't get my purse."

The second young man had a thin scar down his cheek, probably a souvenir from a knife fight. He was out of breath.

"You shouldn't come down here, it's dangerous. You were lucky," he said, as he helped her up.

The two of them looked like archetypal hoodlums and here they were thinking they had saved her.

"Gosh lads, thanks."

Then the boys insisted on walking her back to the main path and Kal let them.

Down at the bus stop, a man stood up and gave her his seat, and she noticed how he was careful not to make eye contact. Sure, she looked a mess and she was giving off a vibe because the thug had made her angry.

Hired thugs usually rolled over when confronted. It wasn't their bag to put themselves at risk for whoever hired them. Yet he hadn't told her a thing. In fact, he'd fulfilled his contract and delivered the warning.

None of it made sense. Every step she took kept bringing up more questions and the danger level kept upping. Whatever Alesha was involved in, it was big.

Kal was a loner by nature yet she wasn't a fool. She was smart enough to know when she needed help and there was one person she could confide in, Marty, her old girl friend and martial arts training partner.

Back at the apartment, Kal kicked the door shut. Marty's number went to answerphone.

"Hi, Marty, if you're around give me a call. I'm in town."

By the time she walked to the main room, Marty called back.

"Great to hear from you. How're you doing?"

"Mum's gone missing. Someone's stalking me. And I'm in danger of losing it."

There was a brief silence.

"When should we meet?" Marty said.

"Straight away and if I don't get a good kung fu session in, I'm going to explode. Is there a session tonight? Can you meet me at the training centre?"

Chapter Thirteen

Tucked along a suburban street, her old training centre had a new sign, 'Kung Fu and Self Defence–Master LeeMing Yeu'. It had been her club for years, from age six all the way to age twenty and now they had a new lead trainer.

At the top of a ramp, red dragons decorated each side of a swing doorway. Marty waited, with her hair cropped short and wearing those loopy, silver earrings which suited her so well. Kal's heart gave a skip. They'd met at the kung fu club in their primary school years and become friends right from the start. Without Marty, Kal would never have made it, not in one piece anyway. Her weird father, his death, Kal's habit of rubbing kids up the wrong way and always feeling like an outsider but Marty could always calm her down. Could always cut to the chase with no bullshit and she'd lost count of the number of times Marty talked sense into her. Just seeing Marty made everything more bearable. The same way knowing Marty had made her childhood bearable.

Kal gave Marty a long hug, breathing in Marty's musky perfume. They had reported her mother missing twenty-four hours ago and it seemed like a lifetime.

"What the hell's happened? You'd better fill me in, and if some oink is following you, never mind the ethics, I'll tackle them," Marty said.

"I tried already. If I don't hit something soon my brain's gonna fry."

"You wanna talk first?"

"I can't."

Marty frowned. "Okay. We join the session, then we talk."

Both beyond Black Sash level, she and Marty had trained side by side, coming up the ranks together. They'd both competed in the regional Championships and her friend had gone on several times to compete in the national Championships. Now Marty poked Kal in the stomach.

"Maybe you've gone soft," Marty said, her pearly teeth contrasting with her black skin.

"I'll fill you in after."

She could see Marty was keeping herself in excellent shape, despite having a demanding job on the security team at Wimbledon Lawn Tennis Association.

"Okay," said Marty, "and do me a favour and tell me the truth–have you missed me?"

Kal couldn't miss the double bluff. Marty pretended to sound piqued, which meant she actually was. At one time, the two of them had been inseparable.

"Of course."

"I dropped a hot date to meet you," Marty said.

In the past, that would've made Kal jealous and perhaps it still did.

Two other students came up the ramp and squeezed by to push through the dragon doors.

"If you really need that mat session we'd better get a move on. LeeMing hates people turning up late."

"I need your help, Marty, I can't get a grip on what's going on."

"Shit, you're serious, aren't you?"

Kal nodded. But she needed the session to clear her mind. She was getting too wound up to think straight.

The training room was just as Kal remembered. It had been her second home. Old sweat, grubby floor matting and incense, it even smelled the same. A two-hour session would clear her system and burn off the emotion.

The new trainer turned out to be a surprise because she'd been expecting an older man and someone to look up to, not someone attractive.

There was no doubting LeeMing's Chinese ancestry. A sleeveless top flattered LeeMing's chest and musculature. On his way to the front, he glanced in Kal's direction, showing his striking, green eyes.

They worked on the Form, which was a long sequence where the group follows choregraphed strikes and blocks and movements across the mat. The Form had long been Kal's favourite because stamina and relaxation were key and it meant letting go of the crush of thoughts in the mind.

LeeMing circulated to correct them, and several times he kept the whole class fixed in a difficult stance for what seemed an eternity. The exertion made Kal's legs shake and sweat dripped from her brow. She counted the seconds, keeping her eyes trained on the distance as her thigh muscles burned and her system rebalanced itself.

LeeMing came alongside.

"Relax," he said, "don't fight it."

With the practise of the Form over, they moved on to work in partners for combat work and Kal teamed up with Marty.

"Marty's our most advanced student," LeeMing warned her.

Kal took several turns attacking Marty, and Marty dealt efficiently with each assault, the final time landing Kal flat on her back. As Kal rolled to her feet, LeeMing came over and pointed at her.

"Change around," he said, "now you take the defensive position."

Kal tugged down her judo-style top. She and Marty briefly bowed to each other, Marty's expression completely focused and relaxed, and Kal felt a sudden pride in her friend.

At age eighteen, Marty received the offer of a stunt film part in America. It could have been the beginning of a successful career and Kal had been gutted. Not gutted by jealousy, gutted by the idea of losing her one and only special friend. She had made a silent promise that if Marty went to the USA, she'd follow and give up her studies, leave her mother and grandmother, just take off. In the end, Marty never accepted the deal, preferring to pursue her interest in electronics. It was a couple of years before Kal told Marty about that vow, leaving it long enough so she could laugh about it instead of cry.

Suddenly Marty attacked and Kal's attention snapped to the present. She felt her opponent's weight, slightly greater than her own, bearing down on her. She countered, pivoted. Got in a blow under the ribs. Then a second to the solar plexus only it didn't land true. Marty got in two blows to impact Kal's kidneys, followed by a light foot strike to the outside of Kal's calf. Kal felt her leg give way. She landed on the mat, Marty upright and positioned over her. The pulse throbbed in Marty's dark glossy neck as she poised to deliver what could be a deathly elbow strike to Kal's temple.

Having gained supremacy, Marty pulled back, allowing Kal to roll up and prepare for a second assault. LeeMing motioned he wanted to take Marty's place.

Now this could be interesting. Earlier on, she'd seen how he had expertise in several martial arts disciplines, not only kung fu. She'd cross-trained in tai chi herself and spent time learning the Japanese martial discipline of aikido, which had increased her versatility. LeeMing must cross-train too. Several of the more advanced kung fu Masters were adept in all the Chinese schools from wing chung to kick-boxing, to tai chi and weapons work. She wondered which would be his specialism.

Up close, LeeMing's looks were distracting. He must have mixed heritage with those lovely eyes and straight, black hair. They bowed briefly and she shifted her gaze away from his face. As her eyes moved, LeeMing dived with the speed and precision of a snake, to pin both her arms to her sides in a move more like a street attack.

She blocked one of his hands, but he got a grip on her right wrist and her counter-punch didn't hit fully home. He'd come right inside her guard, close to her body which was classic kung fu close combat. He applied a lock to her right wrist, forcing it well beyond its natural torque and she absorbed the strain by bending with the movement, then by twisting her hips and dipping her knees. LeeMing gave her hand a vicious, final wrench before releasing it and they exchanged a rapid series of strikes and upper body blocks. *Pah, pah, pah.*

She was forced to lead with her left hand, because of the residual weakness in her right. LeeMing restrained all his movements close to his body, forcing her to bridge the distance to reach him. Damn him. He avoided everything she threw at him, anticipating the weakness in her wrist. Sensing an opening, Kal stepped wide and low, circling behind. LeeMing countered by continuing the circular motion so he ended up behind her with his arm locked across her neck. He inflicted a talon lock on her windpipe, his fingers gripping tight, restricting the airflow.

The pressure built, threatening to implode her larynx. With a lock like that you could kill someone if you wished. Her vision filled with little dappled lights. Now she was on her knees.

When he released the lock, Kal choked. LeeMing spoke right by her ear.

"Sure you can counter attack, you see, the thing is, I expect more. You don't know me and you were waiting to see what I could do. Wrong move. The key is anticipation.

Anticipate my first move before I even twitch a muscle. Then you'll never even need to be in a fight situation."

LeeMing's green eyes looked down at her, steady and clear. Her old trainer, Master Yeung, had a look with the same neutrality, totally free of aggression. LeeMing's breath brushed the side of her face.

"Anticipate. Stay alive," he said.

LeeMing stepped back. He radiated confidence–a man at ease with himself. At the top of his game.

"Carry on," he said as he moved away.

Marty spoke in a low voice, "Like I said, he's not bad."

Later, in the changing rooms, Kal peeled off her clothes before stepping into the shower.

"If you want my opinion," Marty said, "LeeMing had to work hard to get the better of you, in fact, you kept your end up pretty well. I'm glad to see you haven't lost your edge."

"Wow, thanks," Kal shouted over the splashing water, injecting as much sarcasm as she could.

Marty laughed and it was a frank, open laugh, the type where you tip your head back. In all her assignments around the world, Kal hadn't found anyone to match that. Not that she'd looked very hard because Marty was a difficult act to follow. The session had been a good investment of time and she felt better. Now they had work to do.

Before they left the building, LeeMing spoke to Kal.

"I guess you used to train here?"

"It was my regular club for years. I came here when I was six years old and I've loved kung fu ever since. My name's Kal, well, actually my real name is Karla but everyone calls me Kal and I prefer it, even though in India it's a boy's name and it got a bit awkward when a male Bollywood actor became everyone's heartthrob, maybe you've heard of him–he's called Kal Chandra? He's really famous, but I don't care and…" She made herself stop. She was blathering like an idiot. *Get a grip.* "Are you new to London?"

"Oh no, I was born here and I was lucky enough to have Master Yeung pass the club to me."

She hoped he'd continue the conversation, maybe ask her what she did for her work, except he didn't.

"Nice to meet you, please feel free to come along any time you're in town," LeeMing said, "former members are always welcome."

Kal stared at his eyes and searched for something to say, and for the second time that day, she couldn't come up with anything. She was grateful for Marty dragging her away.

Chapter Fourteen

In the past, Marty had been the only person Kal told about the death threats.

Her friend studied a photograph of the most recent letter. Then they scrolled Alesha's photo file, the ceiling lights glinting from Marty's earrings as she listened to Kal's take on Kealy and Scott and the man in the alley. Marty's frown said it all.

"Mum didn't tell me about the security door and then she didn't tell me she's in love. Why the hell not?"

"This is some serious shit. And you say this Scott checks out?"

"He wasn't lying. He was in love with Mum. What Mum felt about *him* I've no idea."

"And?"

Kal shrugged. "And nothing. I didn't warm to him but why should I?"

"It all circles back to Alesha's photo file. We've got to find out more."

"I'll have a chance to get intelligence on Mayor Vankova tomorrow. Assad will be more of a challenge."

"How are you planning to get information? Oh no, don't tell me, you're using your special tactics, like on your journalistic assignments."

Kal knew Marty didn't like to hear about her borderline strategies.

"Please don't tell me, especially if it isn't legal and definitely don't ask me to join in. On top of my ethics,

Wimbledon Lawn Tennis Association won't tolerate any suggestion of disreputable behaviour. I'd be out of a job in a second."

"I know your code and mine's pretty similar. Nothing I do is dishonest."

"Don't take offence, I admire your work, only you know after my father,' Marty said. 'I can't tolerate anything the wrong side of the law."

Their problems with their fathers had glued them together. They were two haunted children. Marty was dead against anything with a whiff of illegal because her father had been a criminal–break-ins, car thefts, the odd mugging, plus, of course, the horrible way he used to beat up Marty's mother. It went on for years, before Marty's mother succeeded in kicking him out.

"Intelligence gathering is an art," Kal said.

Marty shook her head. "All that brainwashing from Khan, all that stuff he rammed into you, it wasn't right."

Marty always called Kal's father 'Khan'.

"It was a game."

"Most dads take their kids to the park. Khan tutored you remorselessly in weird stuff. If it was such fun, why did you keep it quiet from your mum? It was like bloody abuse."

Kal felt her discomfort kicking up. She tried to ram it down. "I enjoyed it and without it I'd never have made it in my career, not to the front lines."

"Enjoyed it? You're kidding me, right? You were his perfect protégé and he took full advantage. You know, don't you, how victims of abuse are often in denial? It's unnerving how blind you are to it."

Kal was far from blind, only she could never get to the right answers. Who could know the line between free will and force? Especially between father and daughter. She'd agonised over that. Why had it been wrong for her father to teach her? Only, if it had been right, there'd have been no need to keep it secret, would there? Deep down, she knew it was *what* he taught her which was the problem. And there was a dark side to it even Marty didn't know.

"Back off, Marty."

"I can't help it. It was wrong and he gave me the creeps. There was something not right about Khan."

Only Marty would have the guts to say it and only Marty could get away with it.

"You're wrong."

Wisely, her friend remained silent. They were going over old ground.

Kal stared out the window. Her father had dark eyes and black hair and handsome Indian looks. Looking at him you'd never spot anything bad. He'd been demanding with her and he'd expected her to follow his instructions to the letter. And like Marty had known as a child, David Khan wasn't a man you disobeyed.

Marty folded her arms. "Okay, so your mum's smart and she was on to something. We need to figure out what as soon as, and this man here," Marty stabbed with her finger, "Assad. He's a tennis fan. He joins the rich and famous to come to the Wimbledon Finals every summer."

"Got any ideas how I can meet him?"

"No, but one of my team used to work private security for his wives. I'll put the two of you in contact."

"Hey, wait a minute, you said *your* team. You got promoted?"

"Didn't I say? I'm heading up Specialist Electronics with lead responsibility for detection of all devices, meaning identification of bugs and bombs."

"Congratulations."

Marty leaned to look out the window. "The man tailing you is unnerving. Someone watching everything you do? That gives me the creeps."

"I probably put him off."

Kal knew neither of them were convinced about that. She quickly tapped the keyboard to select a subset of photographs.

"Kealy, Vankova, Assad and then there are four I've no names for. They're all taken in London except the Indian man in the last picture. From the background, I'd bet that one's taken in Kolkata, India."

"That's the same place as Calcutta, right?"

"Yup, only they changed the spelling from the old colonial name to Kolkata. And look at this."

Kal zoomed in on the occupants of a car. Mayor Vankova was about to take the front seat. In the rear, a face stared straight at the camera. Kal blew up the image as much as she could.

Marty leaned forward, her dark eyes fixed on the screen. "What the hell's going on there?"

The passenger was a young girl with Indian looks and though the computer enhancement blurred her features, her eyes were two huge orbs.

Marty shivered. "That kid looks scared out of her wits."

Kal bit her lip. She agreed and she'd seen desperation in children's eyes before, at the camp all the time, and in the past when she'd held the hand of a child who'd witnessed the butchering of his entire family. It was an unforgettable look.

Marty pushed the chair away from the desk.

"Send me copies of the unknown mug shots and I'll ask around at work first thing." Marty's voice was grim. "I guess you're not going back to your place, Kal, so you're sure you don't want to come over to mine?"

"I prefer to stay here. I should be around in case Mum comes back or, you know, someone makes contact."

"All right, but make sure you close up tight. I know you're capable and very independent, in fact, too independent and it can get you into trouble, so for goodness sake call if you need me."

Then Marty insisted on checking all the windows even though the apartment was seven floors up. In the hallway, Marty patted the door.

"This is top of the range. I've a bad, a very bad, feeling about all of this–we'd better damn well keep in contact. Promise not to go anywhere or do anything without keeping me up to date."

"I'm glad you're here, Marty. What would I do without you?"

"I know what I'd do without you," Marty said. "I'd live a long life."

Kal laughed. "Yeah, but wouldn't it be a tad boring?"

Chapter Fifteen

With closed eyes, Kal sat on the edge of the bed. Marty had been right, she'd been the perfect pupil, though only because as a child she'd adored her father, and a word of praise from him made her happier than anything. But how could she ever admit the monstrous truth to Marty, or even, to herself? It wasn't only surveillance and infiltration and mind games he taught her.

They made many visits to the concrete bunker hidden in the countryside. Deserted. The security fence and main door mysteriously open for them to enter. The bunker quiet except for their footsteps on the gritty floor.

The first time, Kal clamped her hand over her nose to block out the harsh smell and she hated it. Still she carried on, adjusting her stance, willing her arms to relax, resettling her shoulders, squeezing and resqueezing the trigger as her father encouraged her and coached her. She loathed the acrid smell of the after-shot and the smack of the bullets penetrating her ear-dampers. Then, after each series of shots, the whine of the motor as it propelled the target close up for their inspection.

David Khan took her to that firing range a few days after her twelfth birthday. After months, her expertise finally pleased him. That's when he'd extracted her promise to continue when she was older and he'd given her the name and address of the only place where he'd allow her to do it.

As normal, he'd given no explanation, and as usual, Kal asked no questions. Then four weeks later her father died.

The shame went deep and Kal knew she'd never be rid of it. Never be rid of who and what her father was, and she'd been like a sponge, soaking it up from him.

No surprise that after all her father's psychological training how she'd turned those same techniques against him, to sense and imagine and dig out the part David Khan kept hidden. The part she'd always known was there. The evil part.

Kal put her head in her hands and cried.

Chapter Sixteen

Kal had been waiting for a call from Spinks. Yet when he contacted her, it filled her with dread. The inspector suggested meeting in St James Park, and he even told her which entrance she should take to find him. He would be on the third bench on the south side of the lake.

Many Londoners love St James Park with its weeping willows and pleasant ponds. Tourists like it too, for its view across the lake to Buckingham Palace. Banks of daffodils stood knee high and the spring crocus were in bloom, in a sea of yellow and purple. It took Kal fifteen minutes to arrive at Spinks' rendezvous and she found him in the sunshine, seemingly reading a newspaper.

"Hello, Inspector."

Spinks put aside the paper, not bothering to scan nor even finish a sentence, meaning he'd probably not been reading it at all.

"Good morning, Ms Medi."

Spinks stayed quiet as a couple passed by and in the moment's silence, Kal heard her heart drumming. Did he have news? What had he uncovered?

"I know it's a very difficult time and I want to be straight with you. If you'd allow me to summarise–you reported your mother missing two days ago and according to Sarah Wiseman, Alesha Medi had already been out of contact for two days previous. This has been corroborated by neighbours and colleagues. It would be unusual for any demand or ransom to be delivered longer than forty-eight hours after a disappearance and we're already dealing with a probable four days. Can you confirm you've received no contact relating to your mother whatsoever?"

"None."

"Secondly, the letter. The paper and ink are standard and therefore untraceable. There were no prints on it other than yours and Alesha's. Thirdly, the apartment–forensics found no trace of organic or inorganic material to indicate violence. In conclusion, my investigations so far have drawn a blank."

Kal's unease grew. Marty had urged her to tell Spinks about the photo file only she couldn't bring herself to. Not until she knew more, because those people were invincible and she didn't have a shred against them. With her mother's life at risk, she only trusted her own hands.

"Where does it leave us?"

"I'll be continuing my investigations and if there's something to uncover, I shall uncover it. It's a question of being thorough and persistent."

Spinks' hands rested on his thighs and he looked straight at her.

"I'm impressed with your work, Ms Medi. Your photographs from the refugee camp had a big impact. I felt I knew those people and knew their stories and the terrible journey they'd taken to get to safety. They must have trusted you tremendously."

Kal shrugged off the compliment.

"Have you found any more information on the death-threats?" Spinks asked.

"I tried. Nannie wasn't well."

"It's important so please keep trying. Now, there's another matter we should discuss and it concerns your grandfather and your father and the records of their deaths."

The spring air felt suddenly crisper and clearer. Kal stared at Spinks and at the dark pores on his face which later would reveal afternoon shadow.

The coroner returned a verdict of death by natural causes for grandfather Sunni and the police conclusion on her father's motorbike crash had been accidental death. She stared at Spinks' chiselled features.

"What the hell is that supposed to mean?"

"I feel it's wise to update you on all the facts. First of all, I checked your grandmother's accident. There were very few notes on the house fire and I've no evidence to suggest it was malignantly set. However, your grandfather's death is another matter. The coroner found traces of a foreign substance which he said could have been a residue from the breakdown of your grandfather's medication. However, the rate of decay was much slower than he would have anticipated. Given the lack of any additional evidence, it was concluded your grandfather's cardiac arrest was due to his diagnosed heart disease."

"Then his original conclusion is still valid."

"The coroner is retired now, although I managed to trace him and he specifically told me that in a current case we'd have the means to detect whether the said substance was deliberately and malevolently introduced."

Kal stopped her lip from trembling. "Meaning he had suspicions about Grandad Sunni's death?"

"Precisely."

Oh god no. Then a horrible thought occurred to her. What if Nannie had lied about the fire being her fault? What if Nannie had been targeted too?

"Your father's motorbike skidded out of control and impacted at high speed. He was mortally wounded and died instantly. There were no suspicious circumstances. However, I do have a couple of questions about David Khan."

Kal stared at Spinks.

"How did your parents meet?"

"That's got nothing to do with it."

"I need you to cooperate with this investigation, Ms Medi. Tell me what you know."

"It won't help." She shook her head. "Okay. In the days before Mum got her lucky break she worked freelance. One of those early assignments took her to Pakistan to interview women villagers. I think they'd formed a co-operative and got micro-credit from a UK charity to plant cotton in place of poppies. It was Mum's type of thing because they were going against tradition and wanted a better life for themselves and I'm sure you know the heroin trade is rampant in the border region between Pakistan and Afghanistan. Governments are always trying to wean villagers away from lucrative, poppy propagation. Mum met Dad there."

"Your father, David Khan, he was a journalist too, wasn't he? Do you know what he was doing at that time?"

"I can't remember. He was in the same foothills, I think maybe investigating the network of laboratories turning out raw heroin. Mum told me the two of them met again once they came back to England and their relationship went from there."

Kal could see he hadn't yet got to the point of his questioning. She could feel it coming, like a crushing wave rolling in across the ocean. She braced herself.

"I know you were only twelve. Please think back, Ms Medi, what was he working on at the time he died?"

At the time he died. Her brain picked out the words and amplified them to huge. Out of Spink's line of sight, Kal's hand curled around a slat of the bench and gripped it tight.

At the time he died, she had been having a perfectly ordinary day, until her mother met her at the school gates. Kal guessed the terrible news from her mother's expression.

She had fled because facing him being gone was like having part of her cut away. A part she couldn't live without. Her father didn't have to be perfect for her to love him. For all his faults, when she was with David Khan she felt special. He shared his real self with her, his real passion, and dark or light, that passion meant something. Of course, questions had been forming in her mind. Questions and suspicions that one day she would've put to him. One day, she'd have found the courage, right? And when that day came, her father would have given her sound answers–guileless, proper answers that would've put everything straight in her head about what he taught her and how he knew the extreme things he knew. When David Khan died, he robbed her of that hope.

Kal gripped the bench tighter. "Sorry, I've no idea what Dad was working on, only Mum might know."

Spinks' eyes drilled into her. "I see."

As if anticipating she might start interrogating him, Spinks stood to leave.

"All in good time, Ms Medi. I can't answer any of your questions right now. I'll be in touch as soon as I have the full picture."

Spinks tossed his newspaper into the bin and off he went, the dark tails of his jacket flapping in time to his steps.

It was only once he was out of sight Kal let her emotions well up. Had Grandfather Sunni been targeted? And what about Nannie? Her whole life was crashing down around her.

Chapter Seventeen

Kal stood at the entrance to the National Gallery where columns stretched the length of the facade, creating a lookalike of the Greek Parthenon. She leant her hand on the cool stone. That night, her mother's voice had called to her in her nightmares. A frantic feeling of searching stayed with Kal, and it was making her shaky. *Stay on track*, she ordered herself, *make the encounter with Vankova pay.*

She had practically a one-hundred-and-eighty-degree view of Trafalgar Square below. A light drizzle fell and she scanned the crowds. All the way here, she knew covert eyes spied on her. It had been impossible to pick out her follower in the crowded underground, and now they most likely mingled with the tourists in the square. As the drizzle turned to a steady shower, Kal moved into the shelter of the pillars.

Dressed in a navy-blue trouser suit covered with a fluorescent cycling vest, Selena Vankova pedalled to the steps. The Mayor of London often liked to vaunt her green credentials by arriving at official functions by bicycle.

The fourth most visited Art Gallery in the world, the National Gallery today hosted a posse of media for the opening of a Special Exhibition. Camera at the ready, Kal trailed behind with the press. Wrangling a place at this event had taken one short phone call, thanks to her photojournalist contacts.

Vankova shook her brown, bobbed hair and turned to address the crowd.

"Today's event marks the Fiftieth Anniversary of the Special Exhibitions Wing."

In her late forties and trim, Vankova had an innocent appearance and her neat hair style and blue eyes added to her air of openness. According to the press, Selena Vankova's china doll face hid a woman of masterly strategy, the youngest ever to become Mayor of London. Vankova spoke with the enthusiasm of a good orator.

Once the Mayor finished her address, the entourage of senior staff and press shuffled inside. They would take a thirty-minute private tour of a selection of Van Gogh's works, so Kal judged her chances of wrangling a conversation with Vankova as high. They continued at a snail's pace, Vankova in the lead, chatting with the gallery manager.

Kal trailed at the back. Despite its polished presentation, Vankova's internet site was jammed full of promotional shots that were predictable and static, which was good because Kal was counting on it as her way in.

They reached the exhibition hall. With a high ceiling and doctored acoustics, the space gave the impression of a palace full of treasure. The group clustered around Vankova as the gallery manager started a commentary on the first of the masterpieces. Kal edged forwards, clocking the Mayor's body language and observing her mannerisms.

Once they'd studied three of the paintings, Kal broke away and went to a seating area in the middle of the room. Shrugging off her jacket, she tugged down her dress a couple of centimetres. Today, she'd chosen a red velvet number. She extracted her laptop, at the same time listening to the Gallery Manager as he detailed the major, tragic events in the artist's life. In a few clicks, she loaded up the shots she'd taken so far, intending to wait for a chance to bring the screen over to Vankova. Only she didn't need to.

As the others trotted to the next painting, Selena Vankova detached from the group and came over.

Vankova shook her head lightly before she spoke, so that the bobbed edge of her hair swished from side to side. An orchestrated move, Kal thought, in order to appear younger and less sharp.

"Good morning, have we met before?" Vankova asked.

Kal stood up. When Vankova had first spoken, a flicker of recognition passed over her face. How could that be? Kal had never met Vankova. Now, the tiniest suggestion of a contraction started below the Mayor's left eye. It told Kal Vankova used to have a tic. She must have trained herself out of it for public life. Only a deep-seated anxiety would bring that back.

"I don't think we've met," Kal said.

Vankova spewed a few sentences about her interest in the arts and the importance for London and Kal saw the woman scouring her memory for the time and place where they'd crossed. The more Vankova searched, the more the tiny muscle under her eye strained. Finally, it gave in and twitched. What was it that so disturbed her?

Kal lifted up the laptop. "Here are some shots I took this morning - you arriving in a rush with the rain spraying from your front wheel, you speaking to the woman in the queue as you chained your bicycle and the two of you laughing, then a shot of water running down the statue in Trafalgar Square. You see how easy it is to capture dynamism? Images like this mirror your energy and enthusiasm as Mayor. Don't you think they'd look good on your publicity?"

"Why? Are you pitching for a job? What's your name?"

"I'm freelance, so I'm always looking for interesting employment."

Kal smoothed her hair, pulling it over her shoulder and Vankova's eyes widened. Yes, the Mayor must have met

Alesha and maybe the contact had been brief because the generation difference was fooling her.

The gallery manager came over, ostentatiously checking his watch.

"Selena, will you be rejoining us? We don't have long before I need to open to the public."

"I'll be with you in a moment, give me a couple more seconds," Vankova said.

Kal's eyes didn't leave Vankova's face. Time was running out, and the chances of tempting the Mayor into a private meeting to discuss publicity seemed slim, because Vankova's suspicion would prevent her accepting. She needed to get some juice, to squeeze Vankova and see what came out.

"One thing though, perhaps you met my mother, her name's Alesha Medi."

She spoke loudly, firing out her mother's name and there came the giveaway – Vankova's tic fired twice.

"You're correct, we've never met. I made a mistake."

This was the precise moment to press her advantage and she injected venom into her voice.

"Oh, but I think you met my mother, didn't you Mayor Vankova, only you'd rather forget it."

As a red flush raced up the woman's neck, Kal leant forwards, well inside the Mayor's personal space. She could add a great deal of menace to her manner when she wanted to, and to Vankova's credit, the woman didn't back off.

Kal spoke directly in her face. "I know what you're trying to hide."

It was a complete bluff but Vankova's pupils dilated. An extreme anxiety reaction.

"I don't know who you are or what your game is." All pretence at civility had fallen away and Vankova raised her voice. "I'm ordering you off the premises right now!"

The others in the group turned in their direction.

"Don't ever come near me again!"

Vankova gave Kal a look loaded with hatred and stalked away. Bribes, sex, extortion, drugs? With her squeaky-clean image, what would be Vankova's worst nightmare for a journalist to discover?

The manager detached himself from the group and sidled up, blinking apologetically. He was a timid man and his fingers fidgeted with the frame of his glasses. In trying not to stare at Kal's breasts, his focus settled somewhere in the vicinity of her left ear.

"I'm sorry but, er, I shall have to ask you to leave."

"That's not a problem."

She packed up and walked back to the entrance. At last some progress - she was digging in the right direction.

Chapter Eighteen

Marty let the dragon doors swing closed behind her. *Pam, pam, pam.* Kal was kicking the life out of the training bag. One glance at her friend and Marty almost took a step backwards. No one in their right mind would want to be on the wrong side of Kal in a mood like that.

"Wo- ah. What the f– has happened?"

Kal dealt out more blows. "Vankova." *Pam, pam, pam.* "I've got more bits of the puzzle."

"And now you want to kill her?" Marty didn't mean it completely as a joke.

Kal leant breathless against the wall.

"Mum knows plenty of trustworthy photojournalists, so why did she call me at the camp?"

Marty judged it best to keep quiet.

"I went to the Mayor's press conference. Vankova came up to me because she thought she recognised me. I realised she must have met Mum. Anyway, Vankova was really rattled and she's got this nervous tic which she must have spent *years* training herself out of. It came back when we started talking. Only a deep-seated anxiety would bring that back."

"And?"

"Her pupils dilated when I said Alesha's name."

"Doesn't sound too serious to me."

"But it is. It means everything. Underneath her cool exterior, as soon as she realised who I reminded her of, the Mayor was shitting herself."

"Yes, but it's only a couple of nervous-"

Kal rubbed her knuckles. "Listen to me. Blackmail, pornography, extortion or maybe hard drugs. She's covering up something serious. Something which would rock the headlines. I know it."

"Are you sure you're not grabbing at straws?"

Kal pushed back her hair and took a swig of water. Of course it sounded far-fetched. Crazy. Whacko. Because the twisted workings of the criminal psyche were not her friend's domain. The only person in the world who would have agreed with Kal's conclusion would be her father.

"What about the death threat?" Marty asked.

Good, Marty was on the ball and Kal needed that.

"You're right, the death threat is a wild card and I've no idea how it fits in. But I'm going to find out."

What she needed was action because the big problem was, how was she going to find proof?

"I'm going after the tail again tonight," Kal said. "And this time I'm prepared to damage him to get more. You up for it?"

Later that evening, they joined another of LeeMing's sessions. Kal found it hard to focus. Twice in the Form she hesitated over the correct sequence. Shit, everything was messing with her mind.

In the combats, she went onto automatic, bowing without properly seeing her opponent. *Pam. Pam.* Her opponent was skilled and his strike whistled past her ear. Kal heard her own breathing mixed with the sound of her father's motorbike engine, the throaty rev turning into a high-pitched overdrive, as he spun out of control. *Pam.* Her opponent's fist struck her torso and Kal felt the air gush out of her. She threw a return strike and misjudged the punch.

Her fist sank into her opponent's abdomen full force. He doubled and for a split second she thought she'd taken out his spleen. Crumpling to the mat, he began retching. LeeMing sprinted over.

"Oh god," she said, "we should call an ambulance."

She avoided LeeMing's glare as he examined the student and put him in the recovery position.

"You're lucky. Very lucky. Check his status every few minutes." LeeMing's tone was curt.

Strict code within the club dictated all students restrict themselves to light contact, especially senior members. The other students had stopped to stare and Kal felt her cheeks colouring.

When the man finally sat up, she breathed a sigh of relief.

"A blow like that can cause internal injuries," LeeMing said. "I'm sending you for a full check up at casualty. And you," LeeMing pointed at Kal, "get changed and see me at the end."

She sat out for the rest of the session. What excuse could she give? She knew there was none. When training finished and LeeMing came over, she screwed herself up inside.

"You should know better. When you let emotions interfere, it always affects judgement. The discipline of martial arts is maintaining clarity and the more advanced you are, the more important that is."

LeeMing was angry. Heat flushed Kal's cheeks again. She should have refused a new opponent and paired up with Marty instead.

"My predecessor, Master Yeung, spoke highly of you," LeeMing said, "and I'm sure he'd say what happened tonight was out of character."

Kal pressed her lips together. So, he'd been checking up on her.

"Yes, I took the liberty of speaking to Master Yeung. When someone with your level of skill comes to the neighbourhood, I make it my business to keep up-to-date." LeeMing pulled on a sweatshirt. "For you to mess up like that there must be a real problem up here." He tapped the side of his head. "What's going on?"

It took her off-guard. LeeMing spoke as if he expected an answer and if it had been Master Yeung, Kal wouldn't have hesitated. The Master, or Shifu, of your club, commands the greatest respect and students follow their instruction, emulate their conduct and rely on their knowledge, just as she and Marty had done with Master Yeung. Alongside combat skills, all students learnt the strict moral code passed down as part of the Shaolin Temple Tradition–respect, ethics, correct behaviour.

Kal scuffed her foot against the mat. Though a great deal of the respect she held for Master Yeung transferred to LeeMing, not all of it did. The other students filed into the showers and the room fell quiet. As the Shifu of the club, she knew LeeMing deserved an explanation.

"I've *never* misjudged like that and I know there's no justification. Thing is… my mother's missing and the police are trying to find her. And on top of that someone's following me."

Being stalked messed with your mind–she knew that. Putting a stop to being tailed would give two important results–it would give back her space and it could provide intelligence.

"That sounds serious, though if you're looking for an excuse, I'm telling you now, nothing justifies your lack of control."

Kal could do nothing except squirm.

"So–any ideas where she's gone? Do you think you being followed is linked to your mother's disappearance?"

He didn't ask if she was sure she was being followed, which would have been most people's first question. It was a curious omission.

"I don't know. They've been watching Mum's apartment too and I tried to catch them and they got away."

"What do the police have to say about that?"

"I didn't tell them. I want to know *why* someone's following me because I'm sure it will help me find Mum."

"Which explains why you decided to deal with it yourself." LeeMing crossed his arms. "Take it from me Kal, martial arts can't protect you from everything. Going after someone is a huge risk. Was Marty with you?"

"No."

"Master Yeung told me how the two of you worked your way up the ranks together. It seems to me the logical step is to try again with Marty helping, I'm right, aren't I? And I hope I don't have to remind you that as senior members who've earned your Black Sash, you're both ethically bound to avoid harming other people. Am I making myself clear?"

"I know and Marty does too, of course we do. But I need anything that can help. Can you understand?"

"Of course, and understand this–it's my job to make sure you don't overstep the mark."

His eyes were clear and calm.

"You're not against it then?"

"I'm not against it and I'm certainly not for it," LeeMing said, "although I don't think my opinion matters, does it? I think you've already made up your mind."

A bunch of students exited the changing rooms and called out a friendly goodnight. LeeMing gave a nod in their direction and waited for the dragon doors to clack shut.

"The most important thing for me is protecting the reputation of the club–which is why I'll be coming along to make sure things don't go off track."

Kal bit back her protest because LeeMing's remark was not a request.

Back in the changing rooms, Marty rolled her eyes. "Why on earth did you tell him?"

"I owed him. You saw what I did."

"Listen, we all make mis–"

"Don't, I don't deserve it. LeeMing'd be within his rights to boot me out in disgrace and I'd never be welcome in a kung fu club again. I don't care if he wants to come along as a monitor, or a minder, or whatever, and, hey, look on the positive side, he might be useful."

"LeeMing's got a girlfriend you know."

Marty knew her too well. Marty was good at relationships, it was one of her strong points. Whereas Kal considered herself terrible at them, and only good at the sex side, after which, everything went downhill. As soon as anyone got close it made her edgy. Maybe that's why she'd chosen a profession which made any meaningful relationship pretty much impossible. Of course, that never stopped her wanting it.

"I'm not telling you because I'm jealous," Marty said, "it's to stop you getting hurt."

"Shit, Marty, relationships aren't exactly my strong point and I know that."

"We all know that."

"I'm better off on my own, I prefer it that way."

On that one Marty made no comment, not even on how good a liar Kal was.

When they walked out to the training area, LeeMing sat waiting.

She'd already planned an idea to share with Marty and now she shared it with both of them. By the end, they were in agreement.

As they left, LeeMing wished her good luck and somehow Kal couldn't quite kick the idea he'd been involved in similar interceptions.

Outside the training centre, they split up and she headed off alone.

Chapter Nineteen

Kal felt the anticipation. It was an intoxicating high because at last she was going to get answers.

She found the beginning of the footpath for crossing the Common. At weekends, scores of nature-lovers came here to walk to Wimbledon windmill, with the sporty ones continuing for miles, taking advantage of the vast expanse of heath. Hardly anyone took this route at night because the residents were too sensible to tempt fate.

A quarter moon glanced through the clouds and she imagined her pursuer becoming bolder as they left behind the bright lights. Whoever tailed her was persistent. She hadn't put them off in the alley at all.

The footpath quickly turned to mud. Up ahead, deep in the Common, came the haunting call of an owl and around ten minutes walking was enough to feel she had entered a world far away from the city. Behind her came the sharp snap of a twig and Kal froze. Crouching low, she waited, breathing in the smell of wet leaves and imagining her pursuer pressing themselves into the undergrowth.

The chase—one mind against another. Your skill and nerves against theirs.

Her father set her the challenge of tracking him at Victoria station. She followed him from the overground rail lines into the underground system. In the thrill of the pursuit, she believed she was on his trail.

People pressed close on the platform, wearing their office clothes and smelling of after-work sweat and faded-out perfume. Cigarette fumes clung to jackets. She picked her way, weaving, ducking down whenever she thought her father spotted her.

After a few minutes, she lost sight of him. She started sweating, and the point when she began to fear failure was probably when she got confused. The mind works like that. A while later her father crept right up behind her, unseen and unsuspected. When he put his hand on her shoulder she bit back a scream.

She'd been ten at the time and a woman nearby had given her father a suspicious look and he'd disarmed the woman with one charming smile.

When the moon came back into view, Kal continued down the path.

The windmill was in the middle of the Common. Originally for grinding corn, it now served as a coffee shop. The dark, stubby building loomed in a clearing, while against the night sky, the four sails marked a giant, black 'x'. A couple of barns sat to the side. Kal ran beyond the buildings and continued into the undergrowth.

Now the thrill escalated to excitement. In a moment, she would double back and Marty and LeeMing would close in from the opposite side. Choosing a good spot, she crouched beside a tree. Though her breathing came lightly, she covered her mouth with her hand to block every tiny sign of her presence.

Patchy cloud had moved in and whenever the moon slipped from view, she was plunged into darkness. She'd have to rely on her hearing to detect her pursuer's approach and, since no wind rustled the trees, any sound would carry a long way.

As clouds passed over the moon, Kal heard a light rustle ahead of her. Perhaps it was a deer. There were plenty on the Common, though on a still night like this, wouldn't it have been aware of her and kept away? As she strained in that direction, a small suspicion began to form. At Victoria station, the hunter had become the hunted. Why had *that* lesson in stealth come to mind?

Her excitement died, and in the hollow it left behind, apprehension crept in, and with it a twinge of fear. Wait. What if there was someone sneaking up from the other side? The hairs on Kal's arms stood on end because no way could the person following her have circled the windmill so quickly without giving themselves away.

Your skill against theirs. Your strategy against theirs.

Her apprehension grew. Some who hunted preferred to work alone whilst others operated in packs.

Call it off, said the voice inside her head, *something's wrong*. Her friends were close, hiding by the outhouse behind the windmill, waiting for her signal. She shouted at the top of her voice. "It's a trap!"

Crrassshhh. Something came out of the undergrowth and charged with speed straight at her. *Get out of the way!* Her muscles reacted before her mind. A crushing head-butt impacted her torso. Connecting with her nerve centre. Threatening her internal organs. As her feet left the ground, air fled her lungs.

She landed with force onto her back. In the darkness, she didn't struggle. *You know how to fight with your eyes closed.* It was true, they'd practised with Master Yeung in the dark. He'd taught them how to sense the enemy's intention from the shifts of their body mass, from their changing grip.

A man was on top of her, holding her down. Strong hands grasped her head and bashed it viciously against the ground. Once. Then drew her head back for a second smash. An instant before the impact, Kal threw her weight to the side and, in the black, she struck up with her palm to where she knew the face would be, catching the septum of the nose and powering her palm upwards to break it. Warm blood gushed down. *Strike to his groin.* He anticipated and caught her leg, grasping it and twisting her knee. *He's got combat skills. But he's too rigid. He doesn't absorb.* Her pelvis and torso spiralled into the twist and now her face grazed the dirt and jagged edges of stones dug into her eye socket.

Her opponent lost his hold. *Get to your feet.* Kal heard shouting and the sounds of fighting. She rolled to crouching in a bed of leaves and the moon slipped into view and her opponent threw a punch. She snaked her upper body out of range. *Fluid—arcs, circles, spirals. Draw him in.* Block, strike, block.

"Kal!"

She heard Marty's shout and it was followed by a guttural smack as someone took a blow. Then came a horrible splintering of branches. Or bone.

In a disciplined stance, she moved back, keeping her body weight close to the ground. Then, at a ninety-degree angle, she felt a second attacker closing in. Two against one. But the ultra-low stances of the Hung Gar style had always been a favourite of hers and she waited, judging her moment, then with explosive force launched at her second assailant. She felt his instant of surprise and it gave her the advantage. Something flashed in his hand. A weapon. Aikido style, she somersaulted, escaping the arc of his arm. Surely the moon would disappear soon and she anticipated the blackness, crouching like a tigress, ready to spring.

Then, from nowhere, she sensed a lull, as if the attackers were a highly trained force used to working together. Someone, somewhere, had called it off. They were melting into the trees.

"They're getting away!" The warning came from LeeMing.

Kal recognised LeeMing's silhouette as he took off in pursuit. Taking a burning gasp, she followed. One eye was blind. She ignored it, pushing through branches to reach the path.

Ahead, LeeMing took a running dive and brought someone down and the two of them thrashed on the forest floor. She was five seconds behind, four, three and closing. LeeMing was poised above his opponent, and with a jolt, she recognised the type of hold LeeMing had on the man. LeeMing's lock was Dim mak style. Her father's style. Then a deafening noise rang out. *Gunshot.* The sound ricocheted through the woods.

LeeMing released his hold and his opponent scrambled up. She could see the man's hands as he ran away and there was no gun. So where had the gun shot come from?

Sudden terror flushed her mind blank. Where was Marty? Had the shot come from behind? What if Marty had been…

"Marty!"

Silence.

"Marty!"

She stumbled this way and that, panting and losing all sense of direction.

"I'm over here," Marty called.

Her friend walked out of the trees, standing upright on her two legs–in one piece, not blown apart, not missing a limb, not bleeding to death from a bullet.

Kal could feel sticky blood running down her own face. "Oh god, I thought you'd been–"

"Shot? Oh no, don't worry about me," Marty said. "He fired into the air. Thank god you shouted because it gave us enough warning to save our skins. Hey, it's okay, everything's all right. We're all okay."

Kal let her head flop. Yes, of course, it had been a coordinated team, maybe six altogether, she should have realised sooner, and their attackers had been much more accomplished than she'd anticipated. They'd stepped up their game since the alleyway. This has been an ambush.

LeeMing came over and stood with his hands resting on his knees.

"Why the hell did you let him go!" she shouted at him.

"Because of the gun shot, idiot. You want to get us killed? Marty said he fired in the air so they meant it as a warning, but if one of them carried a gun you can bet the others did too. This wasn't an amateur operation, it was planned and executed meticulously. They had the upper hand all along. We thought we had the jump on them when we were out-manned and out-smarted from the beginning."

She could hear the anger in his voice and she didn't blame him. Kal felt sick and for a moment she allowed the pain in her head to overwhelm her.

"You're right," she said, "yeah, I know you're right, they weren't at capacity, we didn't beat them, they decided to pull back."

"Those people are professionals and I'm not talking ex-police or private detectives who follow the rules. No, they were the type you don't want to be messing with," LeeMing said.

Now his calm manner in the planning of tonight made sense to her, and so did the Dim Mak hold he'd had on his opponent's neck. LeeMing must have connections with the underworld.

"How the hell do you figure that out?" Marty demanded.

"I make my living legitimately through martial arts but for generations my family have been part of the Triad and plenty of my contemporaries are active members. Ever heard of it?"

"The Triad—you mean the Chinese mafia, don't you? Best known for protection rackets and gambling dens," Kal said.

"Aren't the Triad the ones who cut people's hands off?" Marty said.

"You should know better than to perpetuate stereotypes, Marty," LeeMing said. "The Triad believes in swift justice, which is extremely effective in keeping order in the Chinese community. It's thanks to the Triad we've one of the lowest crime rates in the city. I'm no longer an active member though in my time I came across plenty of weaponry and vicious, merciless types and I can tell you, those people weren't the sort you want to mess with."

"Are you saying they were prepared to shoot us? I find that hard to believe," Marty said.

"Then you'd better wake up–this is much worse than you imagine. You don't carry a gun unless you're willing to use it," LeeMing said, "I think you'd better start telling me exactly what's going on."

Warm blood oozed down the side of Kal's face and she pressed the wound shut with her fingers. Never underestimate your opponent–it was one of the cardinal rules. She should have known better.

By the time they got back to 701, Marty's neck was aching like crazy. LeeMing sat tight lipped on the sofa while Kal told him about the death threat, her mother's photofile and the details on Kealy, Scott and Vankova. Of course, Marty didn't add the merest whisper about David Khan. Keeping silent about Khan had been an unspoken agreement between her and Kal since childhood.

Marty made hot drinks. There was no point in trying to talk sense into Kal and she'd learned the hard way how her friend wasn't someone who easily accepted help. The best thing Marty could do was stick close.

"One of my colleagues identified two others from the photos," Marty said, as she placed mugs on the table, "and you're not going to like it. They're Randall Greeves retired High Court Judge, and Aaron DeVille, Hollywood producer who loves England. We're dealing with people with an enormous power base."

"Not to mention professional hit men," LeeMing said. "Good job you've got us on your side."

"I didn't ask for your help."

LeeMing massaged his leg. "You're welcome," he said.

If her face didn't hurt so much, Marty would have laughed at the way Kal scowled.

"We need a plan," LeeMing said, "and one which is much smarter than tonight's."

Kal was about to shoot back a comment when her phone buzzed. The look on her friend's face made Marty slop hot tea onto her own hand. "What is it?" she asked.

"Shit," Kal said. "Spinks has found a body."

Chapter Twenty

"A neighbour alerted police," Spinks said. "Thank you for coming so quickly. The victim's name is Derick Sanders."

Spinks made no comment about the nasty gash at Kal's temple. She'd barely had time to clean it.

Derick Sanders, yes, she knew Derick. He was a photojournalist.

A patrol car sat outside, its blue light flashing in the dark street. The inspector's steps sounded greasy on the pavement and Kal followed Spinks through the taped-off front entrance.

In a newly converted warehouse, Derick's apartment had a kitchen and bathroom on the lower floor. It smelled of spicy food, maybe take-out Thai, she thought.

They took an open staircase to an upper mezzanine which was full of people processing the crime scene. The mezzanine was an open plan lounge with a sleeping area. Derick had decorated the tallest wall a bright red and another in sunset orange and for the ceiling rafters he'd chosen a see-through blue wash. That was where they had found him and she could see the length of rope the paramedics cut to get him down. The wrapped body lay on a gurney, ready to be taken away.

Kal held back as Spinks approached the body. But he knelt and beckoned her forward.

"I want you to take a look," Spinks said.

The room seemed suddenly crowded–ambulance crew, the coroner's staff, forensics team, two more police officers downstairs craning upwards to catch the action. Kal felt their eyes on her.

She had seen dead bodies in Eastern Europe and in Africa, though resulting from war or disease and always anonymous. She had only met Derick a couple of times, although her mother had talked about him. It was more terrible when it was someone you knew. She tried to walk normally, ignoring her spaghetti legs.

Spinks peeled open the top of the body bag and she saw how Derick's eyes bulged. The flesh of his face was purple.

"This was staged to appear as a suicide and for now I'm keeping an open mind. We'll know more after the post-mortem. The body has been identified by a neighbour, tell me, do you recognise this man?"

Kal stared down. If the body had been identified, why was Spinks asking? Why had he called her here in the middle of the night? Except she knew why, it could only mean one thing–she was a suspect.

"Yes this is Derick Sanders, he worked with Mum plenty of times."

Derick had joined the newspaper less than a year ago, moving down from Glasgow. Young, and a risk-taker, he'd become one of Alesha's favourites. Her mother said Derick had a quick mind and an even quicker eye for the action, though Kal suspected Alesha also wanted to give him a hand up the ladder.

If it hadn't been Derick swinging from a rope, would it have been her? When Kal didn't return in time, had Alesha involved Derick instead? Were the surveillance photographs his work?

"What's your take on it?" Spinks asked.

He watched her with that hawk gaze of his, as if she was a mouse running for cover with nowhere to hide.

"My gut tells me Derick wasn't the type to do this." She waved her hand towards the blue beams. "He had too much going for him–talent, a new job, a nice, new place. It doesn't fit."

No, nothing about this was right. This wasn't suicide, this was cold blooded murder and it seemed Spinks had added her name to the list of those under suspicion.

Chapter Twenty-one

"We've got twenty minutes to be in and out," Kal said.

Marty was far from happy. "You'd better bloody well watch each other's backs. This is crazy. Derick Sanders is dead and I don't want you going the same way."

Kal tied back her hair. "If we don't take chances we'll get nowhere."

"Yes, it's risky but our priority has to be getting hard evidence and facts," LeeMing said. "Intuitions aren't going to cut it."

In the dark of the Common, Kal had been glad to have both of her friends as back-up. She'd expected LeeMing to tell her she deserved to get her head blown off. Instead, he had joined forces with them.

"Don't feel obliged," Kal had told him.

"I don't."

Marty had rolled her eyes and thanked him.

Kal slammed the car door and she and LeeMing walked to the end of the road, leaving Marty on look-out.

"Breaking and entering in broad daylight will be a challenge," LeeMing said.

"Technically it's not breaking and entering because the security guard leaves two doors open for her coffee-break exit to the garden. Plus, Marty supplied me with a neat device that'll interfere with the security cameras so the wireless network'll be overwhelmed, at least for a while."

"How will we know it's working?"

"We won't," she said, "so don't think about it. And we struck lucky with one of the ex-military types on Marty's team. She's worked security for Assad's wives and she gave me a lot of intel on the household. The guard on the top floor is a smoker and Assad bans it on the premises. Apparently, our real estate baron is a tyrant and he's got a temper. At break time, the guard'll take the risk because Assad is out of town, so at three-thirty when the others go to the kitchen, she'll sneak into the garden for a cigarette and she'll exit into the courtyard. That'll be our way in. And Marty's box of tricks will fuzz the security circuit while we're at it."

At this Kensington address, Assad's five wives lived in luxury. Once a Victorian residence consisting of a main house, servants' quarters and stables, it had been converted into interconnecting apartments with an interior swimming pool, sauna, fully equipped fitness studio and gym, private cinema and garage space for ten cars–the list of top-end facilities seemed endless. Assad stayed on occasion and his five wives lived here permanently.

"Today one of the wives is in New York and another is visiting family in Saudi Arabia. Out of the three others, two of them have a regular shopping date at Harrods, which leaves only one wife in the house," she said.

Arranged around a cobbled courtyard, the property had privacy and seclusion despite being in the heart of London. Kal checked her watch.

"With one bodyguard on duty in New York and one at Harrods, that leaves only two at the house."

"It sounds exotic only working private security is boring as hell most of the time. Believe me, those guards aren't going to be hyper-vigilant," LeeMing said.

"Exactly. We're heading for the far left-hand corner. Let's go."

Kal switched on the device and marched straight through an archway. As she'd been informed, the guard had left the far door on the latch.

Inside the house, they paused. There was no sign of anyone–no creaks, no noise from a television, just warm air and a flowery fragrance and underfoot a thick, cream carpet.

A hallway ran the length of the house. It linked all the apartments and ran along the long side of the courtyard. Kal pointed down it with her open palm and then up, to indicate a staircase. One part of the complex remained out-of-bounds to everyone–Assad's private quarters–and that's where they were heading.

Dressed in black all the way to his leather gloves, LeeMing moved with the poise of a cat. Illicit entries weren't Kal's favourite mode of operation and she wondered just how many LeeMing had been involved in. Judging by his level of ease, quite a few more than her, she'd guess. He was certainly turning into a surprise.

They ran lightly to the end of the corridor, then up the stairs. Assad's quarters occupied the top floor of the far spar, over the garage. At the entrance to the spar, the guard's chair was empty.

Ahead of them, the corridor had four identical doors, two on either side. Kal tried the first one and found it locked. Just as she turned to try its opposite number, LeeMing's hand came down hard on her shoulder. Kal's pulse spiked. The handle of the far door was turning. Both of them pressed against the wall. She dropped low and LeeMing kept high. With no time to run and nowhere to hide, they watched the door swing open. LeeMing's hand flew from her shoulder and she imagined him behind her, ready to take action.

Out came an Arabic woman, probably fifties, with her feet in thick, woolly socks. The woman trod each step slowly and carefully. The smart thing to do would be to knock her out before she screamed and brought the whole household running. That's what protocol would mandate, act now, think it through later.

Presumably one of Assad's wives, the woman was dressed in jogging pants, a pink sweatshirt and a matching scarf, and she was a bit overweight. She was so intent on coming out quietly, she didn't glance up. Fumbling in her pocket, she took out a key ready to relock the door. Then she looked up and the key fell to the floor. LeeMing sprang forward and clamped his hand over the woman's mouth.

Kal had two thoughts. First a random one about how she'd presumed Assad's wives would all be models in their twenties and then secondly, and more compelling, how strangely the woman had been behaving. And what about the expression on the woman's face? The woman's initial astonishment was replaced by guilt and then by fear. How odd fear came second. And what had the woman been doing? Was she sneaking around Assad's quarters?

It would explain why the woman came out of the room so cautiously, slightly crouched, holding her breath. Probably the woman knew the guard's habits as well as they did.

Kal held her finger to her lips.

"Sssshhh. We're not here to hurt you, though if you scream my friend will knock you out."

The woman was shaking.

"Do you understand?" Kal asked.

The woman nodded and Kal exchanged a glance with LeeMing. Slowly, he eased his gloved fingers from her mouth.

"No sudden moves," LeeMing whispered in the woman's ear.

"I got it. My husband hire you? To check on us?" Her words came out with a strong accent.

"No, we're not working for Assad," Kal said.

The woman assessed Kal and then twisted to look at LeeMing, and Kal wondered how many times Assad hired spies to watch the activities of his wives.

"Then what you want?" asked the woman.

Strange. Maybe they didn't look like the usual types Assad hired. But if not, what could they possibly want except to steal? Or injure? Kal chose her words with care. "We're here for... information."

"Information? Help?"

The meaning was far from clear. To be on the safe side, Kal nodded.

The woman hesitated, then pointed at the far door on the other side of the corridor. To emphasise her meaning, she jabbed her finger twice towards it. The woman had a large chest and it was heaving double time. The woman's fear was flowing–which made it unlikely she had enough thinking capacity to trap them. No, Kal didn't think this was a ploy.

Then the woman did something very odd. She grasped her hands together in a prayer position and raised her eyes to the skies in an imploring and unmistakable 'please.'

"What?" Kal asked.

"Help us," the woman whispered, jerking her head towards the far door.

"Help you with what?"

The woman shook her head and refused to answer.

Could it be possible that, like the downtrodden people Kal had spoken to in hellholes, this woman made a snap judgement and sensed them to be human beings she might be able to trust? Was this woman in trouble?

"Are you in trouble?"

More head shaking and more pointing towards the far door.

"Don't take your eyes off her," Kal hissed, and she stepped past. The woman was no threat–

she was soft and doughy and smelled of soap.

Now the woman mimed turning a key in the lock, meaning perhaps 'the door is locked.'

Kal tried it. It was.

"What's in there?" Kal whispered. The woman's eyes got bigger and rounder.

"Tell me what's in there. You want us to help you, don't you? I can see it in your face. That's what you hoped for. What were you doing up here?"

The woman mimed again turning a key in a lock.

"Were you looking for the key to this door? Why, what's in there?"

Kal dived for the key the woman had dropped and tried it in the lock. It didn't fit.

The woman said nothing, which suggested either she didn't speak much English, or she didn't want to. LeeMing's hands were on her shoulders and she patted one of them and then brushed both off. Stepping with surprising agility to the door they'd seen her creeping out of, the woman nodded at LeeMing, opened it and flicked the light switch.

It was Assad's office. Kal was behind them in an instant and she scanned quickly—main desk, two computer screens, filing cabinets, a huge bookcase, two leather armchairs, a lot of framed photographs of Assad with various dignitaries, including one of him with the Prime Minister.

"What were you doing in here? Were you snooping on your husband?"

The woman wrapped her arms across her chest.

"You were looking for the key, weren't you? Except you didn't find it." The way the woman chewed at her own lips told Kal her guess could be right. "LeeMing, keep a look out." Kal pointed to the woman. "You and I will search again."

Kal didn't expect the woman to comply, but the woman did. Together they pulled out desk drawers, ferreted in the filing cabinets and under sheaves of papers stacked on the desk, searched under the carpet and amongst the books. Nothing. Kal scanned the papers, finding nothing of note. She noticed the woman was shaking so hard, her whole body trembled.

"Where did you get the key for this office, did you take it from Assad?"

The woman didn't answer.

"What's in the other room?"

The woman didn't answer.

"Do you know Assad's computer password?"

Silence.

"I can only help you if you give me information. What is it you're frightened of? I know you're terrified except I can't help you if you don't tell me more."

The woman shook her head.

Maybe Assad didn't keep the key in the office. Though if the wife was willing to risk herself by coming up here to search alone, then it suggested she believed he did, and Kal assessed this woman to know everything about how the household and her husband functioned. Or maybe the wife had been searching for something else?

Too soon, LeeMing peered in. "We're out of time."

Damn.

"We've got to get out of here," hissed LeeMing.

Kal tucked her hair behind her ear, went to the far door and pressed her ear against it. She couldn't hear a thing yet she imagined another person, crouched just like her with an ear pressed against the other side. Her blood started pounding in her temples.

"Is anyone there? Mum?"

Assad's wife looked like she might have a heart attack. Her breathing was a bit wheezy. Kal grabbed the woman by the shoulders and gave her a light shake.

"I can help you. Tell me what's in there!"

The woman eyes were wide. From her behaviour, Kal knew the woman had gone way over her threshold of risk already.

In the distance, a door slammed. The guard was returning.

Kal couldn't tear herself away from the door. If she left now, she risked leaving whoever or whatever was behind it to their fate. She simply could not do that.

"LeeMing, help me, we need to break in."

He grabbed her arm. "Kal! We agreed on stealth. We're no good to anyone if we get arrested."

"What if someone's in there. Imprisoned."

The blood drained from LeeMing's face yet he didn't budge.

Shit. She was trapped. That was the problem when you relied on other people. LeeMing was the same as Marty, he wasn't fully convinced these people were guilty.

Another door banged and for a moment she considered fighting him off. Then the wife flapped her arms in alarm, pushing Kal towards the exit and LeeMing dragged her back the way they came, and they both ran, leaving Assad's wife behind them.

Chapter Twenty-two

The ScottBioTec Gala was hosted at the iconic Dorchester Hotel. A venue famed for attracting celebrities, the Dorchester overlooked Hyde Park. As Kal arrived, a melee of press and public clustered at the entrance, making it difficult to get through.

Not everyone was here to celebrate–a bunch of people carried banners with the word 'Mengele' written on them, a reference to the deranged Nazi scientist who used live humans for his sadistic experiments.

A security guard came down the front steps to greet her. "Good evening, Ms Medi, please let me accompany you to the foyer, Dr Scott is waiting for you." He cleared a path through the crowd.

It was quiet inside. With marble flooring and subtle lighting, this was a high-class location. Kal stared straight past the concierge, clocking the way he discreetly scanned her. She had chosen an off-the-shoulder, electric blue, satin dress. She wore her hair loose and had borrowed a gorgeous, turquoise necklace from her mother's collection. Playing the game of elegance was amusing and she was sure it convinced most of the people here. It was a good disguise.

The protestors must be annoying Scott because when the security minder made to stay with them, Scott flicked the man away with a frown.

He bent to plant a kiss on Kal's cheek. "I'm so glad you could come."

"Me too."

Scott wore an immaculate grey suit and his stylish appearance got the attention of every woman around. That she had to fake a smile reinforced Kal's first reaction to Scott. He had all the correct patter and the looks and he left her cold.

"My security chief advised me not to go near the front entrance," Scott said. "He wants me to keep a low profile, though I'd prefer to confront those imbeciles." He offered his arm to escort her.

"What's going on, I spotted some placards?"

"It's a bunch of self-righteous morons claiming to be children's rights experts. It's a cheap stunt."

"I saw something on the internet, don't they claim ScottBioTec's profiting from families in poverty?"

"They should inform themselves of the facts. My company is helping people. If they weren't so blind they'd see we're the solution, not the problem."

She feigned ignorance, keeping her arm draped through his. The solidarity group claimed the high number of children born with limb deformities in Kolkata was due to industrial negligence. An American company, WainChemicals, had owned a chemical plant and though they had long since pulled out, they'd left the ground contaminated, polluting the water supply. There were allegations ScottBioTec was complicit in drawing out the legal proceedings in the US and India so a proper clean-up had been delayed for literally decades in the courts.

On their way to the ballroom, people cast glances their way. The two of them must make an interesting couple to stir up such a wake of curiosity and envy. Kal adamantly refused to think about her mother, who should have been the one here with Scott. If she did that, she might not be able to get through the evening.

They went to the front of the grandiose ballroom. On his arm, Kal felt like she accompanied a celebrity, and with its cabaret layout of round tables decked with silver cutlery and wine glasses, the evening had the air of an awards ceremony.

There were around two hundred guests flaunting designer evening wear and expensive jewellery. Scott shook hands as he passed by the tables. Everyone wanted to congratulate him, and the two of them were amongst the last to take their seats. Scott had the place of honour in front of the stage. A waiter swooped to pour drinks and Kal noted the three places set at their table.

"Is somebody joining us?"

"I invited a Russian colleague. I'm about to sign a multi-million deal to supply Russia's military hospitals and Boris is my contact. He's their top man and without his support, it wouldn't have been possible. I hope you don't mind me mixing business with pleasure."

Scott rested his hand on her arm and gave a small squeeze. Kal forced herself to flash him a smile. Having a third person at the table would complicate the dynamics, so she had better move fast on Scott while she had him to herself. Time to shake him up and see what came out.

"Of course I don't mind, although I was hoping to ask you more about Mum."

The overhead lights dimmed, revealing flickering candles. The chink of glasses and a hum of muted conversation floated from the surrounding tables.

"I was looking forward to getting to know you," Scott said, "and I'll try to answer as honestly as I can. I've been thinking about how to explain the way I feel about Alesha and I've no idea where to start. I never knew I could have such strong feelings."

"No one has an explanation for attraction."

"It's much more. I want you to know meeting your mother changed my life. I knew it the moment I saw her."

A compere took to the stage to welcome first the audience and then Richard Scott. A spotlight fell on Scott and he got to his feet to acknowledge the applause.

"Ladies and gentlemen," Scott said in his deep, smooth voice, "this is ScottBioTec's thank you to all our sponsors and supporters. Please enjoy the evening."

As Scott sat down, Kal leant forward. "I didn't realise you were a celebrity."

"It's the price of success and I don't enjoy it."

On stage, the compere continued her introduction to the evening and Kal blanked out the woman and trained her concentration on Scott. He took a sip from his glass.

"The evening starts with a film outlining the background to our research. The more interesting part comes later so we can talk freely until then." His grey eyes rested on her. "Alesha is an extraordinary woman. She has a wonderful passion for life. Let me give you an example of how she changed me–I was so wrapped up in my business, I'd hardly stepped out of a boardroom in the last twenty years. Whenever I travelled it was for ScottBioTec–New York, Paris, Malaysia, Japan–none of my trips were for pleasure. Your mother introduced me to the joys of travelling for fun. In fact, she took me to Varanasi in India. I'm sure you know it."

A sudden jealousy flared. Her hands lay on the table and she was careful to keep them relaxed, careful to hide her dismay and astonishment–Varanasi was her mother's favourite Indian city and Kal's also.

Her mother had taken her there as a first introduction to India. Home of the silk trade, Varanasi was a mystical town bordering the sacred Ganges river. The banks of the river were covered with tiered terraces of red stone, split into sections called Ghats. In the mornings, the misty Ghats were packed with hundreds of Indian men, women and children who came to bathe in the purifying Ganges and meditate and chant standing deep in the water. Once visited, Varanasi was a difficult place to forget.

Why the hell had her mother chosen to take Scott there? It made her almost hate him.

She was careful not to let her lips tighten. "You liked India?"

"I'll always remember that visit and your mother and I have so many more plans."

She had no desire to hear Scott talk about Varanasi nor of his plans with Alesha. Not today, not ever. Jealousy was one of her weak points and she knew she mustn't let it get in the way.

Kal shifted her position, the candlelight picking out the angle of Scott's jaw. Time to take the conversation on a different tack.

"I know this might sound strange, but ever since Mum went missing I've had this weird feeling someone's following me."

She watched carefully. Not a fibre moved in Scott's face.

"Are you sure?"

"I'm certain."

"Goodness, that's strange and very worrying."

"Yes, I know." She leaned across the table. "Though this might sound even stranger because I've been wondering if… maybe Mum found something out."

Scott's face remained mask-like save for an artery which pulsed at his right temple. The scent of his cologne drifted towards her.

"I suppose that's possible," he said.

"I've been thinking perhaps someone's tailing me to see what I know or because…" she dropped her voice lower, "…Mum hid evidence."

Scott cleared his throat. "Evidence of what?"

His voice sounded treacle smooth. Kal took a sip of water and glanced towards the stage, where the compere now laughed along with the audience. She left Scott's question hanging and he steepled his fingers, sapphire cufflinks glittering a beautiful blue in the candlelight. His next words would tell her so much. She could see him turning it over. What direction would her idea take him in?

"I can hardly get my mind around what you're saying. What would Alesha leave evidence about? One of her investigations?"

"Mum's work covers a wide field. There are many possibilities."

"Do you have any hunches?"

"Not… really."

She injected the tiniest nuance of doubt. A man as astute as Scott would sense it, just like a piranha senses a drop of blood in a pool of water.

Kal took another sip from her glass and dabbed a napkin at her ruby-coated lips. On stage, the film detailing the history of ScottBioTec's rise to fame had begun, and around them, the audience sat quietly. Scott took his elbows from the table and as he did so, the fingertips of his right hand strayed upwards as if to brush his top jacket pocket.

He's unconsciously drawn to that pocket. What's he checking? What's he got in there? Does what I've said make him think of calling someone? Or am I letting my dislike cloud my judgement? Am I hunting for something to pin on him simply because I can't stand him?

"I know a little about your mother's recent discoveries."

Even a great poker player has a 'tell' and she watched for a sign in Scott's manner. She allowed a good few seconds before picking up his cue.

"Really?"

"I know she's been carrying out surveillance on an Arabic businessman called Farouk Assad," Scott said, "he's a man worth billions."

"I think I've heard of Assad. Did Mum tell you why she was interested in him?"

"No, although if your mother found evidence of some kind of transgression she could have been in a lot of trouble. Assad's not a man to tolerate interference in his affairs. He has a reputation for being ruthless."

Yes, of course Assad would be ruthless to protect himself and his secrets. Kal didn't have to fake a reaction. She had always thought of her mother as unstoppable. Alesha had worked her way up from nothing. Against the odds, Alesha had made it in a cut-throat profession, exposing corruption and rooting out the truth for the under-dog. Perhaps it was the shock of realising even her mother was vulnerable which made this so hard.

"I don't want to upset you. Maybe we should talk about something else?"

"I'm fine. Please, what were you saying about Assad?"

"I said he has a reputation for being formidable. I hope you told the police about this, and I'm wondering if Alesha left any specific information about Assad?"

She shook her head. "I'm as much in the dark as you."

Scott's perfect teeth glinted. "That's a shame, it would have given us something to work with. What did the police say?"

"I told them about being tailed and Spinks is on to it. The rest is only a hunch."

"I've got to be honest, my first priority is to keep you safe. I'd imagined Alesha had simply gone undercover, or… I don't know what." Scott ran his fingers through his hair. "Let me arrange a bodyguard. Consider it done." And he reached to his trouser pocket and pulled out his phone.

Kal held up a hand to stop him. "No, I mean, thank you, only it's not necessary."

"I insist. It's for your own safety."

So she gave him one of her best smiles. "No need to fuss. Like you said, I wasn't one hundred percent sure and Detective Spinks will handle it."

"I'm not convinced. If anything happens to you, your mother would never forgive me."

At that moment, a waiter deftly slid the starter plates in front of them. Despite her scrutiny, Scott had passed the test. He seemed sincere. If Scott were faking it, he was one hell of a master trickster.

"This looks delicious."

"I'm glad. It's difficult to enjoy ourselves in the circumstances I know, but we shouldn't let it spoil things."

As Kal took a bite of seafood terrine, Scott picked up his fork to begin eating, and it was at that moment she noticed a tiny shift in him, like a tension creeping in. The shift was significant, because when most people start eating, their body unconsciously relaxes.

"Your mother told me a lot about you and as I said before, she's very proud of you."

She pretended to be engrossed in her food.

"Alesha told me about you signing up at age eighteen to study journalism without telling her, and about how you junked the course in favour of hitch-hiking around the world."

Scott said it as if he recounted a family anecdote, with a smile and a light tone, his fork poised in the air.

"Oh gosh, that was ages ago, surely Mum didn't bore you with that?"

"After months of travelling, she told me you started taking photographs to earn money to get back, and those first photographs sparked your interest in photojournalism."

It annoyed her Alesha had shared details with this man. But why shouldn't she? It was natural to talk about your own daughter, wasn't it? Kal gave a small laugh to hide her discomfort.

"I know too about the time you got arrested concealed with illegal immigrants. They were trying to cross the channel from France to England and you documented their story."

Scott was well informed. The illegal immigrant project was her first success and something in Scott's tone told her that, though this was the point in any polite conversation when he should stop, he meant to continue.

"Mum told you that? I'm surprised." She took another bite of starter.

"Alesha told me much more."

Was the resonance in his voice ambiguous? Not just humour and not camaraderie? A prickle ran up her spine.

"I know about when you were accused of stealing at school and you took the blame even though you weren't the culprit, and how the head teacher threatened you with criminal proceedings to get the truth."

She wanted to tell him to shut up. Surely her mother wouldn't have told Scott that?

"Goodness, I didn't know Mum had such a good memory."

"What about your first national Championship kung fu semi-final? You were fifteen and you'd been up all night vomiting with a stomach bug then you lied to your trainer so he'd let you compete. You collapsed in the third round."

Very few people knew why she had collapsed–Master Yeung, Marty, Alesha, the medic team on site.

Her blink rate had picked up. It was one of the hardest reactions to control. Scott might notice and she mustn't let him know he'd got to her. She brushed her eyelashes with her fingertip, pretending to check non-existent mascara, and then reached for her glass of wine. Was Scott toying with her? Was she imagining it, or was he purposely needling her?

The wine tasted like vinegar. *Be very cautious*, said the voice of her father. The warning made her over-grip the stem of her glass.

Scott smiled. Kal stared at him and had the illusion of being caught in the gaze of a predator. A few angry words almost slipped out. Unwise words that would reveal how much he disturbed her. Except she was saved, because at that point, the public relations film finished to loud applause and the rear curtain lifted to reveal a backing band.

Kal sat back and joined in the applause as a singer walked to centre stage and launched into a jazz number.

"Quality entertainment as well, gosh, you know how to throw a celebration," she said, and somehow she managed to keep the façade going. Either she was being paranoid or he was very, very clever.

At that moment too, the Russian guest joined them and electricity ran up her arms. He was on her mother's list.

His entrance broke the remains of the spell, snapping the strands of the spider's web Scott had been spinning around her.

The new man was noisy, talking about how he'd been caught in traffic. Though over six-foot tall, he had a poise about him. Dressed in a dinner suit jacket and bow tie, his dark hair contrasted with his porcelain-white complexion.

"My apologies for being late, especially to the lovely lady," the Russian said.

"Not at all, Boris. Make yourself comfortable and may I introduce you to a good friend of mine, Kal Medi."

All of Kal's appetite evaporated and she didn't bother to finish her starter.

Scott and Boris talked and Kal played along with joining in, dividing her attention between their conversation and a presentation on stage where ScottBioTec scientists portrayed their work.

The first up was Christina, Head of the Technical Unit, responsible for developing the micro-electrode array and chip technology which allowed the patient's own brain waves to control their artificial limb.

The second presenter was Dr Mark, Head Surgeon, who summarised his work in brain surgery procedures. Successful implantation of the pea-sized array had taken several years of experimentation pioneered at ScottBioTec in Kolkata. By the time the waiter cleared their plates, the two scientists had given a full overview of their work.

"They're fascinating, aren't they? Both brilliant," Scott said. "Though the next guest is the real star of the show."

"Who is it?" Boris asked.

"You'll have to wait and see."

After a musical interlude, dessert was served, then there came a dramatic drum roll. The audience craned towards the curtains at the side of the stage where the material swayed. Then, the backing band played a fanfare and out came the compere followed by a small girl. The child wore a skirt, clearly displaying her artificial leg as she walked to centre stage.

Scott and Boris rose to their feet applauding, and Kal joined them, as did the rest of the audience.

"Wonderful," Boris said.

"Her name's Rani. We flew her in from India for the occasion."

The girl spoke a few words into the microphone and she explained how, due to her disability, she'd been living on the streets, begging for food, until ScottBioTec offered her the opportunity of a replacement limb. Now she had the chance for a brighter future.

"You're a mastermind," Boris said, "this is a marvellous, public relations moment."

After her turn on stage, the spotlight followed Rani's steady footsteps down the flight of steps to the dining area where she was joined by a nurse. Scott got up to meet them and he was pulled into having his photograph taken with Rani. Afterwards, Rani and the nurse joined their table while Scott was caught in a shower of praise from fellow diners.

"Hello Rani, you were wonderful," Boris said, "tell me what's your favourite ice-cream. Let me guess, is it strawberry?"

The Russian's hand slid down the girl's back. The motion lasted a couple of seconds and to a casual observer it would signify nothing. To Kal, it gave a warning. The quality of the gesture was wrong. The girl had said she was eight years old except Boris didn't display a fatherly touch, rather, there was a feeling in his hand that was unmistakably tactile. His hand lingered too slow. Too sensual.

Kal suppressed a shiver. The atmosphere closed in, turning sinister and contrasting with Rani's bright laughter. How do you recognise a paedophile? That's the problem, you can't.

"Come and sit by me," Kal said, and she patted the chair beside her. Rani scooted over and swung in beside Kal, her eyes shining and her hair smelling sweet.

Kal observed the Russian more closely. On his right hand, he wore an ornate ring on his thumb and a second on his first finger, inset with a massive diamond. On the middle finger of his other hand, he wore a huge signet ring embossed with a symbol she did not recognise. Aside from that, he appeared utterly ordinary.

Scott rejoined them and the male singer came back on stage. He was surprisingly good, however, after a couple of songs, Scott pushed away his dessert.

"It's a habit of mine to leave before the other guests. Will you accompany us, Kal?"

She had been considering her strategy. Though all her instincts screamed to get as far away as possible from Scott, she must manoeuvre closer. The children and Scott were connected. Boris and Scott were connected. Just how those dots joined up, she intended to find out. And Rani had given her an idea to buy her way in. Kal picked up her camera.

"Yes, I'll come with you, only let's not scurry out the side door like rats, let's go out in full glory." She winked at Scott, knowing how it riled him to have his event spoiled by hecklers. "Rani can help us, trust me on this one."

She gave it a good injection of confidence and that, coupled with his own arrogance, allowed Scott to be won over.

Kal told Scott, not the nurse, to hold Rani's hand, and their fellow diners got to their feet with some even giving polite cheers as Rani walked past. Their little group left the ballroom and headed straight for the lobby.

When the security chief tried to usher Scott to a side exit, Scott brushed him off, and at the sight of them, the doorman hustled his staff to swing open the main doors.

Out in the cold air, a bunch of people still waited and now they roused themselves. Kal saw the faces of people ready to hurl abuse at Scott, except when they spotted Rani it stopped them in their tracks. What protesters would shout down an eight-year old, disabled girl? Scooting to the side-lines, she took shot after shot of Scott's triumphant face and Rani's beaming smile with the banner-holders awkward and confused in the background.

Once free of the crowd, she showed off the shots to Scott.

"That's a powerful media opportunity you created and you've captured it so well. You've got a talent."

Scott's limousine rounded the corner. As the valet leapt out and held open the door, Scott turned his back on the man as if he was an insect.

"Kal, you know I'm winding up for a big publicity splurge for the new launch and we're always on the lookout for fresh ideas. I could do with a mind like yours on the team. What do you say? You can name your terms."

Perfect, she thought and part of her wondered if Scott was engineering the same opportunity to get closer to her. To scratch further at her weaknesses. She waited a few minutes while Rani, the nurse and Boris got into the car.

"I'm sorry, I've never worked on a commercial project."

"Nonsense, you've an eye for the unusual and that's a rarity. You don't know your own value."

"Gosh… I suppose I could give it a try."

"Wonderful. Consider yourself hired."

Chapter Twenty-three

Hunched at the top of the ramp, Kal waited with her back against the dragon doors. Marty came jogging along the pavement.

"What the hell's happened?"

"Marty, listen, I've changed my mind."

"About what?"

"About what we're doing–wait, hear me out–Derick, Scott trying to undermine me at the Gala and whatever the fuck's going on at Assad's house–it's getting too dark. It's better if you stay out of it and I'm not saying this as a knee-jerk reaction, I've given it a lot of thought."

"We've already agreed and you know me–I don't go back on my word."

"Don't you get what I'm saying? It's dangerous. Mum would never let this go, not if children were involved. Except we've got a choice, we don't have to go further."

"Yeah, only you're not talking about 'us', are you? You're talking about me."

"What's wrong with that?"

"My god, you are dense sometimes, Kal. You think I'd back out? Like I told you, I can look after myself, and there's not a chance in hell I'm leaving you on your own. That girl in the photograph–her eyes–don't you think I know terror when I see it? I lived it, remember? I don't know if your hunches are right, and I hope to god they're not, but I'm telling you one thing, I'm in this all the way. You always worry about other people, Kal, and you don't need to. I'm going into this with my eyes open."

Afterwards, Kal pretended to start back to 701, saying she needed the walk to clear her head, and she watched until Marty disappeared from sight.

Certainly, she was Alesha's daughter and she was David Khan's daughter too, in ways she never dared to admit. She had gone as far as she could tracking these people. Something was taking place at ScottBioTec. Time to go to the source and use her skills to the full.

Enough going about things the right way, she would have to do better than that and this time she'd be doing it alone.

Chapter Twenty-four

Hot air blasted Kal's face as she stepped off the plane in Kolkata.

Taking a deep breath, she breathed in India. Petrol fumes, dust, the odour of cow pats in the town centre because cows are holy to Hindus and wandered everywhere and couldn't be disturbed, pedal-power rickshaws weaving amongst honking taxis. From poverty to riches, from gold-embossed Buddhas to dirt, India had it all.

Kal had given her tail the slip on her way to Heathrow and left London without a trace.

She had come to India several times since her first trip to Varanasi with Alesha. As the second generation born overseas, visits were important. Kal remembered approaching the first one with a mixture of duty and curiosity, and Varanasi quickly charmed her. It was still her favourite city, with Kolkata her second favourite.

Kolkata–with its love of art and successful cinema industry. In this metropolis of four million people, a quarter lived in poverty either in slum areas minimally supplied with basic services, or in unofficial squatter districts with no services at all.

The poorest inhabitants were impressive. They had an ingenuity, being able to repair and fashion articles for everyday use from other people's discards, whether it be bicycle parts, cast-aside utensils or broken-down electrical goods.

The locals had a deep sense of satisfaction in their everyday lives, so different to the excesses and frequent depression back home. Their love of life and ability to surmount hardships gave the city its alternative name–'City of Joy'–after a celebrated novel which captured the spirit and daily battle for survival in the Kolkata slums.

A clamour of male voices vied for her fare as she exited Kolkata airport. She was surrounded by pressing bodies as they all shouted to get her attention. Kal elbowed her way through the drivers, who wore eclectic combinations of western fashion–jeans and worn out shirts–teamed with traditional Indian clothing–baggy, pale trousers and long, loose tunics. Their insistence was another characteristic of Indian city life. Kal chose one of the drivers and he grinned at her, showing his blackened teeth.

On the drive into town, the scrawny driver chatted without pause and, of course, the car was an absolute shell with barely any suspension. The windows were permanently down, which meant he had to shout over the noise of the traffic. He dropped her in the city centre and accepted her tip with another dark-toothed grin.

Kal checked into a hotel. Then she took a battered bus to the suburbs.

The ScottBioTec Research Institute consisted of a state-of-the-art hospital and a children's home. According to the internet, the hospital had two operating theatres and a complement of one hundred and fifty staff.

They ran a clinic, where any disabled child could present themselves for a free assessment. If accepted onto the limb replacement programme, ScottBioTec gave each child housing until age sixteen, in return for participation in the research. Richard Scott tried to keep his critics at bay by offering the children schooling and skills training.

A ten-foot, wire fence surrounded the complex, and the hut beside the security gate housed a guard who was filling in a crossword. Kal knocked on the window. The Indian sun pounded down, super-heating the metal sill. One touch on that would fry her fingertip. She gave a second rap on the pane. This time the guard slid up the sash.

"Good afternoon, what is it you want?"

"I'd like to volunteer at the children's home."

He took in her worn backpack, t-shirt and dusty trainers. "I suppose you're a student?"

Grunting, he pushed a register and pen towards her. "We run a volunteer programme for those willing to stay a minimum of four months. There should be someone in the main office. You can go there and ask."

The compound was huge. Kal made a thorough recce, before presenting herself at the office building, located at the rear. As Kal had read online, the children's home always needed volunteers and the administrative assistant was enthusiastic.

"We have a house mother for each dormitory and they're always in need of help. I'll assign you to the girl's dormitory for ten to eleven-year olds. We split the children into age groups and mostly single sex, though we make exceptions to keep siblings together."

"Do all the children have artificial limbs?"

"Some have and some are waiting. The children who are actively participating in the research sleep at the hospital and I'll give you the advice I give to all our volunteers and that is, don't ask too many questions because it upsets the children. Now, I'll assign you a room. Please go straight over and meet your house mother."

Kal walked back across the pounded dirt compound, passing in front of the hospital which was a modern, two storey, white edifice sitting on the brown earth.

The children's home was a rambling complex of basic, breeze block buildings, set amongst stubby bushes and patches of pounded dirt. They must have started out small and added on dormitories as ScottBioTec expanded. In all, Kal estimated the home to house around two hundred children.

Committing the layout to memory, she searched for block F. The path was beaten smooth by the passage of feet, and it meandered from dormitory to dormitory before finishing at a large, oval space which seemed to be the main playground. As she reached it, a bell sounded.

Children spilled out of the building in front of her which must be the school. Like at any school break time in the world, the children shouted and ran and jostled, tumbling down the steps, pushing each other. In the space of a few seconds, the noise became deafening. Some children headed for the dormitory buildings, others gathered in the open area to play, oblivious to the heat.

Sweat trickled down Kal's temples and she moved to the shade. Some of the children had artificial limbs, others still had the withered arm or leg they had been born with. Some used crutches, some not, and all of them shouted at the tops of their voices.

She walked across the play area. A stubby-looking tree stood on the far side, and a boy, around seven years old, was bent beside it. The boy wore shorts and a much-washed t-shirt and was barefoot.

Kal recognised the type of bush–it was liquorice. The boy was twisting off a young twig for himself, then he would chew the end to enjoy the taste. Just as he succeeded in pulling off his prize, a man darted out from behind the school building and seized the boy by the ear.

"Leave him alone, you big bully." The words shot out before she could stop them.

The man stared at her. He was Indian, late thirties, thin, wearing a long cream tunic and matching traditional trousers and he wore expensive, leather sandals, marking him out as someone on his way up the hierarchy.

"I'm in charge around here and this tree is out of bounds."

He puffed his chest out with self-importance. Kal recognised the type–he had a small amount of power and he wielded it to the full.

"I'm sorry, I didn't know. My name's Kavita and I'm looking for dormitory F." She glanced back the way she'd come, knowing block F lay in front of her.

The man gave her a look laden with disapproval.

"I suppose you're a new volunteer. Well, take it from me, we have to teach them the rules, otherwise they get out of hand."

He gave the boy's ear a vicious twist and whether the boy fell or was pushed, he landed on the ground. The muscles in Kal's arms twitched.

"Dormitory F is that way," the man said, and he gave her a long, rude stare, of the type some Indian men reserve for women of Indian appearance dressed in European fashion. It was a mixture of disgust and disdain with an undercurrent of fascination.

The man walked off, aiming a kick at the boy's back. Kal sprang forward, her anger spiking, but the boy smartly kept out of the way. As the man disappeared behind the school building, she helped the child stand up.

"Don't let him see you're cross, it's best not to get on the wrong side of Mr Singh," said the boy. "I can show you block F if you want."

"Thanks, and if you want to grab a liquorice stick you'd better make sure he isn't hiding to catch you out."

"Mr Singh has eyes everywhere."

"Then you'd better be more clever than Mr Singh."

The boy grinned. "My name's Ashok. I'll be getting my new leg soon."

Ashok had a club foot. It hung twisted and useless on his wasted leg and he used a crutch to support his weight.

"I thought all the children were given shoes? That's what the woman in the office told me."

"I'm keeping mine for later so they stay in good condition. Besides, they're not comfortable."

The woman in the office had told her that too–that the street kids preferred bare feet.

"I'll take you to my sister, Padma," Ashok said, "we both live in F block and she's already had her operation. Padma says once I've had mine we'll be out of here."

"Okay. Hey, wait a minute, don't forget your liquorice."

As she swept up the twig, she hesitated. Very likely Mr Singh, out of sight, was watching them. So just for the hell of it, Kal bent to the bush and twisted off a stick for herself.

The house mother was a young woman around Kal's age and the two of them were similar with long, black hair, dark eyes and a medium dark complexion. Her name was Jasodra. She wore a traditional long, straight tunic, called a shalwar kameez, over jeans and was married and had three children of her own, none of whom had deformities.

"I was lucky they were born whole," Jasodra said. "Three out of three means I've got good karma."

"I don't believe in karma, in this life we make our own destiny," Kal said.

"You should open your eyes, Kavita. Karma is the guiding force linking the generations and you've got Indian blood so you can't escape it."

Kal smiled. Indian people were renowned for their deeply spiritual beliefs.

"It's the street children who are at risk, Kavita. Their families don't have a clean water supply and many children are born with limb deformities. Sometimes the children are abandoned to fend for themselves and then they scavenge from the refuse dump or go into the city to beg."

"Or come to ScottBioTec."

"Exactly, we're so lucky this place is here, it gives hope to the children and employment to people like me."

"How long have you worked here?"

"Nine years. I arrived with a basic qualification in childcare and I've come all the way up to deputy-in-charge. I learned everything I know from the matron."

Jasodra had an open, sunny face. Her smile disappeared as she spoke about the matron.

"I guess I'll meet her later?"

"You'll meet the new matron."

"Oh, what happened to your mentor?"

Jasodra stonewalled the question. Just pretended it had never been asked. It was the characteristic, local way of maintaining politeness whilst saying 'that's not your business' and Jasodra continued without missing a beat.

"The children will be coming back from the canteen soon. Then it's an hour of homework before bed so please could you tidy up the study area, Kavita, before they arrive?"

A while later, after supper, the little boy Ashok and his sister, Padma, settled themselves in the study area to do their homework. The room smelled faintly of spices and chocolate milkshake. Kal found them practising English spellings and Padma was testing Ashok on his list of twenty words.

"I can help Ashok if you like, whilst you get on with your own studies," Kal said.

Since Kal has stuck up for her younger brother, Padma was Kal's firm friend. All afternoon, Ashok and Padma had trailed behind her, chatting non-stop. She had used their company as an excuse to make a more thorough reconnaissance of the compound and the two children had delighted in pointing out the highlights from their viewpoint. Age nine, Padma had been born with a limb deformity of one leg and a harelip. The two had been operated on by the ScottBioTec medical team. Now Padma gave Kal a lovely smile.

"Please, yes, Ashok needs to work harder on his English and I have some reading for tomorrow. We're studying the *Wizard of Oz*, do you know it?"

At the end of the homework period, as the children were packing up their things to go to bed, Jasodra rang a hand bell and the children stood up, their hands by their sides.

"The matron's coming," Padma whispered.

Everyone listened to the approaching footsteps and when the woman entered the room, every child seemed to stiffen. On her way around the tables, the matron glanced at one or two open homework books and addressed a remark here and there.

In her forties, stout, with her black hair severely tied back, the woman had an officious manner. The silk of her sari swished as she moved.

As she toured the room, the matron kept her back ram-rod straight and her hands clasped in front of her showing off her one extravagance–her bright red, painted nails. It seemed to Kal a restlessness spurred the woman. She watched the woman's eyes searching–scanning the children, their books, then the windows, then the corners of the room. Odd. The matron had a desire to check and re-check, to verify everything was in order. Why?

"Carry on preparing for bed," said the matron as she exited the room. On her way out, the matron's eyes fell to the electricity sockets, then scanned the floorboards.

The children relaxed and a light chatter started up again.

"Does the matron tour all the dormitories before bedtime?" Kal asked.

"All the dormitories, every single day," Padma said.

"Did the old matron do the same?"

"No, she didn't."

Jasodra had given her a first clue earlier when she refused to speak about the old matron. Now Kal clocked her second clue. Very likely the matron didn't know what she was checking for. Most probably she was acting on a nagging sixth sense. A sixth sense which gave her a subliminal message that something was wrong, only she couldn't put her finger on what, so she fell back on efficiency and routine and went around to check, like a lioness who senses danger in the environment and feels a need to prowl the perimeter.

Kal helped Ashok pack up his crayons and she dropped her voice to a whisper. "When did the old matron leave?"

Padma seemed a lot older than her nine years, probably because she had been looking after Ashok for most of her life. Kal hadn't wanted to ask if they had been abandoned by their family, though she guessed it was the case. Before they came to ScottBioTec it must have been Padma who kept them alive on the streets. Now Padma's dark eyes flicked to and from her brother.

"The old matron, Indra Gupta, has been gone for a while. Now, Ashok, hurry up and get to the bathroom or you'll be late for lights out."

Padma hustled her brother out of the room, then she turned to Kal, her eyes wise and knowing beyond her years. A shiver of expectancy ran up Kal's spine. Certainly she'd been right to come here. She bent down so Padma could whisper in her ear.

"When the others are asleep, come and find me," Padma said.

The rough matting of the dormitory pressed into Kal's knees as she crouched alongside Padma's bed. Eleven little children lay asleep, and sounds of breathing filled the room. Beyond the mosquito nets, the warm night air carried scents of cinnamon and dust.

"When I first saw you, I knew you were one of Avalokiteshvara's servants," Padma whispered.

It made Kal smile. She'd studied enough Buddhism to understand Padma's view. Avalokiteshvara was a bodhisattva, an entity of great compassion, who vowed to help all sentient beings, a little like a saint. Buddhism depicted Avalokiteshvara sitting cross-legged on a lotus bloom, with a thousand arms reaching out like a fan. Each hand of the thousand arms contained an eye which saw the suffering of humanity. Many Indian people spoke of the bodhisattvas as a reality rather than as part of a faith.

"That's why I trust you, because you helped Ashok and showed yourself as one of Avalokiteshvara's servants. I think a deeper force led you to us. You've a purpose to fulfil," Padma said.

"Uh huh."

Kal liked Padma. The girl had nothing in life and no one, yet she had spirit and courage and resourcefulness. Padma was the type of child who would make something of her life against all the odds–Kal felt sure of it.

"There are others here who need help, I've got something important to tell you." Padma pushed herself up onto one elbow.

"Go ahead, I'm listening."

Kal shielded her torch and it played a dull yellow light on the side of Padma's bed.

"If you ask, they'll say the old matron, Indra Gupta, left." Padma paused and licked her bottom lip, her tongue finding the remains of the cleft which had been repaired by the surgeons. "Even if you press, it's unlikely they'll tell you more. They won't want to say she's supposed to have doused herself in fuel and set herself alight. That she died from her injuries."

"Oh no."

Self-immolation was sometimes a way out for Indian women. It was a desperate, last-resort after years of torture and abuse at the hands of their husbands and families-in-law.

"Is that true Padma? Did the old matron set light to herself?"

"Her charred body was found. The important thing is the police didn't investigate, they said it was a family matter except I believe the matron was *murdered*."

As Padma hissed the final word, the girl in the next bed stirred. Kal crouched lower and pushed away the memory of Derick in the body bag and tried not to think of the matron aflame, burning to death in agony. Tried not to think either about the fact that the matron was the same ethnicity, and perhaps a similar age, to her own mother.

Once all became calm in the next bed, she moved her mouth close to Padma's ear.

"What makes you think the matron was murdered?"

"I think someone wanted her out of the way and they made it look like she set fire to herself. I know she was happy. She was happily married and everyone knows that. Everyone here loved her. Ashok adored her. She would never set fire to herself. No, she was murdered and no one wants to ask questions because they're scared so they all pretend, they go along with the lies told by the police."

Kal's shirt stuck to her back and not due to the warm, night air. Padma believed what she was saying. When the child in the neighbouring bed muttered in her sleep, Kal and Padma fell silent.

That afternoon, Kal had spent an enjoyable time with Padma and Ashok. Padma was so intelligent and sharp, so witty and astute in her observations of people, their mannerisms and why they did the things they did. She and Ashok had laughed themselves to tears at Padma's characterisations of Mr Singh, the cook and Ashok's schoolteacher. Padma had shown herself to be a survivor and an observer, and her skill in reading people and situations had been sufficiently keen to keep her and her little brother alive.

Kal thought of how Alesha used to put her to bed as a little girl. Her mother hadn't read fairy stories. Instead, Alesha told real tales of children and people she'd met in other countries and other places, and how other people's lives were filled with impossible dreams and ideas and sacrifices, just like theirs. How she'd loved those stories.

Under the sheet, Kal found Padma's small hand and squeezed it. Padma held on.

"I believe you, Padma, and I'm here to find out why someone would want to kill the matron. Can you help me?"

Padma nodded. She tossed off the sheet, sat up, and swung her legs over the side of the bed.

The metal of her artificial leg gleamed in the torch light as Padma pressed her feet, one flesh, one metallic, soundlessly on the matting and in one smooth motion, stood up. Then she put her finger against her lips and beckoned to Kal to follow.

Chapter Twenty-five

Kal shivered in the warm night as pent-up emotion raced around her system. The chirruping of cicadas filled the air. A group of fireflies swarmed around a nearby bush, their bodies tiny dots of red and orange flashing in mad spirals.

After checking no one was around, the two of them broke into a run, Kal following Padma. It felt good to be moving and she was pleased ScottBioTec didn't have guard dogs.

She expected Padma to head for the hospital. Instead, the child took a route threading through the dormitories until they came out at the rear of the compound, in front of the office building. They paused in the shelter of the last dormitory, then Padma ran ahead, scooting around the corner of the office. A row of windows ran along the side. They went to the furthest window, slid up the fly screen and climbed in.

A quick flash from Kal's torch showed they were in a room stacked with cartons. The room reeked of cardboard. This was a storage room, full of school and office supplies. Padma crossed to the door and opened it cautiously. It let out onto a dark corridor.

"This is it, this is as far as we can go," Padma said.

For a moment, Kal wondered if Padma might be playing games.

"And?"

"And nothing. This is as far as we can go. Have a look at this." Padma peered through the open doorway and pointed to the end of the corridor. "That door at the end is locked, don't you get it? There's a whole section to this building that we can't get into and I'll never be chosen because of my harelip, but I've seen children picked to go in there and they *never come out.*"

Kal recalled the outside of the building. There were windows running along the side and they stopped halfway along. Padma was right. The rear section could contain three or four sizeable rooms with no outside access.

"What about the other side of the building, are there any entrances along it or windows?"

"It's exactly the same as this side with no openings at all, silly," Padma said. "Aren't you listening? I've seen children go in there *and they never come out.* They disappear."

There was no doubt Padma believed what she said and she tugged at Kal's arm.

"That's why as soon as Ashok's had his operation, we'll be getting away from here, you've got to believe me."

"Padma, I do." She just needed to find out what it meant.

Propping open the door to the storeroom, Kal stepped into the dark corridor. She put her hand against the door leading to the closed-in, rear section and ran her palm down the surface. It was cold, made of re-inforced steel, and firmly locked. She checked the surround. A metal frame. Somebody didn't want intruders.

Padma stuck to her like glue. As Kal crouched down to inspect the door, the girl whispered in Kal's ear.

"There are so many children here. Some of us go for therapy, some of us go for surgery and after surgery we stay over at the hospital for months afterwards, then we go back regularly for the research programme. Children move around all the time and if you've no brother or sister then who would ask if someone goes missing? They'd just say they've been taken for surgery or physiotherapy or research examinations, or that they've run away, except it's not true."

Down at floor level, a splatter of marks sprayed the door frame, like dark paint. Scratching at one, it flaked away and Kal crushed the flake between her fingertips and then sniffed the residue. It had a distant tang of iron. Not paint. Dried blood.

Thunk. A door swung to and the noise came from close by. Padma snatched in a breath. In one move, Kal picked up Padma and half-lifted, half-threw her inside the storeroom, pulling the door shut. Someone came striding down the corridor, training a beam of light on Kal's face. She raised her arms to protect her eyes.

"Hey!" a man's voice called out, "Who's there? Identify yourself."

It was Mr Singh. Just as good as any guard dog.

"Mr Singh, it's Kavita, the new volunteer, we met this afternoon."

"This area is strictly out of bounds. You've no business down here."

"I couldn't sleep and I wondered if there might be a television in the office..."

"Your job is to assist your house mother. We have sterile areas, sensitive equipment, confidential records, you can't go wandering around anywhere you like."

"Of course, it was silly of me, I'm sorry."

Mr Singh escorted her all the way back to her room. Once she'd heard him stalking off, Kal went to the children's dormitory to check on Padma. She found the little girl safely in bed and she knelt down again on the matting.

"You were smart to come straight back here."

"Be careful of Mr Singh, he's nasty," Padma whispered.

Kal tucked the sheet around Padma's thin shoulders. "Don't worry. I'm not scared of people like him, and when you're older, you won't be either."

"There's something I forgot to tell you," Padma said," and it might be important. The children go missing when we have guests. Can you help?"

If anyone was Avalokiteshvara's servant, it was Padma. Kal looked at her with admiration and she gave the little girl a kiss on the forehead.

"Yes Padma, and thank you, you've been very helpful. Goodnight and sweet dreams."

Chapter Twenty-six

As a new volunteer, Kal was to have an orientation. To start with, she reported to the office and the matron set her up in a side room to watch the same film which had played at the Gala.

After Padma fell asleep the previous night, Kal had located Mr Singh's room, then she had returned to the office and searched systematically through everything. She sat patiently through the film until the matron returned.

"Do you have any questions, Kavita?" the matron asked.

Today, the matron wore a dress patterned with small flowers, belted neatly at the waist. The woman's demand for order was taking over as she pushed at a stack of papers until the edges aligned, then rearranged a line of pens on the desktop. Most likely the unconscious warnings nagging at the woman were causing her to tighten up on her desire for everything to be in its place. Now the matron readjusted the already centrally-positioned knot of her belt.

"I don't think so, though I'm curious about the research work."

"You can ask questions over at the hospital." The matron rubbed a palm across her forehead.

"Do you have a headache, matron? Can I get you something to help?"

"Oh dear, I wish there was something, except there isn't. I've taken painkillers although they won't do much good, you see, I'm prone to migraines and I can feel one coming on. I'd like to spend a couple of hours with you, though I'm sorry, today it won't be possible. I must conserve my energy because we've our Founder planning a visit."

Kal hadn't seen any mention of it the previous night. "You mean Dr Scott is coming here?"

"I received a call this morning and I've a mountain of preparations to make sure everything is exactly as he likes it."

The matron gave her belt another little swivel of correction and then pressed her hand to her brow. "Dr Scott is due tomorrow evening and I simply have to lie down to try to fend this off."

"If I can help with organising the visit, please let me know."

"Thank you. Unfortunately, that won't be possible because Dr Scott will allow only myself and Mr Singh to be directly involved in the arrangements."

"Gosh, that's strict."

"When you're the Founder, you can be as demanding as you wish."

The woman handed Kal a pass.

"This is for the hospital. Report there at four o'clock and they'll give you a tour. Now if you would excuse me. Please take a seat, the administrative assistant is running an errand and when she gets back, she'll go through the paperwork with you, there are some details you still need to provide for us."

"Of course."

Once the matron left, Kal tried accessing the computer again and found the system still locked down. Rifling through the drawers of the desk, she found a large envelope. Grabbing a pile of random papers, she stuffed them into the envelope and sealed it. When the assistant came through the door, she sprang to her feet.

"Thank goodness you're back! There's an emergency! Matron has a migraine and she's gone to bed." She waved the envelope under the assistant's nose. "This is an urgent delivery. You've got to see to it straight away."

The assistant was flustered. "Is it for the Founder's visit?" Her voice squeaked. "We're never going to be ready in time."

"It's got to be delivered straight away." Kal plonked the envelope onto the assistant's desk.

"Who's it for?"

"The family of the old matron have requested important documents. Matron said they must have them this morning."

The woman blanched. "That's impossible. I have far too much to deal with."

Kal waited a few moments and then shrugged. "I don't know the area but maybe... I could help. Do they live nearby?"

"Oh not far at all. You could borrow my bicycle and I can draw you a map. Would you really? That would be wonderful."

"Er, well, I'm not sure if-"

"Yes, yes, really that would be wonderful."

The woman rushed to log herself onto the computer, pulled up the file of employee details and wrote an address onto the envelope. The assistant's eyes had already gone watery and she wiped at them.

"Excuse me being teary. Did the matron explain Indra Gupta died? It was terrible."

Kal nodded.

"Here's a map, it's easy to find and about twenty minute's cycle from here. You can't get lost."

At the doorway, Kal paused. "Matron gave me a quick tour only I think she left out the back of the building. What's down there?"

"Oh, that's Dr Scott's private suite. It's nothing to do with us and no one gets to go in except his personal assistant, Mr Singh."

The family of Indra Gupta lived in a ramshackle neighbourhood with its own water supply and local school. The modest house had flaking, red-painted walls and several scrawny chickens ran in the yard. Kal leant her bicycle against the wall. A patch-it-together bell system hung from a tree over the gate and when she pulled the wire, the bell clanged. Though the door and windows of the house were open, no one came out.

"Hello! I've a delivery from ScottBioTec."

Very likely this was home to an extended family. It would house Indra and her husband, and children if they had any, plus the husband's parents, and maybe nephews and nieces and cousins depending on the financial circumstances of the family. Here, the tradition was that the wife moved away from her parents and came to live with her husband and her family-in-law.

Kal pushed open the gate. "Hello! I've a delivery."

"If you've come to snoop you can get out. And if you're a reporter you can get out too. "

A wrinkled old woman stood at the front door, leaning on the door frame. With white hair and skin the colour of dark earth, she wore a sari which by its faded look she probably wore most days, keeping it on each morning when she took her daily bathe at the wash-stand, as was the custom here. Though she was smaller, the woman reminded Kal of Nannie.

"If it's my son you've come to pester, he isn't here."

Kal walked closer. "I've a delivery from ScottBioTec."

"We have no business with that place. Get out."

The woman had a white cloudiness in one of her eyes, marking her as having an advanced cataract. The other eye was so dark it was almost black and it regarded Kal unblinkingly. Clearly the old woman was angry. For a moment, Kal felt guilty intruding. Being honest would be the best approach.

"I'm a new volunteer at the research institute and I was very sorry to hear about Indra. A little girl called Padma told me what happened and I had the impression Indra really cared for the children and the children felt the same way about her. I wanted to offer my condolences."

"Well now you've done that, you'd better go back."

People who lived from day to day were savvy and this woman in front of her was no exception. She'd get nowhere by being evasive.

"I know there's no reason for you to trust me except I know there's something strange going on and I want to help, and Padma told me she believed Indra's death wasn't suicide."

The one dark eye regarded Kal for a moment, then the woman turned quickly to enter the house, jerking her head to tell Kal to follow.

The interior had rush matting and a collection of furniture which, in wonderful Indian style, would have looked at home in a flea market back in London. Delicious savoury scents drifted from a stove at the rear of the one main room. The old woman indicated for Kal to sit on the threadbare sofa.

"I was just making a cup of tea, would you like one?"

"That's very kind."

"You look very young."

"Not exactly, I'm almost thirty."

Behind the sofa, the old woman pulled a kettle from the stove and took cups and saucers from an overhead cupboard.

"As I said, you're young and I'm eighty-eight and I can see you're no fool. There's a depth in you, it's in your face and in your eyes, and you have a lot of character, but if you're really wise, you'll turn round and head back where you came from. Don't hang around ScottBioTec."

"Why not?"

"Because it's a nasty place. Even talking about it outside my own house is dangerous. The police have spies everywhere."

"Which means you don't think Indra took her own life?"

The old woman scoffed. "No one who knew her would think that. Though you'd never believe the bullying and threats my husband received from the police to push him into confessing to beating her. That's why he's moved away. For his own good."

The cups rattled on their saucers as the woman carried them over. "No, there's no need to help. I can manage."

The old woman set the tea on a low table and took her place in a rocking chair directly opposite Kal.

"So when are you going to tell me why you're really here?" asked the old woman.

"Like I said, I know there's something strange going on."

"That isn't what I meant." The old woman took a sip of scalding tea, her one dark eye staring at Kal over the rim of the teacup.

A shiver ran down Kal's back. Ever since she had heard of Indra's immolation, she couldn't stop thinking about the woman's agonising death and the charred body. Had the remains been verified? Indra and Alesha must have been a similar age. Two Indian women. Please no, surely there could be no connection with her mother's disappearance?

She chose her words with care. "If Indra was murdered I want to find out why. I've come here from England to investigate. My mother has gone missing and the trail points in this direction."

"You've got courage and determination… just like your mother."

Kal jerked her cup, sloshing dark tea into the saucer. "I– I'm sorry, what did you say?"

"I recognised you in the yard. You look like her."

Her heart started hammering. "My mother came here? You met her?"

"Your mother met Indra in the room we are in right now. It was private and Indra only told us she needed your mother's help. I don't even know how the two of them got in contact. What I do know is Indra was scared and she wouldn't tell us why. I think she wouldn't say because she was trying to protect us."

"This is a dreadful thing to ask I know, but… was Indra's body identified?"

The old woman shook her head. "Two witnesses said they'd seen Indra entering the garage shortly before the blaze and the police didn't look for any other evidence. She was doused in fuel and there was nothing left."

Kal swallowed. "I'm so sorry."

"What was your mother doing here?"

"She's a journalist, actually a very well-known one, and she works for a newspaper in London. She was working on an investigation."

Alesha had come to ScottBioTec for Sarah's project. What had her mother discovered which had spurred her to begin investigating the people in the photofile? The old woman sipped her tea. Kal lost all desire for her own drink and placed it to the side.

"I believe in my heart that my daughter-in-law is dead," said the old woman, "and I don't need science to tell me the remains were hers. Someone killed her and those witnesses were paid to lie because for Indra to be in that garage she could only have been dragged there by villains. Someone doused her in fuel and set her alight." The woman leant her bony elbows on her knees. "I wish I could help you more. The only thing I can do is answer the question I see written all over your face. I can see you're frightened for your mother and I tell you, the body they found wasn't her."

Kal realised she was shaking. She never cried in front of other people.

"The last time I saw her, I didn't even say a proper goodbye. She phoned me for help and I put her off, like I didn't even care."

She wiped at her face.

"My dear girl, your mother knows you love her without you having to tell her." The old woman patted Kal's knee. "You have a path to follow and it's brought you here. Trust in yourself and I believe you'll find the truth."

Chapter Twenty-seven

As Kal crossed the compound, the sun shone mercilessly down, pounding the earth. The children were in school and no noise came from anywhere. Even the cicadas were silent, overpowered by the heat.

At the hospital entrance, Kal pressed the pass against a pad and the glass doors slid open. Inside, a welcome draught swept down from the air conditioning. A white man waited in the foyer. In his thirties, with curly brown hair, he wore a blue, nurse's tunic.

"You must be Kavita. Hi, my name's Tommy."

"Pleased to meet you, Tommy," she said, "you sound American."

"Can't hide the accent. I'm from Illinois."

"Oh yes, and how'd you find your way to India?"

"By chance," he said, giving her a mischievous grin.

Tommy was attractive, in good shape, full of personality, and on first glance, most probably gay.

"I'm pretty good at puzzling people out, give me a few seconds, hmmm, let me see… was it by chance anything to do with love?" she asked.

Tommy laughed. "You're a good guesser. I was chasing after a nurse who came to work here. That was two years ago and I'm still here."

"And the nurse?"

"He left. I'm a mental health nurse myself so I stayed on and what d'ya know, I fell in love with the place. I can't get enough of people's honesty and spirituality, not to mention the dahl and curry." Tommy patted his stomach and laughed again. "Come on, we'll start at the top and I'll explain as we go."

They took the stairs to the top floor.

"This is a whistle-stop tour for you to understand the basics. There are five departments–the research institute, specialised surgery unit, intensive care, therapy and technical department. First of all, if children are selected at the clinic, they're put straight on a physical therapy and nutrition programme to prepare them for surgery. Most of the children have been under-nourished since birth, so you can't just wheel them into the operating theatre. It can take up to a year for them to be fit to withstand the procedures."

"Wow. That's a long time."

"Sure, and when a child is ready, a tiny micro-electrode array is implanted in the brain. As you can imagine, the brain surgery is a delicate procedure and the children remain in intensive care until they've been stabilised. After that's successful, the child's limb stems are prepared to be ready to accept the artificial replacements. "

"Does the brain surgery always go well?"

"Mostly, yes. In occasional cases, the children can react badly. It's a highly specialised field and Dr Mark, our senior surgeon, has pioneered the work. In fact, he's become a world expert. Before we started here, implantation of mini electrodes in the brain had only been attempted on animals."

They peered in the window of a ward where four children lay surrounded by machines.

"These four have already completed the brain surgery procedures and they've recently had their lower limbs prepared. That means their deformed limbs have been removed ready for the artificial replacements."

"And the new limbs can be controlled by the way the children think?"

"That's right. The children learn to think in a way which makes the limbs work how they want. The array communicates with chip technology in the limb. The idea grew from the intensive therapy patients undertake after they've suffered a stroke. I guess you've heard of that? When you lose the function of part of the brain, intensive physical therapy can retrain a patient to use new, un-used areas of the brain."

"Right."

"At first it's deliberate and difficult, but the more you do it, the more natural it becomes. The brain pathways actually change. Now if you give someone an artificial limb, the brain can learn to use it too, via the electrode array that's been implanted."

It sounded futuristic.

"Everyone's brain communicates with the body by electrical impulses and the array picks those impulses up. The trick is for the person to learn how that translates into motor action in the limb. What we're talking about is translating thought into action. And, of course, the more refined the mechanics of the artificial limb, the greater the possibility for achieving natural movement."

"Wow. It sounds amazing."

'Yeah, I know."

More wards contained children in bed. Then they came to a number of empty rooms.

"These children are either in physiotherapy or they're taking part in research."

"You like working here, don't you?"

"It's great, though I can't stay here forever, even though I might like to. I'll have to pick up my life at home again some time."

"No boyfriends here, then?"

"Not at the moment and they don't know what they're missing." Tommy spread his hands and laughed as they took the stairs down to the first floor.

"What happens in the research centre?"

"They've their own team of scientists. That's where they make all the advances in chip technology and nerve pathway control. Children have a remarkable ability to learn to move the artificial limbs and accustom themselves to the brain implants many times faster than adults. And you know what? How the brain learns to interact with the chip is still a mystery. Rumour has it they're working on identifying specific cocktails of neurotransmitters manufactured by the brain–it's those cocktails which actually enhance the communication in some way. If those molecules can be identified and then artificially produced, it could help adults to adapt more fully."

Kal watched through the window of a therapy area. It was decked out like a gymnasium and children with artificial limbs practised walking on balance beams and skipped with ropes and bounced on trampolines.

"They make all the physiotherapy fun, you know how kids love to play. In separate rooms there's also work on fine motor-control where kids can see a scan of their own brain real-time and learn to direct the colours in the image. It helps them connect thoughts to fine movement."

"I'd like to see that."

"Sure, we can pass by."

"I think the work here is fascinating, and I read up about your third-generation limb. They say it's top of the range."

"Absolutely, but it's the quality of the communication with the limb which makes any limb special. What's the point of having a top-performing artificial arm if you can't make it work for you?"

Tommy knocked at a room and entered. "Mind if we observe for a few minutes?" he asked, "You won't even know we're here."

A little girl was in the process of threading beads to make a necklace. She had an artificial leg and an artificial arm. Her scalp was wired up to a machine and, in front of the child, a screen displayed an image of the two hemispheres of her brain.

"That's a real-time image of her brain," Tommy said. "You can see the implanted mini-array right there and the colours around represent the associated brain activity. She's being trained to control her finger movements. You see how the colours in different zones are changing? The hotter the colour, the more that part of the brain is active. So that small orange area is the most active and it tells us it's the part of the brain she's using for this task and it's that zone which is affecting the electrode and being picked up by the chip."

"Good Amita," said the therapist, "the hotter you make the spot, the easier it will be to get the thread through the hole in the bead. Let's try to make it turn from orange to red."

"She's around eight years old and probably had her set of operations a few months ago," Tommy whispered, "she'll have worked hard to get this far. As she progresses, they make the beads smaller and smaller."

"Wow, she's really concentrating," Kal said.

"When they first come in here the colours are all purples and blues and the brain activity is dispersed. The children target the coloured area with their own will and the brain itself has worked out how that translates into action in the fingers. Isn't it incredible?"

Kal had to agree it was.

"Next stop is the technical department," Tommy said.

"Seems like it all works well, although one little girl told me children sometimes run away."

"There can be problems, for instance when the limbs are attached there's a need for pain control which can be prolonged. Some of it's what we call 'ghost pain' generated by the brain and not associated to a specific part of the body. That's the team I work in. We think ghost pain is triggered by the area of the brain they implant to. There are several remedies and the most drastic is to adjust, or even remove, the electrode implantation. That only happens as a last resort, there are plenty of methods we employ before we get to that stage."

"That doesn't sound good."

"It's a complex problem because not all the children exhibit it. Apart from that, there's always new technology to be trialled. The research programme takes a lot of time and the children agree to take part until they're sixteen. It's a big under-taking."

"You mean that's why some of them run away?"

"Maybe one or two run off, I've heard of it. You've got to understand there's a massive amount of procedures and technology for them to deal with. The children are adaptable only some of them get spooked. For them, running away would be a natural response and, of course, sometimes they come back."

Tommy pushed through a set of doors. "This is the technical area. The limbs are manufactured in the USA and the final adjustments are made on-site to custom fit to each patient. The equipment here is worth millions of dollars."

"I read about some controversy too, I mean, doesn't the child's agreement to take part in the research programme strike you as odd? They're far too young to know what they're signing up to."

"The ethics did bother me, except I've seen too many miracles and let's face it, most of the children who come here have no adult to vouch for them, so who would we ask permission from? This isn't the United States or England, they're not wards of court, they're street kids, and since the children are growing, the limbs need to be regularly updated so they need regular appointments anyway. Don't forget, here they get good food, a bed and education."

A range of artificial limbs stretched along a shelf. Leg units from small to large. Arm and hand units too.

"Don't touch any," Tommy said, "or the technicians will go berserk."

"Doesn't it bother you there are people comparing ScottBioTec to a concentration camp and the horrors perpetrated by sadists during the Holocaust? When I read that it made me feel very uncomfortable."

"Medical research always attracts strong views, and a lot of crank protestors too. Well, it isn't like that or I wouldn't be here. Mark and Christina are professionals and their teams are run impeccably. There's no Dr Mengele at ScottBioTec, Kavita, I promise you that."

Tommy handed her an object which looked like a mobile phone. "Now this you can touch."

It was the size of her palm. Slim and black and a lot heavier than a phone.

"It's Christina's brain-child. It's a mobile control unit which allows communication to the chip to be deactivated from the outside. So, for instance, if ghost pain is a problem the children can be given total rest without the need for drugs and without the need for unattaching the limb. The idea is that in real life, the limb remains permanently attached, it's not taken on and off like the old-style prosthetics. This control unit is marvellous. The children start with a few minutes' interaction with their new limbs per day and gradually build it up. As they get more experienced, the children take over the use of the control and decide for themselves how much time they spend interacting with the limb. Those experiencing ghost pain often overcome it by their own motivation to succeed."

The tour was coming to an end and they left the laboratory and looped back round to the entrance.

"Is there any surgery takes place outside the hospital? For instance, in the office building?"

Tommy laughed. "Of course not, it's only administration over there. Like I said, it all happens right here."

And she could see from Tommy's eyes he believed it.

After her tour, Kal headed back to her room. It would have been good to chat with Marty though, of course, for the sake of security she'd left her mobile and true identification at the hotel.

It struck her as soon as she closed the door. Someone had been inside her room.

She had only partly emptied the contents of her backpack–half her clothing she'd placed onto shelves and the rest she'd left in her bag.

Kal rested her hand on the pile of folded t-shirts, and then bent to examine her pack. The evidence stood out immediately because the clasp on a side compartment had been hastily closed. Too hastily. The third prong of the clasp had broken off years ago, so only two prongs remained, meaning it was trickier to fully close than it should be. It tended to get stuck halfway. Whoever had last closed it hadn't taken the time to push it all the way in, and that wasn't her.

The most likely suspect? Mr Singh. Checking the rest of her belongings, she found nothing missing, nor out of place, which meant Mr Singh was better at snooping than she would have imagined.

Kal lay on the bed and for the next hour or so, stared up at the ceiling, thinking through her next steps.

Chapter Twenty-eight

Several hours before Scott's arrival, the matron's migraine peaked. From the steps of the dormitory block, Kal watched the administrative assistant sprint across the playground.

The night before, Kal had briefed Padma. So that morning in the school room, Padma fell from her chair, claiming she felt dizzy, which meant Padma had been lying in sick bay since then, situated right next to the office. Kal had discovered the matron liked to keep an eye on children who felt poorly and had the habit of keeping the sick bay door open, making it the perfect place for Padma to spy on the arrangements for Scott's visit.

On Kal's instructions, Ashok went in and out to see his sister and the little boy was keeping Kal up-to-date. She knew the time Scott's private jet would land, when Scott should arrive and the checklist of instructions the matron was following to the letter to prepare for his visit and, of course, she knew the matron's migraine had been getting steadily worse.

Little spurts of dust flew from the heels of the administrative assistant as she ran. Certainly, the assistant had come to summon Jasodra, who, as deputy-in-charge, would be the one to take over.

"Where's Jasodra? Matron wants her urgently." Tendrils of hair fell across the assistant's face.

"Jasodra's in the dormitory. Why, is there something wrong?"

"Matron's migraine is unbearable. There's no way she'll last until Dr Scott arrives. Jasodra will have to take over."

Kal waited while the assistant went inside. She heard a kerfuffle, and then the assistant and Jasodra came outside. From the expression on Jasodra's face, Kal could see her contemplating the enormity of welcoming Dr Scott alone.

Somewhere out in the dirt plane, a lone cicada chirruped. It was important to let Jasodra take the lead, then Kal could step in to be her right hand.

"Kavita, can you manage here for me?" Jasodra said. "There's the dormitories and the lounge areas to put in order and a mountain of clothes to sort. Everything has to be in top shape for the Founder's visit, not a shoe out of place."

"I've been up since six this morning and it's all done. Matron spoke to me yesterday about Dr Scott's visit and I offered to help out, I'm sure I can be more use to you over in the office than here."

Jasodra hesitated. So Kal pushed open the door of the lounge to display the chairs neatly in place, the spotless surfaces of the tables, the crayons and brightly coloured exercise books stacked on the shelves. In the adjacent room, she had already emptied the laundry baskets.

"Matron will be out for the count soon, she can hardly stand. You might need someone you can rely on."

"Okay, Kavita, that makes sense and I'd be grateful, I'm not sure how I'm going to cope. Please come with me."

Over at the office, the drone of a ceiling fan filled the room. Barely able to talk, the Matron clung on. She gripped the armrests of her chair, her magenta-coloured nails making her hands look like claws.

"I'm sorry… Jasodra, you'll have to manage… on your own. Dr Scott's very… picky about arrangements for his… visits. My predecessor left… full instructions. There's a…

detailed checklist and you must go through it... item by item." Matron clenched her teeth.

"Please go to bed," Jasodra said. "I can manage and Kavita has offered to help. We shall be all right."

Matron's eyes flicked to Kal.

Oh no, the woman was about to object. Grabbing one of the matron's arms, Kal instructed the administrative assistant to take the other side.

"There's no arguing matron, you're not well enough." Kal spoke loudly and the matron gave up the battle.

As they hoisted her to her feet, the woman started shaking. Sorry, Kal thought, I had no choice. Early that morning, she had hunted for monosodium glutamate in the kitchen and added it to matron's mug. It had certainly had the desired effect, being known to trigger migraines, and in the matron's case it had speeded it up nicely.

"Can you help her back to her room?" Kal said to the assistant, and she practically propelled them to the door.

"Poor matron," said Jasodra, "it must be the stress of the Founder's visit. I've no idea how I'm going to welcome him, I've never met anyone so important in my life."

Kal squeezed Jasodra's arm. "There's nothing to worry about. We can write out a welcoming speech together, I'm sure you'll be fine."

Several typed sheets lay beside the keyboard. Sensing Jasodra's hesitation, Kal swept them up. Matron had struck through each task on the checklist as she completed them. In the few seconds before Kal politely handed it over, she scanned the list. One item had recently been scored through, it read, 'Mr Singh to prepare The Suite.' Kal noted how Scott planned to tour the hospital and, despite his time of arrival being seven o'clock at night, he wished to see a display of physical therapies performed by the children.

The ceiling fan whirred, ruffling the sheets.

"Let's carry on working our way down," Jasodra said, "the next is, 'meet with Head of Physiotherapy to confirm order of events this evening.'"

"'Then comes, 'Confirm menu arrangements with the kitchen.' I could deal with that. The menu is attached at the back."

She waited for Jasodra to agree and head off for the hospital, leaving her free.

"Good idea, Kavita. Let me know if there are any problems."

From the window, Kal watched Jasodra walk briskly across the compound and when she disappeared inside the hospital, Kal went straight to sick bay.

"The matron's gone, Padma. You did really well and now I'd like you to go back to the dormitory and lie low."

"I can help you."

"You've helped me enough and this could get dangerous."

Padma sat up. "Something tells me I won't be seeing you again."

The girl's pre-sentiment gave Kal goosebumps. She rubbed her arms. It was going to be a big night that was certain and no telling how it would turn out.

"Like we said before, the missing children are my priority, Padma, and in case I don't see you again, will you make me a promise?"

"What?"

"That you'll continue studying hard and if you're ever in trouble, there's an American nurse called Tommy at the hospital. You can ask him for help, he's a friend."

Padma gave the briefest of nods and slipped away.

Beyond the office, Kal pushed through a set of double doors and found herself in the long corridor stretching to Scott's private suite. She ran swiftly, covering the distance in a few seconds. As she passed the door to the stationery store, she pulled up, and then ahead she saw her luck was in, because Mr Singh had been careless. He had left the steel door ajar.

She leaned close and listened. Silence. With her fingertips she gave the door a little push. It swung open to reveal a hallway with expensive, wooden flooring and a single, decorative floor lamp giving out a muted glow. A faint scent of floor polish hung in the air. The private suite seemed to be a luxury apartment.

There were two doors. From behind one, Kal could hear faint sounds–an electrical, rhythmic noise that came closer then moved away, came closer then moved away and each time, the noise progressed nearer to the door. Whatever made the noise sounded like it might be coming out soon.

She chose the other door and flexed her shoulders, her heart rate accelerating. The gold handle was cold to the touch. Swiftly pushing it open, she stepped boldly inside, keeping low, ready for whatever she might encounter.

An automatic ceiling light flicked on and adrenalin pumped round Kal's system but the room was empty. She was in a top-of-the-range bathroom suite, with a huge mirror and a corner tub and shining, double hand-basins. A luxury shower area lay in the corner with a curved, glass door. Something there caught her attention.

Grey slate tiling covered the walls backing the shower and the tiles were large, slightly uneven slates such as you'd find in an ultra-fashionable, Nordic hotel. The tiles were so irregular, they acted as good camouflage. Kal ran her hand over the surfaces until she found a consistent vertical flaw. This was a panel, not a wall.

She gave the edge a smart push. Despite its weight, the wall slid back into a hidden recess, rolling soundlessly on runners concealed in the floor and ceiling. It hid a dim cubicle. The hairs on Kal's arms stood on end.

She took a step inside and faced a smoky window which looked out on a lit bedroom. Through the window, suddenly she found herself staring at Mr Singh and she dropped to the ground, though he passed on oblivious.

Creeping up onto her knees, she touched the glass in front of her. Of course, it wasn't a window, it was a two-way mirror. Mr Singh was in the process of hoovering a large, Persian rug and she could hear nothing from the machine. Mr Singh didn't even know she was there.

A light sweat prickled her top lip. In front of her was an open-plan area which was half-lounge, half-bedroom. Directly opposite Kal, beyond the Persian rug, lay a king-sized bed and alongside was a cabinet. A stainless-steel set of handcuffs sat on top of the cabinet. Kal's blood ran cold only it wasn't the cuffs which gave her the chills, because the cuffs, although small, could perhaps be for a consenting adult. But right next to the them was a bowl of colourful sweets.

For a moment, her vision spun as the shock wave hit her. Small cuffs. Sweets. For children.

A console was tucked into the side of the cubicle. Clutching at the edge of it, Kal fought the urge to vomit, digging her fingers into the plastic until they hurt. When the wave of nausea passed, she forced herself to look again and re-scan the area–Mr Singh, the bed, the cuffs, the bowl. She had missed something. Partly concealed on the bottom shelf of the cabinet lay a slim, black unit. Insert the correct chip into that and, like Tommy said, you could deactivate the limbs of a child. Render them helpless with the press of a button.

Though Kal suspected those on her mother's list could be involved in paedophilia, she'd hoped to be proved wrong. Now, the evidence was like a match to fuel. Her rage flared, forcing its way, white hot, into her veins. She wanted to kick and destroy with her bare hands. She imagined jamming her arm across Mr Singh's windpipe and squeezing all the way and enjoying doing it. It took all her discipline to get herself under control. The exertion of it made her shake.

It wasn't the first time she'd felt a rage forceful enough to commit murder. On assignment, colleagues dealt with facing destruction and crisis in their own ways–depression, drinking, becoming a workaholic. Sometimes Kal picked out her targets, be it politicians or local despots, and she imagined the vulnerable areas on their bodies, which with one shot would bring instant death. It never got beyond imagining, and she had sworn there would never be an exception.

She forced herself to take deep breaths. Singh was a puppet. The sick controller behind this place was the one she wanted.

With cold precision, Kal re-examined the room quadrant by quadrant–two Persian rugs, a couch, armschairs, table, door to the hallway, door leading to an unseen room, a bar. She noted the dimensions and the lay out, storing them in her memory.

Meanwhile, Mr Singh finished his cleaning and wheeled the machine away. Kal wiped her sweating palms down her trousers and turned her attention to the cubicle.

The console equipment was for recording and everything was channelled through a main computer. Bending on one knee, Kal traced the wiring and found ports for a portable hard-drive at the side of the computer where a black lead trailed to the ground, its end hanging empty. Whatever atrocities happened in this room, somebody kept a record.

Mr Singh returned and went into a room at the rear of the bedroom. Kal took the chance to leave, rolling back the panel to its concealed position, careful to leave everything exactly as she found it. With her camera in town it would be difficult to capture concrete evidence of the suite. She would have to improvise. In a few careful steps she was out of the apartment and running along the corridor back in the direction of the office.

They spent the rest of the afternoon working their way down the checklist until, half an hour before Scott's arrival, Kal typed up a speech for Jasodra. Amongst all the running backwards and forwards, she found a gap to sneak over to the hospital to speak with Tommy, and even though she only had a few minutes with him, it had been enough.

At half past seven, a black sedan drove up the track to the compound. Temporary floodlights had been rigged over the parking area and they lit up a cloud of dust as the car engine died.

The children had been assembled and they nervously shuffled their feet. Jasodra wore a lime green sari and the gorgeous silk cascaded over her shoulder as she stepped forward to greet their Patron.

The children had been waiting for over half an hour, stretching in two long rows all the way from the parking area to the hospital. Like greeting royalty, they formed a corridor and stood with hands clasped palm to palm in front of them. Kal had objected to that prayer position.

"We must have the children standing like that," Jasodra said, "because it's what Dr Scott will expect and it's not for us to question his wishes."

Kal had bitten back her retort. Now she hung in the shadows as Richard Scott stepped from the car. A second person got out and Kal recognised the Russian, Boris. From the front of the car, came a chauffeur and a fourth man–both of whom Kal assessed to be bodyguards, and not locals either because they were both white and must have flown over with Scott from London.

Jasodra shook Scott's hand and read the passage Kal had prepared. On cue, the children began reciting a Buddhist chant, their rising and falling voices filling the warm, night air with a message of welcome.

Kal felt like spitting and, as Scott and Boris walked along the corridor, she watched Scott smile, his perfect teeth over-white in the floodlights.

Was Scott as guilty as Boris? Had her mother got close to him as a way of finding out more? She flexed her hands by her sides. Smile on, Scott, she thought, because soon she would find out everything.

Chapter Twenty-nine

The display of physical therapy was scheduled for one hour, followed by a two-hour dinner. Kal wondered how Jasodra was coping. At least Mark and Christina were joining the group, so Jasodra would have help with social conversation.

Time crawled by, so Kal returned to her room and spent a good hour stretching every single muscle in her body. She considered going for a run around the outskirts of the compound but even though it was long after nightfall, the insects would be voracious, it just wouldn't be possible even if she covered herself in repellents. Instead, in the tiny space beside her bed, Kal executed a highly-modified version of the Form, holding each movement to its maximum, one stance flowing to the next, preparing herself for what was to come.

Three hours later, she crouched at the corner of the office block. Grit had collected at the base of the wall and the slightest movement of her trainers would grate like sandpaper, so she kept her body perfectly still. The trick with surveillance was to not do anything and not think anything. You must hang there, conserving your strength, alert but not over alert, saving your energy. She felt detached, almost clinical. Go in clean and swift, get evidence, get out. This must be a precision operation.

The dinner took place in the long dining hall. When finally Mark and Christina came out, they called goodnight to Scott and Kal watched as they returned to the hospital together, the two chatting in low voices. Meanwhile, Jasodra headed back to the dormitory. A few minutes later, Scott and Boris exited, followed by the two bodyguards. Both guards were in excellent physical shape though they trod heavily, their bellies full of Indian food.

Kal squeezed into the shadows. There was no moon tonight which was to her advantage. In contrast to the bodyguards, Boris had a swing in his step and an eagerness which threatened to whip up her rage.

She had a good view as Mr Singh trotted out and intercepted Scott and Boris, and, after a brief exchange, Mr Singh scuttled off in the direction of the hospital. Kal waited for the four to head towards the private suite then she went after Mr Singh, maintaining a stealthy profile, keeping her footsteps light and Mr Singh in her sights.

Mr Singh didn't go to the main hospital entrance. Instead, he headed for the side where a fire exit door had been propped open. A young woman from the hospital staff waited in a pool of light. She was clearly over-impressed by Mr Singh, and bobbed her head in deference as Mr Singh approached. Stopping with her back pressed against a tree, Kal strained to hear what they said.

"Are the children ready?" asked Mr Singh.

The woman bobbed her head. "Shall I bring them out?"

"I hope you impressed on them what an honour this is," Mr Singh said, "Dr Scott wishes to be discreet. He doesn't want the other children to know or they'll be jealous they haven't been chosen. Nobody is to know about this, you understand? That is our Founder's prime concern."

"Of course sir, I didn't tell anyone, and they've been dressed exactly as you asked. They're very excited." The nurse spoke rapidly, barely lifting her eyes from the ground.

"Excellent. They'll be well taken care of and since it's likely the evening will end late, I've arranged for them to spend the night in the children's home. Matron has made the arrangements. Now please bring them to the office building straightaway. Oh, and as a thank you for your help, Dr Scott has agreed for you to take time off to visit your family. They live some way from here I understand, and you have leave to travel to visit them first thing in the morning, Dr Scott will fund your fare."

"Th... that's most generous," the woman stammered.

"Not at all," said Mr Singh, "now please escort the children."

Clever. If any questions were asked the nurse would be off-site. Probably her family lived several day's journey away, which meant the woman would stay three or four weeks since the cost of travel demanded it.

The assistant disappeared inside and Mr Singh checked around, then headed back the way he'd come.

Kal itched to get inside the fire door so badly a muscle in her calf started twitching. Mr Singh passed her hiding place and kept going. She forced herself to count to four and she managed to get to two and a half before she took her chance and ran for the fire exit. Mr Singh's stride didn't miss a beat–his mind fully occupied.

Inside the hospital, she followed the sounds of excitement and found three children clustered around the nurse in a therapy room. There were two girls and one boy and the woman was fussing with the hair of one of the girls.

All three children were dressed in lavish silk, shalwar kameez tunics and close-fitting leggings. One of the girls was dressed in red and the other girl and boy in pale blue. The girl in red Kal recognised as Amita, who she had watched threading the beads. The colours of the silk were lovely and all three children had shining brown eyes, and it was the children's radiant expressions which most caught at Kal because it was like they believed they were going to a party.

She stood firm and solid in the doorway and crossed her arms. "Dr Scott has changed his mind."

The nurse held the hair-brush frozen in mid-air. "What do you mean?"

"Dr Scott wants you to leave the compound immediately to visit your family."

The woman was astonished.

"Your family lives some days away, so the sooner you leave the sooner you'll arrive."

"That's impossible."

Kal produced a fat wad of rupee notes. "Go to the entrance and instruct the guard to call you a taxi and you can wait at the train depot until the morning. I'm sure your train will leave early and you can take advantage to queue for your ticket."

Many poor families stayed overnight at the depot and lots of passengers slept in the queue outside the ticket office.

The nurse's eyes fixed on the wad and Kal waved it backwards and forwards. Perhaps the woman had never been offered so much cash in her life. Probably she earned a paltry wage and normally saw her family once a year, saving solicitously for the trip. Most likely she would pocket the offering and borrow a bicycle to pedal into town, then she could share all her good fortune with her family.

Kal pre-empted the last hurdle. "Don't worry about the children. I've been instructed to take them over to Dr Scott. Quickly now, we mustn't keep him waiting and give me your tunic, I'll put it in the laundry for you. Now go!"

She thrust the wad of notes into the nurse's hand and hustled her out the door.

The three children hadn't said a word. At their big, innocent eyes Kal almost backed out. Almost grabbed them and ran for it, knowing that if she did the abuse would carry on, not with these children but with others. A choice like that could paralyse her. No, she must continue and do everything in her power to make sure this stopped. With corrupt police prepared to overlook the matron's murder she had no other way of closing down the operation except with concrete evidence. She must get her own proof and find out who kept the master record. *Dig deep*, she told herself, *keep your nerve*.

She spoke her promise out loud. "I'm not going to let any harm come to you."

The children nodded in unison, totally out of their depth. Kal wanted to hear their voices, perhaps she wanted to reassure herself everything would be all right.

"How do I look?" she asked.

"You look lovely," Amita said.

With a tug, Kal tightened the knot of her Muslim-style, head-covering.

Back at the dormitory, she had barely recognised herself. She had tucked every strand of hair inside the head covering and folded the fabric so low down her forehead it almost met her eyebrows. And those eyebrows, for the first time in her life, Kal had plucked mercilessly to the thinnest of lines. With just her eyes, nose and mouth showing and her features so Indian, it offered the perfect disguise, and she'd delved into Jasodra's wardrobe and borrowed a plain, cotton shalwar kameez, somewhat dull. Only her accent would give her away. Kal buttoned up the blue nurse's tunic. Perfect.

"Wait here a few minutes you three. I'll be back in a moment," she said.

Kal returned to the fire exit. How long would it take for Scott to get impatient and send Mr Singh to speed things up? Not long, she'd guess. Soon, Mr Singh came hurrying across the compound and Kal placed her body in the shadow, leaving only the bottom part of her leg and foot trailing in the pool of light.

Mr Singh wasn't happy. "What on earth is going on? What's the delay?"

He stopped short when it wasn't the person he expected. Kal saw him double-take, trying to place her. No recognition registered on his face. Good. Her cover was sound.

Stepping forward, she knocked him out with one swift blow. Mr Singh fell like a log. "There's been a change of plan," she said.

On her way past the office, Kal clocked one bodyguard sitting in matron's chair, bored, with his feet resting on the desk. The second guard lounged at the steel door. He could be more of a problem.

As Kal approached the private suite with the children, his eyes tracked her and he licked his lips.

"Hello, my lovely, what have we got here?"

He wore a white t-shirt which displayed his biceps. With a London accent and sharp eyes, unlike his colleague he was alert. He flicked the loose end of her head scarf with his finger. She noticed his powerful neck and thickset hands. Certainly he was someone who had invested in years of sweat down the gym. Bench presses might be his speciality.

"Why the modesty? What have you got you want to cover up?" His eyes trailed over her body.

She considered decking him. It would be possible only the children would be spooked. One of them might scream, and if she didn't get the bodyguard in one, he'd retaliate. Sounds could filter to the suite or back to the office.

"It's the children for Dr Scott and his guest," she said. No fears about him recognising her, he'd never met her.

"In you go then," he said.

As she went past, the man brushed his hand over her breast. Kal stamped down the urge to break his fingers and kept walking. The guard snickered. That punk is dead meat, she thought.

To prevent the children from bunching up behind her, she held the hand of the little boy as they entered the lounge. Before walking across the floor, she took off her long shawl and pulled a chair out, draping the shawl over its back so the fringe trailed to the ground.

Then she walked across the first Persian rug, Tommy's phone bumping against her leg. She hadn't risked telling Tommy why she needed it, just said it was urgent. It had a camera and a limited video capacity and it would be enough. All she needed was to find a way to conceal herself.

Scott reclined on the couch and Boris in one of the armchairs, an empty glass in his hand.

"Come in children and don't be shy. Come and sit on the rug," Scott said. He indicated for the children to make themselves comfortable on the carpet in front of him.

"Where's that Mr Singh got to? I want a clean glass. You," Boris pointed a bejewelled finger in Kal's direction, "get me four glasses."

Leaving the children kneeling on the rug, she walked to the rear of the lounge to the kitchen door. Neither of the men had so far even looked at her. Lowly staff clearly didn't command any attention, which was perfect. She opened the cabinets, listening to their conversation.

"I like the one in the red costume," Boris said.

Kal almost dropped a glass in the sink. The one in red was Amita.

"Sit next to me and tell me your name," said Boris. "Well, Richard, as I've told you before, this is an amazing set-up."

Scott gave a smug laugh and Kal felt like vomiting.

"There are no birth records, the children have no identity and in the eyes of the Indian government they don't even exist," Scott said. "I keep the communication between the hospital and the home deliberately poor. If anyone bothers to wonder, which they won't, they'll think the children stayed at the home."

The fucking piece of shit. Scott was the supplier. She felt like killing him on the spot.

"It can be left indefinitely because nobody cares or wants to ask questions," Scott said. "On top of that, Christina's got her head buried in her research so none of her team want to cause a problem and Mark's having an affair with an Indian doctor, so they're all fully occupied."

So Mark and Christina weren't aware of the existence of the suite. Which meant two targets less. Kal placed the glasses on a tray.

"Only the old matron put the dots together and poked around and it was easy to dispose of her. I was amazed she stuck her head above the parapet, these Indians can surprise you sometimes. A lifetime of servitude and then *blip*, they go right off track. For an employee like Indra Gupta it was totally out of character. I heard she was quite a fighter at the end screaming about the vengeance of the gods and how children are sacred. I had to laugh. And I guarantee you Boris, for the rest of them, their narrow imaginations and tedious pre-occupations won't allow them to consider the possibility. Denial and stupidity will preside," Scott said.

It was going to be difficult to control herself. But with corrupt police willing to overlook Indra Gupta's murder, she had to get hard evidence to take back to Spinks. It was the only way of bringing this to its knees.

Careful to walk modestly and not stride, Kal went back to the lounge and placed the tray on a coffee table beside Boris.

Boris lifted the decanter and poured spirits into four glasses. He had removed his jacket and tie, so his pale skin showed through the open neck of his shirt. He looked like he'd had plenty to drink.

In contrast, Scott appeared stone cold sober. Totally in control. As she stared at the back of Boris' head, Kal had to work hard not to clench her teeth. She knew she must be careful to maintain herself as insignificant and as nondescript as possible.

She loitered out of their direct line of sight and, more importantly, out of range of the mirror and the recording equipment hidden behind it. Even given her position, with a swift and accurate action she knew she could reach and take the life from Boris and not be caught on camera. He'd struggle. He was large but he had little fight in him. He'd go down. Scott would intervene and certainly he'd alert the bodyguard. But she wasn't a killer. Or was she?

"Boris, my private jet is on standby to take you back to London, so leave whenever you wish and Mr Singh will look after your needs. I've business in New Delhi so you can return without me."

As Boris grunted a response, Kal registered a sudden tension in Scott's shoulders. On some subliminal level, he'd picked up a danger signal and his eyes swivelled in her direction. She controlled her breathing and trained her gaze on the children, pretending not to notice his stare.

Meanwhile Boris handed a glass to each child. "Drink up," he said.

Scott's eyes remained on her. Kal could imagine them– grey and dispassionate. The tension mounted as she waited for Scott's brain to work through the permutations. She concentrated on maintaining a low demeanour, letting her chest and shoulders cave in a subservient fashion, keeping any tightness from her features and ready at any moment to respond with violence. Amita raised a glass and looked at her and Kal coyly inclined her head. Scott turned away.

"There's only one piece of equipment you may not be familiar with," Scott said, rising to his feet.

Whilst she had the chance, Kal mimed a tipping movement with her hand, indicating to the children to spill their drinks on the carpet. Now Scott returned with the black control unit.

"I won't spoil the surprise for you, Boris, but if you press this switch it will give a whole new dimension to the word 'helpless'. I think you'll find it most enjoyable."

The room offered few opportunities for a hiding place. What she needed was incriminating photographs. The most convenient would be the spy cubicle though she was betting that's where Scott would be heading. He would put a hard drive in place and remove it later. Maybe he'd stay to watch. She could take Scott out, the problem being it would warn him of a threat. What if he closed down the suite and moved to another location? What if he already had alternative locations set up? Kal considered the other options. Kitchen–no. Entrance hallway–yes. She'd have to take out the snickering guard and that would be a pleasure.

Scott clicked his fingers in her direction. "You, girl, what are you hanging around for? Get back to the hospital."

Kal bowed her head just as the nurse had done in deference to Mr Singh, and she shuffled from the room. In a few steps she was back at the threshold of the corridor.

"Finished already?" asked the guard, and he put his leg out to prevent her going any further.

The man had tone and strength. If he had been less of an arrogant asshole, he'd have been able to use his combat skills too. As it was, Kal had all the advantages–surprise, preparation and a mountain of motivation.

She went for his kidneys. His weak spot. Possibly a genetic tendency and given away by his puffy, blotchy complexion and sagging, purple circles under his eyes. Organ weaknesses and other physiological problems could often be identified by a facial diagnosis.

She got in two full power strikes, right on target. The guard doubled. She followed with an elbow strike up under his jaw, hearing the satisfying crunch of the cervicals at the base of his neck as the small joints whipped out of line. A strike to the temple and he was down. That should keep him out for the count.

Kal spotted the hilt of a handgun sticking from the back of his belt. She yanked it out in disgust. Now she listened carefully. No sounds came from inside the apartment, nor from the direction of the office. Good.

Hauling the body into the stationery store seemed to take an age. She returned to crouch by the door of the suite.

"I'll leave you to entertain yourself, my friend."

Scott sounded close, almost on top of her. *Keep your nerve, he won't exit.* He was pretending to go for Boris' benefit and instead of leaving the apartment, she heard Scott open the door to the bathroom. The gamble would be how long he'd stay in the spy cubicle but she'd have to take the risk.

Neutralise all your opponents, commanded the voice in her head. This time, Kal ignored David Khan. Returning to the office to deal with the second guard would take too much time. Most likely he was snoring by now, and she had left the children for too long.

Kal crept across the hallway. Taking out Tommy's phone, she got down on her belly and using her elbows and propelling herself with her toes, she crawled inside. She knew exactly where she'd have cover from the observation mirror and where not. As she inched forward, the trailing ends of her headscarf kept snagging under her forearms, holding her up. Her clothing felt tight and far too hot. Shit. This was taking too long. *Keep steady, you can do this.* Salty sweat began stinging her eyes.

Once inside the lounge, from her position on the floor, she took a video of the bed and the cuffs. She got in the side of Boris' head. What she needed were the children clearly in the frame.

Over on the couch, Boris was talking to Amita, telling her not to be frightened. If Boris so much as laid a finger on Amita, she swore she'd finish him. Meanwhile, Kal realised the chair she so carefully positioned with the shawl shielding the view to the mirror, had been pushed aside. Damn it! If she crawled further into the room there would be no cover to hide her from Scott's view. Boris had dropped his voice to a mumble. Would the video capture it? She doubted it. It left her no option except to take out Scott. She needed to be inside that cubicle.

As Kal wriggled back towards the door, one of the children gave a frightened squeal. She scooted backwards even faster and just as she regained the hallway, something hard jammed into the back of her rib-cage.

"Get up. Quietly."

The voice had an eastern European accent. It was the second bodyguard, the one from the office.

"What the hell are you doing?" he demanded, waving the gun in her face.

Had he seen the phone in her hand? No, she'd concealed it fast. She made her eyes large and scared, made her lip tremble as she spoke.

"I... I'm sorry, I was searching for the bathroom."

"On your hands and knees, yeah, tell me about it sweet cheeks. Have we got ourselves a little spy?"

He leered close. The skin of his lip was cracked, his breath fetid. The tip of the gun had dipped.

She grabbed his arm and drove his firing hand diagonally across his body and down. Struck him direct to his face then up under the ribs. He fell off balance though he kept an iron grasp on the weapon. It fired. The explosion resounded in the hallway. She kept her grip on the man's firing arm and smashed his hand against the wall. The gun fell though she couldn't hear it through the ringing in her ears.

He wasn't in as good shape as his partner. He had weight around his middle and as he made to push upright she went straight for his stomach. *Pam, pam, pam.* He swung at her with a vicious upper-cut. He must be a boxer. She should watch out. His strikes would come like lightning and full power. Likely he'd go for her head.

He struck again and the edge of it caught her temple. Kal snaked her upper body away so his follow up missed by a fraction. She felt air on her cheek as his fist sped past. A tiny part of her sensed a change in the environment as the bathroom door cracked open and she fired a kick behind her at the floor lamp, sending it smashing to the ground, plunging the hallway into darkness. Then she flew at the bodyguard's legs, pinning his knees together and the two of them crashed to the floor. As Scott came out of the bathroom there was a rapid triangle of light and then the lights inside the bathroom automatically shut off. Scott practically fell over them as he staggered through the chaos of limbs.

"Get to the car Boris!" Scott shouted.

The guard's breathing was laboured. Kal rolled off him and got behind, jamming her arm across his windpipe. He got to his feet and lifted her, swinging her in the air like a marionette. As the guard smashed her head against the wall, she saw dark spots and dancing lights. Boris stampeded out. The guard smashed Kal against the wall again, then one more time and she held on, her head spinning, squeezing her grip to starve him of oxygen.

She kept the lock on the guard until he staggered and fell to his knees. A few seconds more and he crumpled onto his face. Letting go, she checked his heart. Still going.

Taking a jagged breath, Kal raced for the spy cubicle. Scott had pulled the panel to. She rolled it back and bent to the cable. The end hung empty, still swaying slightly from being pulled out of a socket. Scott might have heard a muffled sound of the gun going off. He would certainly have witnessed the Russian panicking and Scott still had the presence of mind to close down the recording operation. Damn the bastard.

She clutched the side of her chest where one or two ribs might be cracked. Then her whole body flushed cold, as if she'd been doused with icy water. A high-pitched wail escaped her lips as she stared out at the children in the room.

One boy and one girl, both in blue, sat side by side on the Persian rug.

Kal slammed herself against the wall to bring back the adrenalin. She flew from the suite and down the corridor. Pounded away from the office and out across the dirt. Past the hospital. Heading for the parking area.

In the distance, she heard the starting of a car. Head flung back, she raced harder, legs working overdrive, chest burning, ignoring the scream of her ribs.

Boris was military trained. Saving his own skin would have been his priority. Had his own perversions been so overriding he had risked his own safety to get what he wanted?

The parking area came into sight. One of the floodlights had been inexplicably left on and the sedan's reversing lights came towards her as it executed one part of a three-point turn. She was too far away. The car manoeuvred for the second section of the turn. She'd never make it. Now it straightened out in line with the exit road. Kal gave all she had for a desperate, last spurt and as the car pulled away, her arm lifted from her side, aiming with precision at the driver's side. Kal tracked the vehicle, her finger squeezing the trigger.

Only a red flash of silk in the rear window brought her to her senses. Her shot wouldn't hit Amita but the child could be killed in the ensuing crash. Her arm fell, as, with a roar, the sedan took off into the night.

Chapter Thirty

It was a long walk back to the centre of town.

Kal started out in darkness and her legs moved automatically, everything numb. Gradually, the sky lightened from black to blue to palest mauve and the sun rose above the horizon. Though daylight didn't bring any comfort.

She had no recall of picking up the gun. In fact, she hadn't realised she had it in her hand until she'd taken aim. Once the sedan was out of sight, she coldly removed the bullets and threw the gun into the ditch beyond the compound. Its taint remained on her skin, imprinted in her pores. Hadn't she always denied what David Khan trained her to be?

A dense fog clung to the streets yet its heaviness was nothing compared to the weight dragging her down. Dewdrops formed on Kal's clothing as she trudged along. When she reached the shanty-town districts, little by little the sun burned away the mist and people stirred. Families who lived on the streets always awoke early to take their morning ablutions at the standpipes, and every small child reminded her of the one she had failed to keep safe.

Before she left ScottBioTec, she returned to the office and had found a blanket discarded outside the building. Whilst she was seeing stars, Boris must have bundled Amita up and carried her from the lounge. The odds of him taking time to snatch the child when his own safety was at risk should have been close to zero. But the proof was there–

Boris had been so fixated on Amita he had not been willing to leave her behind. And in trying to secure the recording as a priority she had failed to keep the children safe. Kal tore at herself in rage. And anguish.

As the centre of the city drew nearer, the morning call to prayer rang out from mosque minarets, stirring inhabitants from their beds, and a while later, people took to their bicycles or opened up roadside stalls selling breakfast chapattis and sweet pastries.

The City of Joy, she thought, where people fought to keep themselves alive. Even when they had nothing, they always had hope. That thought circulated for a while until she became aware of people staring at her as she walked by. Probably she still had blood caked in her hair. Finally, she stopped and took a drink at one of the standpipes and doused her head under the flow. The deluge shocked her into the present. Wallowing in despair and recrimination would not save Amita.

By the time Kal reached the centre of town, she had only one aim–to get back to London as fast as possible. She must gamble they would take the jet and head there with Amita.

From her downtown hotel room, one phone call to the airline confirmed the next Heathrow flight left early evening.

Not bothering to take a shower, she left the hotel to find a juice bar, where she took a seat outside. The juice bar lay on the corner of a large intersection and by now the noise of city life filled the air–revving cars, puttering buses, bicycles ringing their bells.

Freshly pressed orange juice always had a special flavour in Kolkata. Not this morning. It was tasteless and she downed it in one. Smartly dressed men and women hurried in all directions. This was a fashionable district with several international banks. Right in front of Kal, a woman scuttled to cross the road just as the clasp on her bulging briefcase gave way, spilling a sheaf of papers onto the road. The woman scooped up the white sheets. She wore expensive, black shoes, teamed with sombre attire. When the woman re-latched her bag, the logo of the Indian Government showed plainly on the leather case. She wasn't a banker, she was a lawyer.

Kal slammed her palm down on the table, causing the server to almost jump out of his skin. She tracked the back of the receding lawyer as the woman disappeared around a corner.

Kal beckoned over the young waiter. He gave her an uneasy look.

"Is the Kolkata High Court far from here?" she asked.

"It's some way away but you can't miss it, it's a huge, red building, just go straight and head towards Eden Gardens and the Howra river."

She put some money down on the table, then hurried back to the hotel. Now she showered with urgency and renewed energy, allowing the hot jets to revive her morale. After, she pulled on smart clothes and, grabbing her camera bag, headed in the direction of the Kolkata High Court.

At the High Court entrance, two security personnel struggled with the crowd. Visitors were anxious to enter for hearings and Kal found a bunch of people trying to get in at once, clamouring and gesticulating and pushing Indian-style, waving their papers to try to get through the narrow entrance–not an orderly queue such as she'd find in London. She waited for her moment. When both guards were occupied dealing with a man they didn't want to let through, Kal waved a press pass.

"Let me through. Let the Press through."

The melee parted. One guard glanced at the paper in her hand and didn't stop her, as she flashed the old pass she kept in her pocket for emergencies.

The vaulted ceiling of the High Court soared overhead. A check on the internet had shown the building dated from the 1800s and its odd, neo-gothic design was based on a Flemish, historical building. Stone pillars rose to the heights. Court personnel in suits and black gowns rushed past her. Incumbent judges held offices in the building and Kal found the one for Honourable Justice Chatrawalia.

Chatrawalia had heard the case against WainChemicals and passed it up to the Supreme Court and she had some questions to ask about that decision. If the case had been decided in Kolkata it would never have been delayed, WainChemicals would have born the cost of the clean-up and the high incidence of deformities would have been declining by now.

In Chatrawalia's chambers, a male secretary sat in the outer room, tapping at a keyboard.

"I'd like to see the Honourable Justice Chatrawalia, please."

"Do you have an appointment?"

"Not exactly."

"The Honourable Justice Chatrawalia only sees clients who have an appointment. His next available slot is in eleven weeks' time, would you like me to book you in?"

"I need to see him much sooner."

"That will be impossible."

Kal eyed the door to the inner sanctum, letting the secretary see she wondered about barging in.

He shook his head. "The Honourable Justice Chatrawalia is in session all day. Not even his assistant will have access to him until recess at eleven o'clock."

It didn't take long to find a printed list of the day's proceedings in the foyer. The list ran to several pages and she scanned for Chatrawalia's name. Then came a long wait sitting on an uncomfortable, wooden bench outside the court room. Time crawled by and the night's terrible events re-ran. What frightened her most was if Boris took Amita to Russia. What chance would she have of finding Amita there?

At eleven o'clock, Kal heard the scraping of chairs inside the Court and soon after, the heavy doors swung open. The first out was the wigged and robed Judge and he had his head turned to speak to someone scuttling at his side. Then as Chatrawalia looked in Kal's direction, all the accusations she had about WainChemicals fell away because Chatrawalia was the final person on Alesha's list.

Perhaps it was the trace of a smirk at the corner of his mouth which did it. Her self-control was worn right through. The smirk wasn't meant for her, she knew that, it was the judge's characteristic expression, except something snapped. All the night's desperation exploded and she let her self-restraint slip, launching herself straight at his face.

"Filthy, sick pervert! You're an evil bastard and I'm bringing you down! You, and your disgusting paedophile friends."

The judge took rapid steps back, tripping over his own feet. As Kal closed in, two security officers grabbed her from behind and one of them twisted her arm so viciously, she felt it might break. She let herself go limp. No. Now was not the time to reduce him to pulp.

With backup at hand, Chatrawalia recovered himself and he gave her a look of disdain.

"How dare you come in here and accuse *me*, screaming vulgarities. I advise *you* to clear out of my sight."

"Filthy paedophile!"

"Escort her from the building." Chatrawalia spoke as if she were a cockroach.

The guards dumped her on the steps outside, tossing her bag after her.

One of them attempted to peer up her skirt. "Try that again and you'll be arrested. I'm surprised the Honourable Judge didn't order you detained on the spot. You deserve it you little slut."

Her behaviour hadn't been wise. She'd cracked, and why hadn't Chatrawalia called the police? Kal picked up her scattered belongings. It was interesting how passers-by paid no attention. Here, no one wanted to be on the wrong side of the wrong person.

Dusting herself off, she walked slowly down the main road in the direction of her hotel. Alerting Chatrawalia meant he would inform his contacts, though Scott was already alerted, so no difference, she hadn't lost anything.

Kal took a few deep breaths–her head had cleared and she felt calmer. Who said giving vent to emotions didn't make you feel better? They would pay. For all the children.

City traffic flowed in full force. This was a four-lane highway of taxis and motorised rickshaws interspersed with the ever-present haphazard, melee of bicycles. Traffic fumes were already piling up. On the opposite side of the road, two men were shooing a cow down a side street away from the cars. Cows wandered free here, protected by their sacred place in the Hindu religion and the sight of the lumbering animal helped bring back some of Kal's natural optimism. Once in London, she must use Scott to lead her to Amita.

At the intersection, the traffic lights were on green. Kal waited, pressed with a bunch of pedestrians. The smell of sweat and spices was on the rise as the heat mounted. The oncoming flow of traffic came to a stop and the crowd began to move.

She was halfway across when she sensed danger. There came a screech of tyres. Car horns blared, and she kick-started into a sprint before even glancing over her shoulder.

One look back was enough–a small, black car was heading in their direction.

A man shouted a warning and several people screamed. The group crossing the road panicked and ran. Kal veered off from the pack at right angles and went full speed for the side pavement. She knew the car was gaining. Could hear the sound of its tyres getting nearer, gaining on her by the second which meant it wasn't going for the crowd, it was targeting her. It would hit her in the back.

Time slowed. Her own heartbeat drummed in her ears and the pavement appeared unreachable, as if down the end of a long tunnel. Could she jump at the precise moment of impact to lessen the damage? She must try. *Focus. Let your instincts tell you when.* A woman shrieked, high and shrill and never-ending, and somewhere in the middle of the scream, Kal forced her muscles to leap and catapult her body to the side. Her feet left the ground and the bonnet of the car impacted her leg. The car ploughed towards the pavement as she fell to the side.

The car's engine was in a high-pitched overdrive. She caught a glimpse of a shattering windshield as it swerved and collided with a lamp post.

Even as she flew through the air, she understood. It had tried to run her down. And it would have succeeded except for her leap to the side and the fact the car swerved. Why did it go off course? Why had the driver lost control? She had glimpsed the answer. It was because a tiny black hole appeared in the centre of the driver's forehead. He'd been shot.

Kal slammed into the road.

She landed badly and couldn't roll. Pain coursed up her spine. Her eyelids fluttered and she looked up to see a circle of brown faces peering down.

She could smell petrol stink. From the circle of faces, a man came closer, kneeling to check the pulse in her neck. A lock of black hair fell over his forehead and as he bent, a chain slipped from his open shirt, the silver bright against his dark skin. Inches from Kal's face, a medallion swung on the end of the chain–the insignia unmistakable–a crescent moon in a sky studded with stars. She tried to speak except her tongue felt like wood. Her ears filled with a rushing sound and the glint of the familiar insignia was the last thing she saw before everything went black.

Chapter Thirty-one

"You took a jolt to your vertebral column. There's no permanent damage, though you're lucky you don't have a fractured skull because your head took a nasty impact. We'll keep you in for observation overnight."

The doctor took a biro in one hand and her chart in another. The pen scritch-scratched across the paper.

"I have to get back to London."

"You have a head injury, which means airline flight is out of the question."

Whatever the doctor wrote on her notes he finished it, holding the pen poised in mid-air as he looked at her over his glasses.

"I hope you're not going to be a problem patient?"

"Of course not, doctor."

"I'm glad to hear it, now, your knee scans show extensive soft tissue injury, which requires plenty of rest and it may need attention when you return home. Bear that in mind and see your doctor at any sign of continuing pain. We'll transfer you to a ward as soon as we can and meanwhile, you rest here."

The doctor exited with a swish of the cubicle curtain.

Her head throbbed and she lay back on the pillow. The overhead lights glared in her eyes. So she closed them and saw again the silver medallion, swaying as it fell from the man's shirt. The insignia a replica of the one on her father's ring.

She must have lost track of time, slipping in and out of sleep. When a nurse came in, Kal jerked awake.

"What time is it?"

"Relax. It's...." the woman checked, "...almost four o'clock."

"Can you help me, please?"

"If I can, I will, though not if it involves checking out. The doctor already told me he's worried you won't stay, even if it's for your own good."

"It's not about that." Though her sore muscles protested, Kal levered herself up. "When I came in, who else came with me?"

The nurse wrinkled her nose. "Hmm, I was on duty when the ambulance brought you and as far as I remember you were alone."

"There was a shooting, someone shot the driver, the police must have been involved."

"A shooting, oh no my dear, you're mistaken, the driver of the vehicle ran off, as usual around here."

"I saw it–he was killed, I'm certain."

The nurse patted Kal's arm. "No one else was injured in the crash. Don't forget you've had a serious head injury and it can cause muddled memories."

It had been an attempt at a hit and run, no doubt about that. The paedophile syndicate must have put a price on her, presumably after her contact with Chatrawalia. Which meant they acted swiftly and efficiently. So that's why Chatrawalia had let her go, and they had to have deep and powerful networks to make her a target so soon.

How to explain the mark on the driver's forehead? She had saved herself but he could have reversed and run her over. The crowded street, the vicinity of the pedestrians, the angle of the surrounding buildings, all signified the marksman to be an expert. And someone had enough clout to remove a body without a trace.

"Young lady, you lay back and get some sleep. The ambulance crew brought in your belongings and I'll leave them here on the trolley. We'll transfer you to a ward as soon as we can."

She lay back down and closed her eyes while the nurse fussed. A few minutes later there came the swish of the curtain.

Kal counted to ten, then sat back up. Her head didn't feel too bad. Gingerly, she swung her legs over the edge and tested her weight on the injured knee. It held up, so, hopefully, nothing too serious there either. Kal peered around the curtain. All clear. There was one more thing she must do before she made the flight.

Chapter Thirty-two

Hobbling towards arrivals at London Heathrow airport, Kal kept as much weight as possible from her injured leg. Stiff after the long flight, Kal's back ached and her knee was swollen.

After leaving the hospital, she went to find the Kolkata group lobbying against ScottBioTec. The group's organisers were a young couple, both university lecturers. They had a room jammed full of files and documents and they had let her read what she wanted. What she found had been disturbing.

ScottBioTec had sprung up on the site left contaminated by WainChemicals. But it was in the WainChemical documents she discovered something even more interesting.

The owner of WainChemicals, Henderson, was a British man who owned several businesses in the Bengal area of India and he'd died in strange circumstances–Henderson's throat had been cut. No one had ever been able to trace who had done it or why.

Kal knew that type of death was the work of a hired assassin. For someone so wealthy and influential, and a foreigner, such a sentence would only happen for a terrible crime.

One of the businesses owned by Henderson was a boarding school for boys from ex-patriate families and from wealthy Indian families. Henderson had died at the school. What was even stranger was how the head janitor was listed as Sunni Medi. Kal had gone hot and cold when she read it. True, it was a common name, but could it have been her grandfather?

On her way from the plane to the terminal, her phone buzzed. Leaning against a wall, she found Spinks had left a message and he had sent it the moment her airplane landed. So, Spinks logged her departure and her return, which meant she was still a suspect.

Kal rang him back. Detective Inspector Spinks wanted to meet urgently, though he gave no explanation. He relayed an address and, just as she was about to ask where exactly that was, he cut off the call.

London was in the grip of another rainy day, with roads full of puddles and cars slewing through water. Kal took a taxi from the main stand.

"Where to?" the driver asked.

She read out the details from Spink's text. "Do you know what this address is?"

The driver's eyes met hers in the rear-view mirror.

"It's Westminster City morgue," he said.

Her whole body winced, sending a stab of pain down her leg. The driver kept his concentration on the road, until they turned out of the airport exit.

"Everything all right, luv?"

His voice held no hint of pity and only a tad of concern. He must be used to judging people's personalities because he'd got it just right.

The *slap-slap* of the windscreen wipers filled the cab. Nursing her knee, she stared out at the rain. People scurried along with their umbrellas held high and coats buttoned as if winter returned. Never had London appeared more grim, its population a sea of black and grey. The colours of mourning.

"Thank you for asking. No, everything is very wrong," she said.

Kal slumped in the corner, overcome by images of her dead mother.

By the time Kal arrived at the morgue, she had steeled herself for the horror of facing Alesha's remains. Perhaps charred or mutilated and requiring identification. As she walked up the entrance ramp, she had to steady herself on the railing.

A sympathetic employee greeted her. The woman led Kal inside, not being intrusive, nor condescending, giving just enough information to keep communication going. Kal appreciated the woman's professionalism.

"Detective Inspector Spinks is waiting for you," the woman said.

Kal's own response floated in the air, sounding faraway. "Why is he waiting for me?"

"He's going to ask you to identify a body and you have the right to accept or decline. Now, be careful, there's a small step."

The woman pointed to a tiny indentation in the flooring, flanked by several bands of yellow and black tape. Like her, many who walked this stretch must be in a state of shock.

"Does Spinks think it's my mother?"

"I'm afraid I can't answer. The case is held by Scotland Yard so only Detective Inspector Spinks is authorised to discuss it with you."

"Oh."

"I advise you to take your time. Listen to the inspector and then decide what you want to do. Don't rush it."

They arrived at a set of chrome doors, their reflections dull in the metal surface. The woman gave a small smile of encouragement and kept her arms held by her sides, making no move to push them open.

No, she can't help me more than she has already, thought Kal, now I'm on my own. Staring straight ahead, Kal put her hand out and walked through by force of will, every fibre in her body exerting a collective impulse to refuse.

"Ms Medi, thank you for coming."

Spinks stood in a rectangular room. It was a room from a movie set, with dark grey flooring, large drainage grilles and bright overhead lighting and two walls lined with square, silver, drawer-fronts like filing cabinets only much larger.

Kal pulled her gaze away from the cabinets and onto Spinks. Her other senses continued on automatic and told her that, though several degrees cooler than the rest of the building, the air smelled of disinfectant and faintly and unmistakably of blood and other, unnameable body fluids. Meanwhile, Spinks scanned her injuries.

"Don't worry, I'm going to tell you where I've been and what I've been doing, then you'll understand how I got the bruising. First, you've called me here for a reason and I'd rather get that over with."

Spinks offered a chair, which she refused.

"I'll be frank with you, Ms Medi. A charred body was found washed up by the Thames river. A post-mortem has been carried out and the remains are, as yet, unidentified."

She forced herself to speak. "Is it my mother?" Then she counted the seconds, waiting for Spinks to respond.

A colleague had once shown her footage of an immolation. A journalist had been taken hostage, kept for days and then burnt as a 'punishment'. The captors released the horrific video on the internet and she watched it before the authorities took it down. Mercifully, the victim had been drugged but he still screamed in agony. If the matron at ScottBioTec had been lucky she'd have been unconscious first, and Kal hoped her mother would have been too.

Spinks dragged out the silence, as if he turned the ratchet on a torture wrack, stretching her to breaking point. At last, he cleared his throat.

"This is the body of someone much younger than your mother. It's a child. She's of Indian origin and a girl, around eight or nine years old."

Kal staggered backwards. "That's not possible!"

Somehow Spinks managed to position the chair behind her. Kal felt the metal against the back of her legs and she folded onto it. She couldn't speak, couldn't think.

Spinks handed her a glass and the water trembled as she stared at it, unable to fathom what he expected her to do with it.

At last, she put aside the glass. "It's all right. You can continue."

He must hear the tremor in her voice. Facing the body of her mother would have been terrible. Facing the body of Amita would be unbearable.

"Unfortunately, the identification is complicated. I'm sorry to say the body has been burned intentionally after having been doused in inflammable liquid."

Her stomach churned and Spinks raised his hand in a soothing gesture.

"The burning, I hasten to add, happened after death, presumably in an attempt to erase evidence or disguise the victim. A second serious injury also occurred after death and that was to the skull and though the body was found in the water, the cause of death was asphyxiation."

He waited for her to assimilate the information.

"Asphyxiation?" she whispered.

"Yes. There's evidence of a ligature having been tied around the victim's neck. The Coroner also identified small marks scratched close to the ligature at the front of the neckline. Unfortunately, this leads us to believe the ligature was in place for some time and the victim attempted to remove it with her own fingernails."

Kal retched. Seemingly from nowhere, Spinks produced a cardboard receptacle and Kal grabbed it and bent in two. After that, she couldn't help it, she started crying. When she looked up, Spinks offered a box of tissues.

"I really didn't think you would react so strongly. Am I right in assuming you believe you may know the victim?" he asked.

Kal pressed a tissue to her mouth and nodded.

"You must tell me everything, Ms Medi, but first are you willing to proceed with the identification?"

She closed her eyes.

"Ms Medi... are you willing to go ahead with the identification?" Spinks' voice held a trace of pressure.

So she opened her eyes and nodded.

"I must warn you the remains are shocking. The flesh of the body has been carbonised and this extends, in places, down to the bone. The Coroner has accepted there may be sufficient tissue left for facial identification, though if there was any other way of us identifying this child, believe me, I wouldn't be asking anyone to look. Aside from the remains of the face, there is one other identifiable element and you will be shown that also. The rest will be shrouded from view."

Kal peeled herself from the chair. She braced herself.

"Let's get this over with."

Spinks pressed a buzzer and a morgue assistant appeared dressed in overalls. The assistant knew which drawer interested Spinks and he gave a final check to the identification tag and with a light tug, pulled out the drawer. The bearings rolled smoothly out to a cushioned stop. A small form lay beneath a white sheet.

"When you're ready, Ms Medi," Spinks said.

She'd never be ready. She pressed her lips together and gave the man in overalls a nod. He folded back the corner of the sheet to reveal half of the girl's face.

Kal's hand flew to her mouth.

"Take your time, Ms Medi," Spinks said.

Still holding the corner of the sheet, the assistant's hand remained steady on the flimsy material. She stared at his pink, chunky fingers, touching distance from the blackened remains. How could he bear it? Part of her wanted to sob and scream. She wanted to collapse to the floor and never get up.

"Oh my god, no, no."

"Take a deep breath, and tell me, do you recognise this girl?"

Her vision blurred.

"No, Inspector, I can't recognise anything."

The assistant replaced the material and moved to the left side of the body. He again folded back the sheet to reveal what should have been the left arm. Only it was a charred stump. The limb was missing.

"Due to the burning, it isn't possible to know the nature of the limb removal but we know trauma from its removal was not the cause of death. Healing of those wounds occurred long before the asphyxiation," Spinks said.

A thought was working its way into her mind. Her brain must have stalled because she couldn't quite grab it.

"Wait."

"There's no rush, Ms Medi. Give yourself time to get over the shock. If you're not certain and wish to take a second look..."

"What I mean is, wait a moment, you said there was only one other identifiable element?"

"Yes."

"And that's this missing arm?"

"Correct."

"So the girl doesn't have any other limb amputations?"

"No," Spinks said.

"Both legs are there?"

"Both of the victim's legs are intact."

In a rush of dizziness Kal grabbed for support. If both legs were intact, then it couldn't be Amita, though certainly this poor child came from ScottBioTec.

"Ms Medi?" Spinks asked.

The vertigo passed.

"Give me a moment. I can explain everything," she said. "Tell me, did you manage to get any fingerprints?"

"Two partial prints, only we've nothing to match them with because she doesn't figure in any databank. No one has reported her missing."

She thought of the bead necklace Amita had been working on at the hospital and, as Tommy told her, all children with arm amputations would work on as part of their therapy. The children would transfer fingerprints from their intact side, so they should be able to get prints from the necklaces. Which meant they could get evidence to link this child to ScottBioTec.

Kal stared at Spinks. He'd had no idea she might be able to identify the body, which meant he'd brought her to the morgue to jolt her, by letting her presume she'd come to identify her mother. That way, he could have forced an error if she was involved, or lead her to confide in him. What a clever man.

She reached for the glass and the water shook as she took a sip. Kal closed her eyes. Being faced with an impossible choice rips you apart–like in films, or nightmares, where you must decide in a split second who dies–you or your lover, your son or your daughter, your mother or a complete stranger. Who would she have preferred be on this slab, blackened and disfigured? Her mother or Amita? Her mother or this nameless child? The answer could make you go mad.

When she opened her eyes, Spinks was still looking at her. Kal felt sick with horror. And rage. This poor girl had been abused. Then dumped like garbage. Bringing the monstrous perpetrators down was the only thing which mattered. Even if it was the last thing she did.

"I don't know this girl, though I know where she comes from and I know she's received the injury to her skull to eradicate evidence of brain surgery, and the limb amputation is part of the ScottBioTec research programme."

Spinks raised his eyebrows.

"You know I've flown in from Kolkata. I unearthed a paedophile organisation and Richard Scott is the ringleader. He trafficks street children, supplying them to high profile abusers, and this poor girl was one of them. I've a list of his current clients. There's a lot I need to tell you, Inspector Spinks."

She started there and then giving Spinks an account of everything she'd found. Spinks listened to every word. Part of her registered what an experienced detective he must be, logging every element of such a long account. The only detail Kal left out was the medallion, and Spinks commented only once she'd finished.

"This is the second child found washed up by the Thames and both had similar injuries. We suspected a trafficking organisation and I've been putting pressure on my contacts for some time. No one was coming forward and now I understand why. Those people have silenced everyone with their wealth. You took grave risks out in Kolkata on your own, Ms Medi, but you've given us the break we need."

"Does this mean I'm no longer a suspect?"

"Who said you were ever under suspicion? I've plenty of questions and we need to have a proper discussion."

"If you can put up with me limping, then lead the way, Inspector."

Spinks smiled. "That's the first time I've seen you relax your guard, Ms Medi. Solving these terrible child crimes is something which means a lot to me and my team. I hope you finally realise we're as committed as you are."

She gave him a steady look. "Then let's work together."

Chapter Thirty-three

"First you go off on your own, then you tell us Spinks can't make his move yet!" Marty slammed her hand on the table.

"Spinks is concentrating on the London end of the chain, but he's working with an international squad for child crime. Once we can prove paedophilia and trafficking, it changes everything."

"It's a good thing you finally told Spinks about the stalker, that was sensible, it will get them off your back," LeeMing said.

"Bloody fantastic," Marty said, "to be replaced by someone who organises hit and runs and the disposal of bodies from the scene of a crime."

Kal felt herself reddening. Would Marty have guessed a connection between Kal's father and the sniper shot?

"And the marksman? What's your take on that?" asked LeeMing.

LeeMing was no fool. He must know she held back.

Kal squirmed. She couldn't keep lying. "I know you're both going over the line for me and there are some things from the past I should've filled you in with."

"Take your time," LeeMing said.

"It's my father. Whatever he hid from me and Mum had something to do with that marksman. I saw an insignia just like the one he used to wear."

LeeMing and Marty exchanged a glance.

"The sniper might have saved your life," Marty said.

"Your father and the marksman are part of the picture. We won't break the syndicate nor find your mother by ignoring it," LeeMing said.

He spoke as if he was talking about having breakfast or going for a stroll in the park. LeeMing was casual and accepting, and he'd not even mentioned what type of man it meant her father was–a criminal, the lowest of the low.

"We've got to bring down this operation through the British justice system, not take things into our own hands. I'm right aren't I?" LeeMing said.

"Agreed," Kal said, "we've got to outsmart them."

Marty was pacing in front of the windows. "Then we break into Scott's house and search it."

Kal's first impulse had been the same and if they didn't find Amita, then continue the break-ins with Assad next in line. The problem being it would alert the paedophile network and Amita could end up anywhere, most likely at the bottom of the Thames.

"No because Scott has three listed addresses. The first hit we go for has to be the right one. If we go for the wrong one, they could kill all the children in their possession. We want Amita, we want evidence and then Spinks and his squad moves in."

"You're right, we only get one chance," LeeMing said.

"I've got an idea. I've been researching paedophiles. There's massive amounts of information on the web–psychological profiling, habits and behaviour patterns. Paedophiles often have an obsessive personality and get addicted to small details about their crimes. They've been caught because they like to prove how clever they are. They've a desire to show-off. Scott's set up the whole operation and he thinks his network is impregnable."

"And so?" LeeMing said, "What does that give us?"

"An advantage. If I play on Scott's weaknesses, it gives me a way in."

She was clear on the psychological tactic she'd use to manipulate Scott. She'd play to his superiority. Fawn and flatter and pander to his ego. Give him the adulation he craved for his crimes. Eventually, in an urge to vaunt himself, Scott would tell Kal where Amita was. Then, of course, Scott would have to kill her.

"Scott isn't going to roll over and blab. Manoeuvring close to an experienced criminal and extracting information is a task for a specialist," LeeMing said.

"I *am* a specialist in mind games. I can do it."

"We've got to get that hard drive, that's the evidence we need, then Spinks can bring in his team. Your idea is way too dangerous," LeeMing said.

"I don't care–I've got to find Amita."

Marty stopped pacing. "And there's your mother as well."

Save first a child she'd allowed to be abducted for abuse, or find her own mother? The choice was obvious and Kal knew her mother would agree.

"I made my decision at the morgue."

"These people haven't hesitated to kill. Don't think being in London will give you immunity because it won't. We should pass it to Spinks and step away," LeeMing said.

"The police can't go in yet. Amita was taken because of me. Other children are captive and subjected to god-knows what horrific acts. There's a girl lying dead and mutilated in the morgue–you've got to let me try."

"Scott's going to guess it was you at the research institute, don't be naive," LeeMing said.

"I know what I'm doing! Scott will play the game because he thinks I've got something on them. He won't move against me until that possibility is secured."

Her voice had gone up several octaves. If she couldn't convince them, she was going after Scott anyway. Alone.

LeeMing looked at Marty.

Marty gave a small nod. "Then we've got a plan, but only on the *strict condition* this is a team effort. No more going off on your own."

"Okay."

"Don't try to get out of it, Kal. I want to hear it," Marty said.

"Okay, yes, and I made the same promise to Spinks."

"I'll work on locating the airfield Scott uses," Marty said, "and I looked into the background to ScottBioTec."

Marty told them what she had found. She'd discovered the same details about Henderson's assassination and how ScottBioTec sprang up right where the disabled children were being born on the site contaminated by WainChemicals.

"The killing of Henderson sounded strange. Maybe it was retribution for the industrial pollution?" Marty said.

Kal didn't think so. She had another theory. Her leg began throbbing and she stretched it out.

"Looks like the effects of the impact are working their way through your system. You'd better get some rest," LeeMing said.

When LeeMing smiled at Kal, Marty rolled her eyes.

Kal felt the strain lessen. With Spinks on board and her friends backing her up, they had a chance.

Chapter Thirty-four

Scott was calling around his clients, calming them down.

"We should be careful," Selena Vankova said. "She's a cocky little bitch. She's either got a few brain cells missing or she's on to something. It's too much of a coincidence. It must have been her at ScottBioTec."

Scott agreed and it was his job to reassure his customers they were beyond risk. That supply could continue and their habits could be met.

Assad had already told Scott he didn't give a damn. Assad felt impregnable. Whereas Kealy was weak and on the point of cracking. Scott didn't like weakness.

"The girl doesn't know anything," Scott had told Kealy. Down the line, Kealy's breaths made it sound as if he was hyperventilating. Yes, Scott thought, very likely he was thinking about exposure. About personal ruin and the symbolic public hanging.

"It's all under control," Scott said. "Trust me. I have a plan that will shut her up for good."

Yes, it was always important to have a plan to get rid of the scum. Then they could all continue as before, like gods, way, way above the vermin.

Chapter Thirty-five

Where the impulse came from, Kal couldn't say, and she went with it, taking a blue silk, shalwar kameez tunic from Alesha's wardrobe. Kal rarely wore traditional Indian dress. Now she teamed the the tunic with jeans and carefully applied make up.

As she left 701, Spinks called. According to his sources, Boris had returned to Russia alone. She and Spinks agreed, it gave them a higher chance of finding Amita.

Heading for Richard Scott's office, she took the elevator to the top floor. The strategy most likely to rattle Scott would be to keep it light-hearted, as if she didn't have a care in the world.

There was no sign of the personal assistant, instead Scott waited by the assistant's desk. She could see him clocking her mood and wondering what it meant.

"Where on earth did you disappear to these last few days, Kal? You worried me sick."

She accepted Scott's kiss on her cheek.

"Goodness what's happened to your face?" he said.

The bruises from the fight at ScottBioTec were purple and blue. "Oh, nothing to worry about, just a sports accident."

"Did you have it seen to? I've an excellent Harley Street doctor. The last thing you want is any scarring, and I know she'd see you in an instant if I call her."

"There's no need, it was only a little knock."

"Well, if you say so my dear, and I must say, you look very attractive today." He indicated her silk top.

If they were going to play games, then she'd better do it properly.

"It's lovely isn't it? I borrowed it from my mother, although I'm not sure about the colour, I'd have preferred it to be red, wouldn't you?"

Kal watched for Scott's response and he didn't disappoint. A tiny muscle in his right cheek tightened as he stifled a reaction. Yes, she'd taken him by surprise. Every opportunity she had to pull the rug from under his feet, to push him off balance, keep him guessing—she must take it.

Scott cleared his throat. "I hope you're ready? I've an important appointment and I'm so pleased you and your camera-eye can accompany me. It will be a good introduction to how I run my company."

She patted her camera bag. "I've been looking forward to learning how you operate. This is a great opportunity for me. Please, lead the way."

They took a black cab to Regent's Park, where the driver pulled into an exclusive crescent shaped street full of townhouses. Unlike most of central London, here, the iron railings glistened as if newly painted. This area was known for housing wealthy lawyers, and the residents clearly got top-notch treatment from the borough council. Even the pavement appeared to be scrubbed clean.

A liveried butler opened the door and he welcomed them with a formal bow. The entrance was reminiscent of a stately home, with marble flooring and dark wood panelling.

Whilst the butler hung their coats, Kal admired a display of roses. Their lovely scent filled the air and from the freshness of the flowers she supposed the huge bouquet must be renewed on a daily basis. This was a household pampered by a whole bank of staff and local tradespeople.

The butler offered to carry Scott's briefcase. Scott accepted and when the butler enquired if she'd like him to take her backpack, she politely declined and instead took out her camera.

"As you wish, madam," said the butler.

At the base of a sweeping staircase, a grandfather clock swung out its rhythm and she went to admire it.

"It's lovely, isn't it?" the butler said. "It belonged to the great-great-great grandfather of Judge Greeves, who was a clockmaker. We have a number of interesting timepieces in the house from his collection."

As she had guessed, they were in Randall Greeves' house, retired High Court Judge. Sixth on Alesha's list.

Scott cut in. "I suggest we keep the pleasantries for another time."

The butler swept to the front, giving her a wink on the way. "Of course, sir," he said, "if you would follow me."

Judge Greeves sat in the library wearing a green-and-red, tartan-patterned waistcoat over a grey shirt and brown trousers. Navy boating shoes completed his look. Greeves' terrible taste meant he must chose his own clothing, rather than delegating the task to his butler. From his saggy complexion and bloodshot eyes, Greeves looked the type who enjoyed a diet of rich foods. For a portly man, he held himself with authority and it was clear he knew himself to be a man of power.

"Take a seat, Richard, and good morning, you must be the lovely Kal Medi," Greeves said.

His voice had a ring she'd associate with a military officer rather than a retired circuit judge and it made Kal adjust her assessment of him. Probably many people had been thrown off by his eccentric appearance, however, Greeves' tone betrayed him as having a sharp and strategic mind. Probably the type to be an avid war games expert. She must keep alert.

The butler returned with a pot of coffee and a bowl of sugar cubes accompanied by a tiny set of silver tongs. She heard the door close as he left them alone.

"May I offer you some coffee?" Greeves asked.

She declined and Greeves poured for himself and for Scott.

"Richard tells me you've a rare talent and I took the liberty of reading a little about your career. I see you have several scoops to your name, and I must say that's unusual for someone of your age."

"I enjoy photojournalism and it's a profession which depends partly on luck. I've been in the right place at the right time."

"How modest," Greeves said, taking the silver tongs and placing two sugar cubes into his cup, "and I understand, unfortunately, the police have made no progress in locating your mother?"

"No," Scott replied, "it's terribly frustrating. Even the detective agency I employed has come up with a blank."

"How distressing," Greeves said, sipping his coffee.

Behind Greeves' head, rows of leather-bound books filled the shelves. The spines revealed fat lawyers' tomes and compilations of past court cases, as well as a huge collection of fiction. The floor to ceiling library acted as insulation from the rest of the house, muffling outside sounds, as if they sat swaddled in a cocoon. All Kal could hear was Greeves sipping his drink, interspersed with the chink of his bone china teacup on the saucer.

"Perhaps you're not aware, Kal, the Government has announced its intention to set up a Special Commission on Children's Rights and Medical Research. The Commission will draw up recommendations," Scott said, "and they're due to make an announcement very soon on who will be Chair. Randall is tipped as top choice."

She bit back her disgust. Trust paedophile Greeves to be selected. She pretended to be interested in Scott's news and Greeves assessed her, she knew it. What would he come up with?

"If you don't mind me saying, you've dressed most elegantly," Greeves said, "although, in my experience, the choice of traditional clothing often works as a disadvantage for people of… your type of background."

The superiority and veiled racism were unmistakable.

Greeves continued. "I find it interesting you mention luck in relation to your career. In my own progression through the legal profession, I found luck to play no part. In my view, contacts are a person's main asset."

The more he spoke, the more Greeves reminded her of a blood-sucking leech, bloated on the spoils of his career. Kal put aside her camera and all pretence they were here for ScottBioTec. All three of them knew there was another agenda.

"That's an intriguing comment."

"Yes, isn't it?" Greeves said.

The calculating side of her mind inspected each phrase of their conversation. If she was to speculate, she'd say Greeves was leading up to making an offer to a minion. He'd try to broker a deal.

"I never met your mother though she has a formidable reputation as a seeker of the truth. I'm sure when some people think of her name it makes them shudder," Greeves said, "and quite rightly too."

Scott pushed away his cup. "Alesha was a champion of justice, not so different from yourself, Randall."

"Quite right, quite right," Greeves said wiping a dark drop of coffee from his second chin. "However, in my experience it's always prudent to consider if sometimes..." he gave her an oily look, "we should put our own needs before justice for the many. Particularly those of us that start out..." here Greeves scanned her shalwar kameez again, "with a disadvantage."

"Which reminds me Randall, didn't you tell me a friend of yours is on the lookout for new talent? That's why I thought to introduce you to Kal," Scott said.

Her skin crawled.

"Ah yes, you must be thinking of Terrence Humphries, he's always hunting for bright, new recruits. At our Gentleman's Club, he mentioned to me the other day how lacking he finds his top creative team. The poor fellow."

"Terrence Humphries, you mean the head of PrizM with media supremacy in Europe and the prime provider in Hong Kong, Malaysia and Japan?" she said.

Both Scott and Greeves studied her as if she was an insect under the magnifying glass. Kal allowed her fingers to play with the strap of her camera. She licked her lips and made her eyes a little wider as if she was impressed and a bit over-awed.

"Why yes, as I said, contacts are everything," Greeves replied. "In exchange for a little matter of information, well, the world could be one's oyster."

And there she had it. The very reason Scott brought her here in the first place. The idea she floated at the Gala had an impact because Scott suspected Alesha had left evidence. That perhaps she had gathered evidence too at the research institute, and they were willing to trade for it. It was logical to attempt a bribe before giving themselves the difficulty of disposing of another dead body.

She licked her lips. "I don't know what to say," she said, as if they'd de-railed her. As if she might really be tempted by the lure of help up the ladder and the possibility of success and opportunities for the rest of her life.

"Early in one's career is such an important stage, isn't it Richard?" Greeves said. "One tiny misjudgement at such a sensitive time can mean one never achieves one's full potential."

Greeves' tone had changed slightly. Not so oily. A bit tighter.

"We agreed not to be impatient didn't we, Randall? I always believe in giving a person time to reflect on important decisions," Scott said, "and to understand the good intent of her benefactors."

As perceptible as the wind shifting, she felt Scott's energy change, just as it had during his recount of stories about her past at the Gala.

She resisted the urge to wrap her arms across her chest. The leather settee creaked as she uncrossed and recrossed her legs and when she tried to read Scott's intentions, she had a dreadful, chilling premonition. A sudden perspiration flecked her top lip.

The very shelves of the library seemed to inch forward, hemming her in. Scott placed his cup on the table and he stared straight at her.

"I suppose you've always had questions about David Khan."

Her presentiment had been correct. At the mention of her father's name, a cold sweat broke out on her back.

Scott's lips formed into a slow smile.

On her other side, Greeves' eyes bored into her. She felt sandwiched. To control an overwhelming desire to flee, she bit the inside of her mouth.

Scott leaned back in his chair. "I thought that would get your attention. Khan was an interesting man. Tell me, did he ever tell you he wasn't really a journalist? That he worked for the main heroin cartel in Pakistan? That he foiled anti-drug offensives for them? That he succeeded in infiltrating the highest levels of American intelligence services? That he was highly skilled in his field and rose up the echelons to become the cartel's top expert?"

Blood thundered in Kal's ears.

"… as I recall, he was involved in numerous deaths of anti-drug trade personnel…"

The books behind Scott's head blurred.

"… and lethal hits on their families."

She pressed her lips together to stop herself from screaming.

"You must have been consumed since childhood by unanswered questions about his activities. Of course, I don't expect you to take my word for it. Rather, as a token of our goodwill, Judge Greeves and I have decided to offer you the answers you've been looking for."

Scott placed a slip of paper on the coffee table. It was folded in two, so she couldn't see the contents.

"It's the name of a contact. He's based in Soho and I think you'll find what he has to say most interesting," Scott said.

She stared at the paper, understanding she should never touch it. That she should resist the temptation with every fibre of her being.

"Go on, take it," Scott said, "and then I hope we can get all this unpleasantness out of the way. You can give us what we want and we can all carry on as if nothing happened."

Even Greeves seemed to crane forward. Kal fought her own desire, her own longing to stop the agony of not knowing, to finally have the answers she always wanted. A silence fell in the library.

Then with a trembling arm and as if on automatic, her hand reached out and grasped the white slip of paper.

Chapter Thirty-six

If you're going to play games with an evil bastard, you've got to be prepared to see it to the end. Kal stared at herself in the mirror. She prepared with care for the coming encounter, mentally more than physically. Scott had liked her idea of an evening together, suggesting they dine at his Greenwich residence. Spinks and Marty had wanted her to wear a hidden microphone, and she had refused because if things went wrong and Scott got an indication she wasn't moving onto his side, it would put Amita in immediate danger. It was two days after Amita's abduction. Kal took a taxi and headed east across London.

The darkened streets rushed by, until, on the bend of the Thames, the O2 dome came into view. Originally home of the Olympic games, and now an elaborate entertainment venue, the O2's futuristic purple spikes pointed skywards from its green dome. The cab entered the London Borough of Greenwich and soon after they came to a privileged, commuter neighbourhood. They pulled up outside a smart, two-storey house with private drive, a wooden surround fence and a lawn running the perimeter.

Scott greeted her and Kal accepted his kiss on the cheek. Her glamourous outer shell must give nothing away. She must use what Scott wanted against him. Over her shoulder, she heard the taxi tyres gritty on the road as the driver headed back. The street fell silent and she followed Scott inside.

As the front door closed, Kal heard a secure *click*, which meant the door had an automatic deadbolt system. Presumably Scott kept the control in his pocket.

"I'm so glad you were available," she said.

For tonight, she'd chosen a dark red dress, long to the floor, the velvet close-fitting down to knee level, where it fanned out in an elegant fishtail.

The house seemed quiet and her heels tic-tacked on the parquet as she followed Scott down the hallway and into the lounge. He was a picture of composure and confidence, as was she.

"It was such a wonderful idea of yours, Kal, to meet for the evening, and I took the liberty of giving my staff the night off, so we won't be interrupted. My chef has left us a full menu and I do so enjoy entertaining guests at home, it's tends to be much more... interesting."

The twist on the last word sent a tingle down Kal's back. Her whole body was on high alert and she smoothed the sleeves of her dress, waiting for her nervous system to calm.

"Perfect," she said, puckering her lips.

Events had pushed her beyond a mental limit, pushed her more towards being like her father than she had ever been. The game had changed and now she walked close to the dark side where the rule was dare and challenge, and kill or be killed. Perhaps she understood the attraction her father had for living close to the edge after all.

"Without taking risks, wouldn't life be dull?" she said.

Scott laughed and for the first time, Kal sensed he genuinely agreed. Yes, she had been correct. Sadism, abuse, danger–it was the excitement which gave Scott a high. It made him feel like a god and without it, his life would be nothing. Scott didn't live for riches, he lived for pushing beyond the limits with his perversions and getting away with it.

A split-level lounge opened to a dining area and an open-plan kitchen. Scott walked across to the granite-surfaced worktops of the kitchen. There, after a few tugs at a corkscrew, he pulled the stopper from a bottle of wine.

"You've a nice house and this fireplace is wonderful," she said.

"It's nothing much. I bought it years ago when I first started out and I only keep it because it's so convenient for the City."

It appeared top-of-the-range, show-room perfect with tasteful flooring and decor, designer furniture complete with muted lighting and abstract prints on the wall, all chosen, she was sure, by a professional decorator. Just like in his office, the place was sterile and devoid of Scott's personality. No, Scott kept who he really was somewhere else. In the place where he abused the children or watched others in the act.

Logs blazed in the hearth and the flames tried to throw gaiety into the room. Scott handed her a full glass. Kal swirled it, the red wine leaving its waxy patina on the sides, like blood, she thought. Perching on the edge of the sofa, she raised her arm to make a toast.

"Here's to ambition."

"Ambition," Scott repeated.

He took a leisurely sip. Wearing a white shirt and grey, pin-stripe trousers, Scott's appearance was as flawless as ever. The firelight reflected in his gleaming, black shoes.

"I've been considering our conversation at Judge Greeves' house," she said.

"Very sensible."

"I liked your offer, only the thing is... I want more."

She stated it boldly.

"I'm sure we can come to an arrangement. What did you have in mind?"

"Everything Judge Greeves offered, plus half a million pounds sterling."

Scott gave a chuckle. "What would make it worth our while parting with that sort of money?"

Made of several layers of alternating glass and mosaic, an attractive coffee table, like the one in the City, lay between them. Scott placed down his glass and took an armchair directly facing her. The fire crackled as Scott steepled his fingers, regarding her full-face. Just like in a poker game, she thought, he wants to capture my behaviour so he can read me to the maximum.

So she reclined, draping one leg over the other, lightly jiggling her foot.

"You took me by surprise with your revelations about David Khan. I don't want to go into details, but I always suspected my father had an unpleasant side–always travelling, never talking about what he did, keeping things hidden and secret. He was a strange man. He had no friends, never mentioned his past. I was a little surprised, perhaps not that much, to hear his real story. You see, he always terrified me," she lied, "and I can't say I was sorry when he died." She assessed Scott and saw him weighing her words. "Richard, I know you're curious about the information my mother left, so I've decided to be straight with you."

Positive anticipation was always more difficult to control. Scott concealed his expectancy well, nevertheless Kal noticed the tiny signs because the salivation of a Pavlov's dog could never be completely hidden.

"Mum was in the middle of investigating a child abuse ring and she left me photographs taken inside a room. One set shows Farouk Assad with a child and the other set shows Alistair Kealy. Two such well-known, influential men." She shook her head. "And the evidence is damning. Once they're taken into custody, I presume the trail will lead straight to ScottBioTec?"

Scott remained still as stone.

"If the evidence is so clear, why didn't Alesha go to the police?"

She shrugged. "Until I know the reason for Mum's disappearance, I've no idea."

"And why not go to the police yourself?"

Of course he needed to check she wasn't bluffing. He had no way of knowing what she'd collected herself at ScottBioTec, or even if it had really been her. Most likely, he continued to misinterpret her true nature–his assessment falling far short of her capacities for scheming and manipulation. First impressions were so powerful, and the persona she'd been displaying since their first meeting was so winningly feeble.

"There were too many unanswered questions and Mum going missing worried me. I was expecting a ransom demand, only now, I have a better opportunity."

She still kept a faint hope for her mother's safety, a hope which was becoming more fragile the further this sordid case went.

Scott kept his hands motionless, fingertips lightly touching. "Did Alesha reveal the location of the room you're talking about?"

She took a sip of wine. What did he mean? Could more than one exist?

"No, the photographs are of the inside of the room and that's all I have–so I've no clue as to where they were taken."

"I'd like to see them."

"I hoped you might and I'm sure we can come to an arrangement, though of course, I've copied the evidence and placed it in more than one location, and, should anything happen to me, I've given instructions to a friend to mail it directly to Inspector Spinks."

"I'm glad you're being prudent," Scott said.

Kal smiled. "Thank you."

She watched as, like the master he was, Scott considered his hand of cards and compared it to hers.

"I'll need time to consider your request," he said, "meanwhile, let's not allow my chef's preparations to go to waste."

Scott invited her to move to the dining area and she picked up her glass and followed.

"Besides, I make it my business to get to know my associates," Scott said.

Know your enemy. Yes, she made it her business too. "Our conversation has given me quite an appetite," she said.

"I opted for an Indian banquet. Quite appropriate, don't you think?"

As Scott opened the servers, the scents of spicy foods filled the air. Kal made her selection slowly and carefully.

She carried her plate to the table and Scott seated himself opposite.

"ScottBioTec's third-generation limb looks set to catch the headlines and I'd be interested to hear more about it."

"If you like."

Scott began with the new discoveries about brain chemicals and Kal interrupted here and there with questions. Scott appeared to be at ease–enjoying his food, talking with eloquence, gesticulating with his fork. Then at some moment, her eyes strayed to the granite counter-top a good distance behind Scott. Beside the corkscrew, lay a remote-control device, slim and black, like a phone. It was placed slightly to the right of Scott's head.

"Is something wrong?" Scott asked.

She brought her gaze back to her plate. She mustn't stare at it. Without taking the remote in her hand she couldn't be one-hundred percent certain, yet she felt sure it was a remote control unit for an artificial limb.

Scott dabbed his mouth with a napkin. "Is something bothering you?"

"Not at all, please continue."

Scott started talking again and she continued eating, avoiding looking at the slim-line unit. Scott must have positioned it there deliberately. There was not one single item out of place in this house, and he had put his wine glass on the table before she did. He'd planned where she would sit and he'd placed the remote control intentionally in her line of sight. Scott was true to type–a certain sort of paedophile likes to show off, enjoys vaunting his cleverness.

Kal made herself go through the discipline of logical deduction. The conclusion came out exactly the same as the reflex which leapt to mind as soon as she spotted the device– that Scott was hiding Amita in the house, right here, right now. That he'd invited her here for the thrill of having her close to the captured child. As part of his kicks. Her rage flared white hot. In Kal's imagination, a red target mark flickered on Scott's brow.

She put down her cutlery. "Excuse me, may I use your restroom?"

"Of course, it's down the hallway."

As she stood, Scott tugged down the already faultless cuffs of his shirt and she fancied a ghost of satisfaction played across his face. Only force of willpower stopped her from slamming her fist into it.

She made herself walk casually, crossing the lounge and pulling the door softly shut behind her.

The bathroom lay further down the passage. With heavy footsteps, she went towards it and, remaining on the outside, smartly pulled the bathroom door closed. Then in one smooth gesture, she removed her shoes, hitched up her dress and sprinted back along the hallway and straight up the stairs.

On the top landing, the carpeted floor masked her quick footsteps. She would search the whole house systematically. Every quadrant of every room. Perfectly silently. He was a pervert–it was part of his high to invite her here–to have her touching distance from Amita. She was certain of it. Her muscles shivered, full of bodily drugs and the hormones which come with simultaneous fast action and stealth.

First bedroom; two windows both locked, a walk-in closet with no exits, an en-suite bathroom also with no exits. Kal ran her hand down the walls, checked the carpeting for any marks where it might habitually be pulled aside, examined the skirting for tell-tale signs of scuffs or scratches from over-use, scanned the ceilings. Nothing. No hidey holes, no hidden recesses.

Second bedroom, same story; no marks, no give-aways, no tiny clues on door frames or inside closets. Third bedroom, ditto. No attic openings. Smooth, painted walls. Be meticulous, she commanded herself. Don't miss any detail.

Next a luxury bathroom; large tub, glass-enclosed shower unit, tiled walls. She checked the tiling. There was no secret panel. She ran her hands over the flooring and along the side of the tub. Nothing.

Time ticked on and her frustration kicked in. She judged she had a couple more minutes before Scott might wonder. Then he might exit to the hallway. No matter. She could deal with him.

Fourth bedroom and fifth; windows locked, walk-in closets with nothing amiss, no signs of any underfloor entrances, no indication of a trap-door of any kind, no cupboard spaces or under-beds she hadn't checked. No one could be hidden up here, not even stuffed into a tiny space but Amita was here, she knew it. She could smell it. Everything pointed in that direction.

She stopped. *What have I overlooked?* Yes, she should verify the sizing of the rooms. So she paced the length of the walls and referenced them inside and out to check for any compartment hidden between rooms. Nothing. Yet she felt sure. Scott was true to type–Amita was in the house.

Running back down the stairs, her heart went double-time. She made for the first door opposite the lounge. In one movement she opened it and switched on the light. A bureau. One patio window, locked. Book shelving on one wall, completely solid. A parquet floor. Kal got down on hands and knees to examine the flooring, testing with light taps of her knuckles–no hollow sounds, no signs of imperfection, no hidden cupboards. She listened, straining for any slight sound, any indication of Amita signalling for help.

Leaving the bureau, she headed for the door further down the hallway. A key sat in the lock and her hand hesitated. Why had Scott left the key there? She took it out, in case he decided to try locking her inside, then she opened the door.

It was a double garage with a metal door to the exterior. There were three blank walls of bare bricks and a concrete floor, recently swept. Kal ran zig-zag across the concrete, starting one corner and working her way across, checking for signs of wear, unusual tags, anything suspicious, any sign of a concealed entrance. Nothing. No cellar. Nothing underground. Dammit.

Closing the door, she replaced the key. The hallway held no other doors and no hidden entrances. The parquet flooring as perfect as it was in the bureau. She dived into the bathroom and locked the door and examined the enormous restroom, full of luxury fittings, complete with a mirrored make-up area. Nothing. Her frustration was sky-rocketing and it made her breathless. Keep it under control, she commanded herself. So she stood for a moment and closed her eyes–Scott invited her here, he left the remote in clear view. She could swear he was keeping Amita in the house, or, wait.

Her eyes sprang open. What if Scott was jerking her chain? Was she so desperate to locate the child, he could make her run wherever he wanted? Toy with her as a cat plays with a mouse. Opening up her avenues of weakness? Outpsyching your opponent was an effective tactic in breaking someone down. Used consistently, it could bring hardened professionals to their knees. Certainly she'd rattled him in penetrating to the heart of his set-up in Kolkata. A man like Scott would delight in spinning out his revenge.

Putting her shoes back on, Kal brushed concrete dust from her calves and checked her hair in the mirror before walking back to the lounge.

"Did you find what you wanted?"

The arrogant son-of-a-bitch.

"Do you always feel the need to be so cautious?" she said. "It's as if you're scared. Why not be open?"

"It's unwise to show all one's cards before the right moment."

"It's only unwise if you feel threatened. A master at his game is beyond petty anxieties, my father told me that. Which I guess means you're not yet a master."

"Whereas your father was?"

"Perhaps, in his own way."

"So young, and so naïve. It's a shame he didn't teach you how the world really works."

Scott toyed with a dessert spoon, "You were twelve, weren't you, when your father died? Your mother told me she met you at the school gates. You guessed she'd come with bad news and you ran to a friend's house. She found you there hours later."

She stared at him, her mind tagging red target marks all over his body.

"What was the name of that friend, wasn't it Marty King? Are you still in contact with her?"

Her back flashed hot. "That sounds like a threat."

"Goodness, Kal, what an imagination. Why would I threaten your friends?"

Her chair scraped against the parquet. "Whilst you might think a lot of people are stupid, don't make that mistake with me."

Fury shot through her system. One blow to the face and Scott would be down. Hadn't her father trained her to be a killer? She could feel it in her veins, in her boiling blood. One shot to the forehead, or the heart. Or for a slow and painful end, a hit to the stomach and watch him bleed to death. Kal's chest and arms shook with the strain of holding it in. Stalking across the room, she swept up her coat.

"Leaving so soon? How disappointing, and I was about to enquire about the health of your grandmother."

Her answer came out like a snarl. "Come back to me on the money and don't push your luck."

Kal marched down the hallway and heard the *click* as, from his position at the lounge doorway, Scott casually unlocked the entrance bolts and allowed her to exit.

Running down the street and around a corner, Kal fumbled for her phone. LeeMing answered straight away.

"LeeMing, listen!" she shouted.

"I'm listening. What's happened, tell us clearly and precisely."

"Nannie's in danger, she needs protection! Scott's targeting her and…"

LeeMing cut her off. "Calm down. I already took care of it. My contacts have been watching the nursing home and your grandmother is perfectly safe."

"And when exactly were you going to tell me!"

"Take it easy, and it's okay, you can thank me later."

She swore at him and demanded to speak to Marty.

"Watch your back, Marty. Scott made a threat against you and he means it."

"No sweat," Marty replied, "we've been waiting for you to phone. Sounds like you had an eventful evening."

"Damn Scott, Marty, damn him! He's stringing me along. He's got me running in circles. He's a clever bastard. Clever, calculating and deadly."

"Yes, we knew that," said Marty softly, "and remember, so are you."

Chapter Thirty-seven

A bitter wind swept across the tarmac. Kal pulled her woolly hat down as far as it would go. Laid out in front of them like a child's play set, the private airfield consisted of a runway, one hangar and an office. The only sign of activity was a light in an office window.

"Scott makes all his flights from here and, according to my source, he flew to Kolkata yesterday and is due back tonight," Marty said.

"With another victim to supply to a customer?" LeeMing asked.

"When the flights are logged, the details of the passengers are left out," Marty said.

"Of course they are, except why else would the bastard go there so soon?" Kal said. Lying out flat on the top of a grass embankment, Kal examined the landing strip through binoculars. "Those perverts think they've got it all wrapped up."

By her side, LeeMing lay stretched on his stomach. "Keep it steady, Kal. As soon as Scott makes a false move, we've got him. Don't let it be us who breaks first."

LeeMing didn't mean 'us' breaking first, he meant her. "Don't worry, I'm not cracking."

"Marty," he said, "you've got useful inside contacts, how so?"

"I've all types on my team at work, including plenty of ex-police and ex-army. They're as keen as I am to see paedophiles behind bars. It only took a couple of discreet questions to get information on Scott's air-time."

"We've got to be ready to intercept any child," Kal said. "Did you get the merchandise, Marty?"

"Yup, all I need to do is conceal this baby on the car." Marty waved the box under Kal's nose. "Remember, this equipment cost thousands of pounds and it's strictly on loan." Marty pushed the tracker back into her jacket. "I'm going down by the gates. I want to check my bearings for when it gets dark."

"We'll sit tight," Kal said.

Once Marty scrambled down the embankment, LeeMing spoke. "Marty's very protective of you. I guess it's because you've known each other a long time. Or is there more to it than that?"

"You choose your moments for the personal questions, don't you?"

"Now seemed as good a time as any."

She rolled to face him. "Marty and I have been friends since way back, though we were never together, if that's what you're asking."

"Right."

"We're close and Marty will always be special and, if you haven't heard, Marty has relationships with women on occasion, which isn't a secret from anyone. That's not a problem for you, is it?"

"Of course not."

"Then why are you asking?" She couldn't deny she felt drawn towards LeeMing.

"Why not hand the case over to Spinks? Why keep taking so many risks?" he said. "You're getting yourself in deeper and deeper. Those people are ruthless. Why keep going like this?"

"Because my mother's life is at stake as well as innocent children."

"Not because you're running away from something, and you can ram it down by constantly placing yourself in danger? I've seen people who act that way and I wouldn't like you to be one of them."

No, and she didn't think he'd like it either, if she turned out to be a nasty blueprint of David Khan.

"What does it matter to you?"

"You don't need to play games with me, if you got to know me better, you'd know that."

"Is that an offer?"

"Of friendship, yes. As you probably know, I've got a girlfriend."

It was a perverse relief to know he wasn't interested. "Great."

"She and I have known each other for years. Our parents knew each other in Hong Kong before our families even moved to London."

That's bloody fantastic, she thought, only please don't kill me with the details.

"Then tell me, do you keep secrets from her?"

LeeMing's whole body twitched. "Excuse me?"

"I said, do you keep secrets from your girlfriend? Don't get me wrong, I don't play around with men who're already taken, I'm asking because that night on the Common you had a Dim mak hold on your attacker. I'm guessing your girlfriend doesn't like the Triad and I think you promised her you'd leave, except I'm not certain you did."

"Are you saying Master Yeung taught you Dim mak? I really doubt it."

"For your information, my father taught me."

"I thought David Khan sounded, shall we say, unusual. He must have been one hell of a father. Actually you're right, my girlfriend doesn't like the Triad though that's not the reason I left, and I certainly don't lie nor do I keep secrets."

Marty arrived in a rush and threw herself down on the ground. "Not interrupting am I?"

"Of course not," Kal said.

For an instant, she imagined she could tell LeeMing everything and she finally realised what a relief that would be. Then, rolling back onto her stomach, Kal clamped the binoculars hard to her face and the moment passed.

It was a bone-chilling, fifty minutes before personnel ran out from the office. A plane appeared in the distance, levelling out for landing and at the same time a black sedan drew up at the gates.

"That's my cue, "Marty said.

"Ours too," Kal replied, "good luck."

With dusk falling, she and LeeMing squirmed down the near side of the embankment and ran low across the open space. They hid as close as possible to the hangar entrance.

Meanwhile, the sedan approached along the interior road and with a crunch of tyres it pulled up close to their hiding position. The driver got out and Kal recognised him as the boxer–the second bodyguard she had fought at the suite.

The private jet approached the runway and the wheels contacted the ground, bounced, then squealed on the tarmac. Then came the roar of the reverse thrusters. As the plane's speed dropped it oriented towards the hangar and Kal caught the whiff of rubber and aviation fuel.

No more mistakes, she thought. Grab any child. Straight in and out. She flexed her fingers and her shoulders. The staff were wheeling over a set of steps. If it took an out and out fight to get hold of a child, they already agreed it's what they would do, then call in Spinks' team to mop up the mess.

LeeMing opted for a crouch position, plastered low to the ground. With the guard close enough he would be alerted, neither of them spoke. The guard lounged by the sedan and lit a cigarette and she heard the *click* of the lighter and the suck as the man inhaled. The red end of the cigarette glowed. Around them, night had fallen.

The airplane door swung aside and out came two adults. Scott first, and behind him, a man Kal recognised as one of the perpetrators on Alesha's list, Aaron DeVille–the Hollywood producer who loves England. Yellow light spilled from inside the plane and she waited for another figure to come into view, a smaller one. None did.

Scott and DeVille headed towards the car.

"I can only apologise again, Aaron," Scott said, "The operating problems will be resolved very soon."

"I hope so."

The bodyguard ground the remains of his cigarette underfoot and leapt to open the car door.

"I trust you had a good flight, Dr Scott?"

"Indeed we did and I shall be joining Aaron for dinner. Please take us straight there."

Not long after, in the back of Marty's car, LeeMing removed his gloves and leaned between the seats to place his hands close to the heating.

"There were no children which means we move to plan 'b'," he said.

"Give me the laptop," Kal said, "there might be a way of getting to DeVille's house ahead of them. Take a left here, Marty, and go faster."

"Okay, you're the boss," said Marty, and she spun the steering wheel, expertly controlling the rear skid as the car took the corner at speed.

"You two are full of surprises," said LeeMing, as he braced himself against the door frame.

Close to DeVille's mansion, they left the car concealed and sprinted the final stretch. They had got there first and somewhere to their right, the roar of the sedan approached down the main road. The three of them reached the bushes at the side of the electronic gate moments before it began sliding open, and slightly ahead of the sedan. The car drove straight through, leaving them time to sneak in. Then they accelerated along the gravel drive, the three of them at full stretch, pounding alongside each other. Kal smelt the lingering exhaust fumes and by the time they neared the house, a sharp pain jarred her leg at each step.

Scott and DeVille had already gone inside. Kal massaged her knee and caught her breath, examining the exterior of the mansion. Twelve windows on the ground floor and though the windows had old-style, diamond leaded panes, on close inspection, they were modern, high-security look-a-likes. Likely DeVille's mansion boasted a range of up-to-date security systems, not to mention plenty of domestic staff. The staff would be pattering backwards and forwards to cater to the arrival of DeVille and his guest. It would make access without detection a challenge.

"Let's check around the back," she whispered.

Sure enough, at the rear, they found a second entrance.

"That's for tradespeople and deliveries and it's my way in," she said.

Marty's eyes flicked to Kal's knee. "Wo-ah, wait a minute. It can't be you who goes inside, not with Scott in there."

"We already agreed on our strategy and I'll be staying well away from Scott, don't worry."

LeeMing placed a hand on her arm. "Marty's right. Our ideas didn't involve Scott sitting at the dinner table. If he identifies you, we'll have much less chance of releasing any child. One person's got to get inside, remain undetected and search the entire house."

"Let me do this."

LeeMing shook his head.

"Marty, back me up on this one," Kal said.

In an upstairs room, someone turned on a light, throwing a rectangle of yellow on the ground.

"Keep your voice down," Marty said. "I've only got one question…"

"What?"

"Why are three of us here?"

"What the hell's that supposed to mean?"

"Don't you get it? Team-work. Like I keep saying, you're not on your own, and with Scott inside and that knee of yours, are you really the best person for the job?"

"Shit. Damn you, Marty."

"Yes, damn me and that's what friends are for."

Marty's voice didn't carry any trace of victory though Kal noticed LeeMing smiling.

"What the hell are you laughing at?"

"I'm not laughing, I've got an idea. Sometimes you just have to fall back on those caricatures. Give me a minute."

A brick wall hid a bin area. LeeMing disappeared and they heard him ferreting amongst the garbage.

"What the hell is he doing?" Marty hissed.

LeeMing reappeared holding a cardboard pizza container. "Anyone for a deep-pan with extra cheese?"

"Have you lost it?" Marty said.

"What this means is Chinese boys like me often deliver pizza. If I turn up at the entrance and announce a delivery, they'll probably let me roll right on in. The name and address of their usual delivery place is even printed on the carton."

LeeMing unzipped his jacket and gave them a big grin, holding out the carton. The effect was surprisingly convincing.

"It's only the stereotypes playing in your mind," he said.

Marty groaned but Kal nodded. "This might work," she said.

"Kal, once I'm inside I'll check the house, you have my word. If I can make it out in secret with any child, I will. If I need back-up, I'll give a signal."

Yes, she knew he could do it and, more than that, she knew he would go all the way. The children in Kolkata, the girl in the morgue–it had gone deep. It had affected them all. LeeMing was as committed to stamping this out as she was.

"Holy shit, this is getting surreal," Marty said.

Marty tossed LeeMing the car keys and he came back a few minutes later driving Marty's car, having been allowed entrance at the main gate. They watched from the shadows as LeeMing sauntered to the rear entrance. When he neared the door, automatic security lighting lit up the flank of the house.

"Do you think this is going to work? I mean, usually you hand the pizza over on the doorstep, you don't go inside. All he's got is an empty carton," Marty said.

"Don't forget LeeMing was a member of the Triad. He'll find a way."

"As long as he doesn't end up in a goddam body bag."

"No chance."

LeeMing pressed the buzzer.

"Do you think good men have secrets?" Kal asked.

Marty's gaze swung away from the door. "What?"

"Do good men have secrets?"

They heard a scraping noise as someone slid back the security latches.

"This is about David Khan, isn't it?"

The final bolt released with a *thunk* and LeeMing stepped forward brandishing the carton and disappeared inside.

It had been threatening rain and now the grey clouds gave way.

"Let's find shelter, or we'll get soaked," Marty said.

They tucked themselves into an evergreen hedge. Marty turned off her flashlight and they waited in the dark. Kal listened to the rain and a few minutes passed before Marty spoke again.

"So what's this about your father?"

"You've never called him that before."

"I know," Marty replied, "it seemed time to stop punishing a dead man for what he did to my best friend."

Kal was glad Marty couldn't see her face. "You were right about him. I loved him you see, and that meant I forgave him. I never told you he took me to a firing range, even made me promise to take lessons."

Twigs snapped as Marty lost her balance. "Shit."

"At Judge Greeves' house, Scott told me details about David Khan's activities. I think it could be true."

"And it could be a pack of lies designed to break you down."

"I don't think so. I can't bear to tell you more, Marty. It's too dreadful."

A raindrop trickled down Kal's neck. It made her realise she was shivering violently.

"Listen Kal, whatever David Khan might have done, he isn't you. Whatever type of person he was, you're different, you're someone deep down good. I know you better than you know yourself and don't you forget it."

"I'm frightened, Marty. Sometimes I don't trust myself. It's like I've been poisoned by him."

"Your father used you. He poured all his sick shit into you except he didn't make you who you are."

"Didn't he? Are you really sure about that? And what if he was a killer, a cold-blooded murderer? What would you think then?" Kal dug her fingernails into the rough bark of a bush and tore downwards. She hoped she'd make herself bleed. "Part of me is like him. I know it, I can feel it inside. And if he's as monstrous and evil as I think, what does that make me?"

"That's bloody rubbish! It doesn't make you anything."

"I've got to know the truth–not knowing is driving me mad. I'm going to check out what Scott told me, and it's something I have to do alone."

Marty thumped the ground. "Fuck it, I knew you were going to say that. Just remember I know you Kal, and whatever you find out, however bad it is, don't ever forget I trust you."

Almost one hour later they heard the door latches being pulled back again. Crouching at the ready, Kal could hear Marty's quick breaths as they readied themselves.

"It's LeeMing," Marty hissed.

"Looks like he's alone."

The three of them ran for Marty's car and Marty started the engine.

"Let's get the hell out of here," LeeMing said.

"Tell me what you found!"

"I searched thoroughly and there are no children I promise you, although there was this, I found it under a bed."

Kal scrutinised LeeMing's face. His lips were tight and she had never seen him looking so drawn. He threw an object onto the seat and Kal reached over to pick up the black, remote control unit.

Chapter Thirty-eight

Known for its risqué vibe, Soho was one of Kal's favourite haunts in central London. Soho included vibrant Chinatown, and though it covered only one square mile of the West End, Soho didn't waste any space. The narrow streets were packed with bars, food venues and nightlife. As a centre for the sex trade dating back two hundred years, Soho also hosted sex shops and burlesque shows, even though it was situated a few minutes' walk from the up-market theatre district.

The man Kal came to meet had the unlikely name of Dante Jones.

Walking down Wardour Street, Kal passed her favourite Chinese restaurant. The Wong Kei's modest window gave no hint of its capacity to seat five hundred diners. After their first regional tournament, Master Yeung had brought the kung fu club here to celebrate and they'd had a wonderful evening. Were the good things all in the past? Would her meeting with Dante alter her warm feelings about Soho for ever?

Kal turned down a back alley. She had never tried one of the sex venues before, still, there was a first time for everything.

Flashing lights ran along the outside and the smartly dressed doorman looked her up and down.

"Can I help you?" He had a South American accent, probably Peruvian.

"I've an appointment with Dante Jones."

Entering a dark corridor, she could hear pounding music and she followed the sound into the back. Passing through a nineteen-eighties-style bead curtain, she entered a dimly lit bar area arranged with small tables. No naked women pranced on a catwalk, rather a fully clothed, female singer entertained the audience from a front stage. The woman was singing a jazz number.

Kal counted about twenty people, most of them sitting alone. The clientele seemed to be mainstream members of the London population.

The doorman had called ahead and a high-heeled waitress approached her.

"Dante is expecting you. Please would you follow me?"

On stage, the singer completed her song to a round of applause.

"Who's up next?" Kal asked the waitress.

"It's Roxy with a burlesque number, you can watch later if you like."

The waitress tossed her red hair and strutted off. When they reached a rear door, the red-head knocked.

"In you go, don't be shy."

The door swung open to reveal a huge room. Kal scanned quickly–orange washed walls gave it a Moroccan feel, a giant flat screen television, two three-seater sofas, a snooker table set up for a new game, no windows to the outside.

A man, tall and wide-shouldered, sat behind a gigantic desk. A Miro print hung behind him, the print a swathe of blue with a red heart and a moon, half white half black, and part of Kal wondered if it might be an original.

She walked towards Dante. The room reeked of drug culture. Impossible to put her finger on exactly why, she could just smell it, as if the walls had witnessed countless extortion deals and threats of violence and absorbed them, and the man sitting behind the desk was stamped with the mark of dirty money.

When she had spoken to Dante on the phone, she'd heard the vigilance in his voice which was the wariness of someone who had earned too many enemies. Dante said he'd been expecting her to call. He said Scott had asked him as a favour to meet her and that, yes, he would be delighted.

A hefty, white man, Dante had the build and appearance of a gangster from a seventies movie. He wore his hair gelled back, which created a suave effect, and in his younger days his looks were probably striking. However, time and neglect had taken their toll, and now his sallow complexion and soul-less eyes betrayed his allegiances, showing how something inside had been destroyed and could never be rebuilt. Nevertheless, Dante affected a coating of style, with his expensive suit and cologne. He must be a senior member in his organisation. A hardened man.

"Kal, what a pleasure to meet you, you don't mind if I call you by your first name, do you?"

Dante walked around the desk and bent his large frame into a half-bow.

"You're as lovely as your father boasted. Please, take a seat."

A soft knock sounded and the waitress entered and placed two glasses delicately on the desk. Kal hardly wanted to breathe the cologne-laden air, let alone ingest the contents of that glass. She sat bolt upright in the chair opposite Dante. She'd chosen black, flared trousers and a dark purple jumper reaching to her thighs. Sweeping back her hair, she looked straight across the desk.

"I want to know the truth about David Khan."

"A bold statement. I like that, I like that very much indeed." Dante rested his elbows on the desktop. "And what makes you think you don't know the truth already?"

"I'm here for information not riddles. Richard Scott made serious accusations against my father and I'm here for facts. Now in what capacity did you know David Khan and what can you tell me about him?"

"I've no intention of patronising you."

Dante opened a drawer and pulled out a fist-sized, cellophane bag and a buff file. The plastic bag landed with a clatter, closely followed by the file. As Dante extracted a sweet from the bag, she caught a whiff of peppermint.

"I'm giving up smoking for the millionth time. Would you like a mint?" Dante asked.

"Please get to the point."

He popped a sweet into his mouth. "You have Indian ancestry, so I'm sure you're aware the links between the Pashtun people in Pakistan and those in northwest India run deep. It was the British who partitioned Pakistan from India in the nineteen forties, cutting across ancestral allegiances that existed for millennia. The Pashtun people of Pakistan also have deep tribal links across their northern border with Afghanistan. Let me paint a picture for you–the region includes the Hindu Kush, the Himalayas and the Khyber Pass and the extensive foothills are home to the poppy harvest, principally on the Afghan side. Each year the poppy harvest is taken across the border to Pakistan to be processed. The heroin is produced in hundreds of ramshackle laboratories hidden in those foothills. The poverty, the power and allegiances of the tribal leaders, and the difficulties in accessing highly remote areas, all contribute to record harvests and production which international agencies struggle, and mostly fail, to limit."

When he paused, she could hear the crunch of Dante's teeth against the mints.

"That's my world–the drugs world. Merchandise is trafficked from Pakistan and northern India to the American and European markets." Dante reached for another sweet.

"As a freelance journalist, your father investigated the tribal factions in the remote areas, back in the days when the tribal leaders in Afghanistan were called upon to be freedom fighters. David Khan became familiar with the Pashtuns, probably got to like them. There's plenty to like in their warrior spirit and their fierce love of their land. "

A faint scent of peppermint wafted across the desk.

"I knew your father from his early days. I suppose we started out in the business around the same time. He was talented and ambitious. He started by passing on information he picked up about planned raids on the cartel's activities. Having an uncanny ability to gather intelligence, he quickly rose up the ranks and used his cover as a journalist to travel freely. The cartel nurtured his talents, backed him, invested in him. In short, in the space of a decade, he succeeded in infiltrating the highest levels of anti-drug operations and became responsible for neutralising threats to the cartel in whatever way was necessary. He had the Baron's resources available to him at all times, though he mostly worked alone. He was what we call a 'lone wolf'–carrying out his operations in Pakistan, India, London, the States–wherever it was required."

Dante opened the file and splayed a sheaf of photographs on the desktop.

"Didn't you ever wonder why your father died as he did? David Khan was an excellent bike rider, and of course, he used a motorbike frequently in the Pakistan foothills, it's one of the most practical means of transport, aside from trekking the passes."

Kal stared at the photographs. They were of a man and a woman, lying in a pool of blood in what appeared to be an extravagant home, in somewhere like Malibu beach.

"I don't understand."

"David Khan was killed by the British secret service, MI6 as the public like to call them. His death, and the manner of it, is the strongest evidence I can give you of his activities. It was a perfectly orchestrated hit, and one which the police will never make progress with. Khan's death was carried out largely as a favour for the Americans, because Khan's last job had been the assassination of a senior, American intelligence officer and his family."

She stared at the photographs. They were taken from various angles, of a man slumped on a sofa, and a woman lying face up on a crimson-stained carpet. The room didn't indicate a struggle, though an arterial spray was splattered across one of the walls.

Dante pointed to the dead man. "This intelligence officer, Todd Cartwright, had been responsible for masterminding some of the most successful raids on the cartel's activities. Cartwright's network was working its way closer and closer to the heart of our organisation. Your father had been shadowing Cartwright for some time, and then one of the Baron's sons was killed in New York and the finger was pointed at Cartwright's team. I'm sure you can imagine the Baron's reaction. It meant Cartwright had to be eliminated, though first, he had to be forced to tell about his sources, because it seemed we might have a high-level leak on the inside."

Bile forced its way up Kal's throat.

"There's not much more to say. David Khan had been responsible for the deaths of many people over the years. The Baron made the elimination of Cartwright a top priority. He wanted one of his top men, and he chose your father."

"How do I know what you're telling me is true?"

Dante swept his hand to indicate the photographs. "What I'm telling you is the truth. Special forces arranged your father's death because of his activities for the cartel."

She forced herself to examine the file. Picked up the sheaf of photographs and flicked through image after nauseating image. Then scanned newspaper articles on the deaths. The articles cited the Cartwright killings as a drugs related assassination. There was a printout of an internal document from the CIA which ran to several pages and she turned them like a robot. One small paragraph stated there had been a survivor. A young child had survived the shooting.

The room fell silent except for the crunch of Dante's peppermints. There was no way for her to check this information. Though Dante was undoubtedly a professional liar, she detected no blips in his story, no tell-tale signs of an emotional snag or oversell, no unconscious errors.

More importantly, her own instincts told her she finally faced the truth. The truth beneath the excitement and the daring and the discipline she had shared with her father. That's why her heart had gone so hard and cold. As if her spirit had shrivelled up and died.

"You said my father boasted about me. Did he ever show you a picture?"

"I never saw a photograph. We were professionals in passing, each with our own areas of expertise. Though I remember a Christmas celebration in India one time, in some colonial-style mansion full of important guests, where politicians rubbed shoulders with dirty men like me and pretended we were all friends. Your father and I ended up side by side at the bar. He told me how he'd just chosen a martial arts club for you. In Battersea wasn't it? He'd seen the Master of the club give a demonstration in the States, and he'd been so impressed he tracked him down in London, and you know what an expert your father was in martial arts, so he recognised expertise when he saw it."

Master Yeung. Her father told her he had seen a martial arts display on his travels and that's how he chose Master Yeung. Her ears rang as the blood drained from her face.

"What about my mother, what was her part in it?"

"Since he was a master of deceit, I'm sure your mother knew nothing about Khan's activities."

"She's missing."

"That's not something I can help with."

"Then tell me about this," she said, slapping a picture down on the desk. She had designed it herself–a crescent moon and sky studded with stars, just as the man had worn in Kolkata. For a micro-second, Dante's teeth paused in their crunch.

"The pieces bearing this insignia are fashioned on the Baron's instructions, by an artisan at the historical bazaar in Peshawar. I once watched the silversmith melting the silver in the fire. I caution you not to show this in public. The Pakistani mafia is strong in London and they would react unpredictably. The insignia is the personal mark of the Baron. He gives such pieces only to his favoured operatives."

"So where's yours?"

"I lost it."

"Which tells me it was the cartel who shot the driver in Kolkata. Why would they do that?"

"The Baron has his reasons for everything. Perhaps we were reminding Chatrawalia and the other judges to keep in line, or maybe it's because, as I said, your father was a favourite."

"And he was killed undertaking your business."

"There's nothing unusual about that."

"Isn't there?"

The photographs stared at her from the desktop. She felt utterly sick to her stomach. Had David Khan tortured the Cartwrights? What about the other people her father killed? She felt contaminated, yet, part of her had always known the truth and always denied it. Never wanting to face the fact her beloved father had been a highly skilled infiltrator and a trained killer who enjoyed his work.

"Why did you agree to see me? Why are you doing a favour for Richard Scott, he can't be anything to you."

Dante flicked his hand. "The activities of his organisation are of no significance. His network is a ripple in the pool and those with such vices only open themselves to the Baron's use."

Kal stared across the desk. "Maybe the Baron owes my father. Maybe you agreed to see me to close the circle after my father's death, and this interview is to do with my father and with me."

"If that's true, then any debt has been repaid, hasn't it, in our intervention in India? Really, was it a good idea to meddle in affairs that are no business of yours? It was unwise to travel to Kolkata."

"I want the cartel to help find my mother."

"That's a big ask. Besides, you should be careful what you wish for."

She banged the flat of her hand on the desk. "I want help! I'm making a request, dammit."

"I could put it to the Baron on your behalf, though I caution you to consider carefully because firstly, I'm sure the answer will be negative, and secondly, it would be better, much better for you, if it was."

"What the hell is that supposed to mean!"

"It means if we do you a favour, then someday a favour will be asked in return, and you will have no choice. You will be placing yourself in our debt."

She didn't care. It was Alesha's last chance. They were out of time. Once Spinks closed in, Scott and the syndicate would do everything in their power to destroy anyone and anything that could be used against them. Including her mother.

Dante leaned back in his chair. "Are you certain about your request?"

"Yes."

"Facing reality is always the best way to move forward, Kal. I'm glad we had the chance to meet."

Dante got to his feet and she stood, steadying herself on the back of the chair and for a moment, the blues and reds of the Miro print swum together. Dante didn't move a muscle as she swayed, righted herself, then turned and walked towards the door. It felt like it was miles away. Only once she was safely on the other side did Kal let herself cave.

She had so wished her father to be a hero, and he was simply a vile criminal. David Khan had been insatiably ambitious and dangerous as a viper. That her father was operating as a lone wolf for the cartel, was in perfect keeping with his profile. He was a murderer. A killer. It was the final, dirty truth.

Chapter Thirty-nine

She must get back to the sanity of Marty and LeeMing.

The Soho streets were full. It was around six thirty in the evening, and scents of Chinese food hung in the air. People were already heading for the Chinatown restaurants. Employees from all parts of London, Chinatown residents, and an amazing mix of tourists, all mingled in the streets.

Kal hurried towards the underground entrance. *My father was a murderer.* Marty would help her. *He killed innocent people. Women and children.* Mary could save her. Only Marty.

There was a crowd going down the steps and someone bumped into her and then apologised. A few seconds later, her vision started to blur and Kal grabbed for the handrail. Shit. No! She had been compromised. Someone grabbed her arm, whispered in her ear. Kal tried to twist to face them except her legs were giving way and the noise and swirl of people and coats filled her head. Then everything went black.

She awoke groggy and feeling sick. She was hanging from her wrists, with her arms yanked upwards. Her toes brushed the ground, giving her no purchase to take up the strain. Her wrists burned and Kal peered upwards and saw a thick rope and the rope attached to an iron ring. The ring was embedded in a bare, brick wall. The fog in her mind kept pushing her to phase out.

They must have pumped her with chemicals. She could use the burn of the rope to work against it. Grinding her wrists against the bindings, it made her feel like vomiting and it also increased the pain and her adrenalin levels, cutting through the fog.

She was alone in a dim chamber. It had a subterranean feel to it, with brick walls and a curved, brick ceiling, much like a chapel. Bricks formed the flooring too, red, oblong, London building bricks. The chamber lay bare except for a wooden chair, and it smelled dank. What was that smell?

Grinding her wrists again, she brought back the nausea, the tendons in her shoulders screaming. No, not seaweed. Something similar. More rank. She half expected to hear the drip of water, although listening carefully there was no sound at all. The mind fog started to roll in again and she fought it off.

At that moment, she heard footsteps, and as the *tap, tap* echoed from the domed ceiling, the answer came to her. It was fetid water. Sewers. Was she in the sewers?

Two men came down a ladder. One of them grabbed the chair, scraping it across the floor to sit in front of her.

"It's difficult to judge the dosage required to knock someone out and we often overestimate, I'm glad you've revived at last."

He didn't give a nasty smile and he didn't gloat. In fact, his face displayed no emotion whatsoever. This was a normal day's work for him. He was a professional, just like LeeMing said.

"Who are you?" Kal asked.

It came out as a croak because her throat was so dry.

"Don't worry about that, we've got more important things to discuss."

He leaned forward and opened his hand. On it lay two silver hoops. The jewellery looked fragile against his meaty palm. One of the hoops was snapped off at the top, where the ear-attachment should be. A terrible sensation crept into Kal's guts and her bowels threatened to turn to water.

With all her will power, she fixed her face into a groggy expression. Let her eyes blur so all he'd see was her straining to focus. He stood up and jabbed the earrings under her nose.

"Recognise these? We ripped them off the dead body of that black friend of yours."

"Don't know who you mean."

"Yes, you do, and she put up quite a fight. A spirited one she was, wouldn't stay down, fought like a mad woman. Strong too. Marty King she was called, remember her now?"

Fear swept through Kal.

"My point being," he tossed away the hoops and they landed with a *plink* onto the brick flooring, "she's now out of the picture."

Kal kept her eyes downcast. One of the earrings had landed at the seam of the wall where a small amount of debris had collected in the crack. Alongside the silver hoop, there was something else. It was a fragment of material, tiny, no bigger than a thumbnail. A torn scrap of orange silk. Identical to the material of one of her mother's favourite dresses. It swept away the effect of the drugs. Her whole body began shaking and Kal couldn't tear her eyes away. She felt like she couldn't breathe.

"How much of that stuff did you pump her with?" the man snapped to his partner.

She clocked the shift in his body position–telegraph, combat fighters called it. A subtle movement, usually of the trunk or side of the body, that precedes a brutal action and signals, or telegraphs, an attacker's intent. She braced her abdominals as the full force of his hand impacted the side of her face. She swung suspended from the ring.

"Wake up sleeping beauty, we've got work to do." He addressed his colleague over his shoulder. "Are the waterworks ready?"

"Ready and waiting, Klaus," the second man replied.

Klaus lifted her chin and his hand smelled of soap.

"Listen up. We want answers. You've got information and we want to know where you've stashed it. If you co-operate then we won't need to use force, will we? Do you know what I think?"

He kicked the chair back across the floor.

"I think you're a very clever girl, though you know what, like it or not you're going to tell me the location of that information."

Klaus nodded at his partner.

In the distance, she heard a sound like the wind in the trees. Or the rush of water.

"Did you know the London sewage system is pretty damn amazing?" Klaus said, as he walked away. "This part of the network is kept dry by a control system of locks and a mere tweak of a computer sends a deluge to flood this chamber. Just holler nice and loud when you're ready to talk."

The two men exited back the way they'd come, up the ladder. She watched their legs and feet disappear as they climbed. Meanwhile, an oily rush of water flowed towards her, cascading into the chamber, gallons and gallons of water pumping in each second. The sound of splashing filled the air, and the bottom rungs of the ladder disappeared under the flow.

Chapter Forty

The debris at the crack was caught up and the tiny scrap of orange swirled before it got swept away. Her eyes followed its path. Her mother's dress. Marty's earrings. Fear had her in its grip, threatening to trap her in shock and horror. No, she must fight for herself. Fight for them. The water formed an ever deepening pool.

The water was already at her knees and the chair fell with a splash and was washed to the side. Soon it would be floating on its back.

She mustn't give up. There was always hope. *Kick your mind back on line. Find a way out. Work at it. You can still save them.*

Whichever man had tied her wrists had done an excellent job because Kal couldn't work any slippage. She searched the room for any sharp object she might use. There were none. Now the freezing water reached her thighs. Should she call them back? She was helpless trussed like this. Could she manipulate them into cutting her down? Could she scheme and lie and worm a chink of an opening to give herself a chance? Studying the chamber, she realised it wasn't a dead end because although the water flowed in, it also flowed out somewhere behind her and to her left. She twisted as far as she could and caught sight of an exit tunnel. A surge of water swept into its dark mouth. The chamber was connected.

The water was beyond her waist. Soon it would lift her off her feet. Oh god, they were going to drown her, she felt sure of it. Maybe they would let it happen and then revive her as a torture treatment. Kal twisted again to examine the tunnel behind her, and as she did, the back of her hand scraped against something. She peered upwards. A rusty metal bolt protruded from the wall. The iron ring she hung from was attached to a metal plate and four bolts attached the plate to the wall and one of them stuck out a little. With her weight dragging her down she would never have reached it. With the water buoying her up, she had a chance.

She must wait until the water lifted her more. *Control your panic. Stay disciplined and wait.* When the oily surface reached her armpits, Kal trod water and as she raised her body upwards, the tension let out of her arms and blood rushed back. She gritted her teeth, ignoring the agony as circulation resumed in torn tendons and starved muscles. She must try to cut through the rope before it got wet.

Rotating herself in the water, she placed her wrists against the rusted edge of the bolt and sawed backwards and forwards. The rusted thread was jagged and it frayed off the strands one by one. The water was now so high she could brace herself with her feet against the wall to put strain on the rope and get more force against the cutting edge. At last the bindings gave way and Kal flopped into the water.

Which escape route? She must choose wisely before the men came back. If she went up the ladder, she would encounter them on their way down. Could she handle them? Perhaps–but it would be close. She was weak and the drugs were still circulating. Maybe it would be better to take her chance in the tunnel. Surely it would lead somewhere? Though complex and running beneath the whole of London, the sewers weren't dead ends because that would defeat their purpose of channelling away the waste.

It was a gamble. She knew she wasn't just physically weakened but mentally weakened too. Yet the tug of water flowed that way. It must be flowing to an exit. Wouldn't it be her best bet?

She made a quick decision and went with it, kicking out with her legs. As she entered the tunnel, it became quickly dark, then absolutely and totally pitch black. How would she locate an escape route if she was blind? Reaching her arm above her head, Kal tested for the roof. Her hand didn't make contact. She must hope the water didn't reach the top and cut off the air.

She concentrated on going with the current and swimming at a steady pace. When she looked behind, the light from the chamber had already grown faint, indicating the water must be running fast. She strained for the echo of voices to show the men had returned and she heard nothing except the lapping of the water along the sides of the tunnel and the splash of her own strokes.

In the dark, a terror started to take root that she would never make it. It grew quickly, infiltrating like an infection. If this tunnel went all the way to the east side of London to the treatment plants, she'd drown from exhaustion way before she got there.

She must conserve her energy. So she stopped swimming and instead kept afloat, moving along by the force of the current. She removed her shoes, jumper and trousers because their weight would fatigue her faster than anything. After, she trailed her left hand along the wall. She could feel the texture of the bricks and realised that the level of the water no longer rose because her hand kept along the same row of bricks. She could only cover one wall because the tunnel was too wide to trail her other hand at the same time, but if there were any side tunnels or changes in the brickwork to signal an escape on this side, she would be able to feel them.

The water had already sucked all the heat from her body. Kal alternated floating on her back and then on her front. She wracked her brain for information on London's sewer system–built in the Victorian era, before its construction, the Thames had been an open sewer and parliament, sitting right on the bank of the Thames, had to practically close down during the summer of the 'Great Stink'. As she tried to recall more details, she felt a change in the current, telling her the tunnel branched and just then her fingers caught on something. She stopped, working against the flow and bringing both hands to examine the wall where she found four, smooth cables running parallel along the length of the tunnel. She vaguely remembered a news item about a fibre optic company running their cabling system in the sewers. Which meant there would be maintenance access to the cables.

She tried not to think that it might not be for several miles. Her fingers were numb and she couldn't feel her feet. But the four cables offered a chance.

She had no idea how long she swam in the dark. There were several changes in the current which meant junctions and she always stayed with the four cables. Her mind clung to the broken silver earring and the orange fragment and those images kept her going.

After an age, as the hope of finding an escape dwindled, only a few thoughts remained. Dear Marty. Had she fought and lost? Was she dead? The scrap of material meant Alesha had been in the chamber. Was her mother dead too? Were they both gone? The torment circled around and around, unanswered and unanswerable, like a ring of vultures closing in on their failing victim.

The life got sucked out until she could no longer recall the shape of the ear-rings. Exhaustion turned her mind to mush. The orange lingered on as a haze. She would swim for an eternity to grasp that scrap from her mother's dress. As if she was reaching for her mother's hand. As if she could grasp her mother and pull her back from whatever abyss she teetered on. Or was it Alesha reaching out to her, to save her from drowning?

When she had no more strength, a faint, insidious undertow tugged at her legs. With a *splosh*, her hand fell from the cables. It startled her, jolting her back to the present. She inched along the wall, groping for those four lines of hope. They'd disappeared.

Clawing against the brickwork, Kal dragged herself back one brick at a time. One brick. Then one brick more. Then one more. She wouldn't be able to continue. She wanted to give up. Her head went under and she took in a lungful and fought spluttering to the surface. Her legs felt like lead. She was going down. *Come on, one brick more.* Then her fingers found the smooth plastic of the cables and she realised why she had lost track of them–it was because they took a turn upwards.

She clung to the bricks with her fingers, her nails, searching, pressing her cheek against the rough surface. It was her elbow which hit something first. Something hard jutting out of the surface of the wall. She clung to it like the lifeline it was and hauled herself onto that first rung of the ladder. Then up, up, in the pitch black. Her body felt like a dead weight. Her arms and legs shook and above her she could see a faint something which, as she climbed higher, turned into the merest crescent of a sliver of light.

When she reached the manhole cover, it took her several heaves to push the hatch, and when she eventually managed to force it open, she crawled out and collapsed on a suburban roadside.

Chapter Forty-one

It was a deserted housing estate, with lamp posts shining on a line of parked cars. Kal lay on the ground, and when she had strength, she kicked the manhole cover back in place. The last thing she wanted was her captors finding their way to her.

She wondered if she passed out, because next time she looked up, a middle-aged couple approached. They were hesitant, then they picked up their pace and ran. She felt cold, so very cold.

"What the hell!" the man said.

"Trevor, call the police!" The woman's voice was shrill. "And call an ambulance!"

There was a trace of alcohol on the man's breath, and judging by the woman's dress, they had been at a dinner party.

"I'm all right, there's no need, it's not like it looks."

Kal got to her knees and tried pushing up to stand and didn't make it. The man took off his jacket and placed it around her shoulders. He helped her up, then held her steady.

"You're freezing. Take it easy now," he said.

"I know something dreadful has happened," said the woman, eyeing Kal's underwear. "You don't need to say, but the police will help you and we need to get you somewhere safe and warm. You can come back with us, can't she Trevor?"

"Of course she can, come on love, we don't live far and I'm not letting you walk around in a state like this."

Her teeth were chattering. "That's very kind only what I need right now is to get to my friends and family. It's an emergency."

The couple looked doubtful. Kal put her hand on the woman's arm. "Really, I'm all right, it's not what you think. There's no need for the emergency services. Please, can I use your phone?"

Kal managed to walk a few paces away. As she dialled, she checked the time on the screen. It was three o'clock in the morning.

Marty's number rang and rang. The longer it rang, the more panic clawed at her. The next number she tried was LeeMing. He picked up straight away.

"It's me, it's Kal."

"I've been looking for you for hours and Spinks has got the whole police force out searching. Are you safe?"

"Yes, I need you to pick me up. They held me prisoner."

As she heard LeeMing hesitate, her whole body went rigid.

"Something terrible has happened, hasn't it? Please just tell me straight."

"They made a strike on the nursing home and the Triad warned them off," LeeMing said, "there's no way they'll try that again, don't worry, your grandmother is safe."

There was more, she could sense it.

"Spinks has posted an officer outside Nannie's room, a woman of course, and your grandmother found the whole thing exciting…"

That was a diversion, the happy news before the bad, she could hear it in his voice. LeeMing took a breath, exactly the same as she did when she needed to compose herself.

"… prepare yourself, I've got bad news…"

Kal heard the man coughing behind her.

"… they attacked Marty."

Her knees buckled and the couple rushed over and propped her up. Kal pressed the phone to her ear.

"She's barely alive. She spent six hours in the operating theatre and the doctors don't know if she'll regain consciousness, and if she does, then there'll be the question of brain damage..."

Chapter Forty-two

After her escape from the sewers, LeeMing had driven them back across town. His knuckles had been tight on the steering wheel.

"They beat the life out of her," LeeMing said. "Probably they intended to capture her and when she fought back they went for the kill, no question. It's her own skill which saved her. That, and the fact they must've decided a gun shot was too risky in a built-up area. They left her for dead. Marty definitely had luck on her side because it was a man walking his dog who raised the alarm, and then he stemmed the worst of the bleeding until the ambulance arrived."

The good people of London–Samaritans at heart. Like the couple who had found her, who insisted on taking her back to their house for dry clothes and then plied her with soup whilst they waited for LeeMing.

No, no, not Marty. A desire for revenge arose, screaming like a Valkyrie, tearing Kal's insides to shreds.

That night, the streets around the Training Centre were quiet as Kal pushed open the dragon doors. She clicked on her flashlight.

Outside the shower rooms, a trophy cupboard displayed the club's successes. It held shining cups and photographs of club members celebrating their victories. It was much too small to house all the mementos and photographs spilled out onto the adjacent wall. Kal's flashlight reflected from rows of glass and gilt frames.

She scanned for her favourite. It was a shot of her and Marty arm-in-arm, laughing their heads off. Marty clasped a gold medal from the area Championships and the runner-up medallion hung around Kal's neck. They'd been fifteen and drunk on elation. They knew they were coming into their own and felt the freedom of adulthood beckoning them on. She remembered their plans, imaging where they'd go and what they'd do, but in that picture it was Marty's laugh, captured in the moment, which Kal loved the most. A wonderful moment never to be forgotten.

Kal blinked, and an image of Marty lying in a hospital bed imprinted itself on her eyelids. Hours earlier she had been there with Marty's mother who had kept her head resolutely bowed, lips moving in prayer. In the background there had been the sucking sound of the ventilator and the bleeping machines which were keeping Marty alive.

Kal smeared at tears with the back of her hand.

The wall itself had been repainted more than once in its customary cream colour. She knelt, and took a chisel and a small hammer from her pocket.

'Keep it safe,' David Khan had told her, 'and always be ready.'

The third brick from the door frame, floor level. At twelve years old, this was the safest place she could think of and she'd stuck with that first choice. *Chink. Chink.* The sound of the hammer rang out.

It only took a few taps to dislodge it. It had once been a ventilation brick and all that time ago she'd replaced it with a normal one, hollowed out at the back.

Kal pulled it free. A neat package nestled behind–a wad of fabric wrapped around an object. She unwound the protection, then balanced the cold metal in her hand, before curling her fingers around the grip, feeling its compact form, designed for a woman.

Her father had left strict instructions which gun range to practice at in the UK and which one in the USA–those ranges and only those ranges, and Kal had kept her promise to perfect her skills. Both ranges were strange places full of people she didn't want to know about. The one in the USA even kept a weapon exclusively for her use, left for Kal by her father. Kal felt the weight of the gun one more time.

Always be ready, said her father's voice.

Yes–she was. This was for Marty, and for Alesha, and Amita. She put the gun in her pocket.

Chapter Forty-three

Click. The dead bolts on Scott's front door smacked home behind Kal's back. Scott wore immaculate trousers and a grey shirt, looking as if he'd moments before stepped from an expensive, Saville Row tailor.

Senses on high alert and nerves taut, her heels tapped loudly as she walked down the hallway. The air smelt of burning wood and very faintly of aftershave. In agreeing to come here, she knew Scott meant to kill her. Time seemed to slow, elongating each moment.

"Good evening," Scott said, "you're as elegant as ever in that dress."

She had chosen a gold, off-the-shoulder number, which hugged her legs to mid-thigh. One of her favourites. Wasn't it always best to go down in style?

"I chose it to mark the occasion."

Scott smiled. On some level they both had the same understanding. This would be their last encounter, winner takes all.

Scott led them to the lounge, and Kal studied the set of his shoulders. No tension, no stress, Scott walked with confidence.

In the lounge, a fire blazed in the hearth with flames dancing red and orange. She scanned the room, her body so reactive, hot and cold flashed across her back. Tonight, Scott was going to display who he really was.

"I hope you have the money ready?" she said.

"Half in cash and the rest to be transferred to an account of your choice at the touch of a keyboard."

He continued through to the kitchen, where two glasses gave a bright *ting* as Scott placed them on the counter top, right next to the black control unit.

"Before we go ahead with the transfer of funds, I've something you might want to see."

His voice had changed. Yes, here it was. He would expose his true nature.

The menace had no effect on her, though for a moment it reminded her of the line she'd been forced to cross. She felt bold and sure, every inch of her David Khan's daughter. The gun tapped lightly against her inside leg, strapped against her thigh. Of course, Scott's arrogance meant he had not searched her. Her act at being helpless had left its mark.

Scott uncorked a bottle and the wine gurgled as he poured. She thought of Spinks and his team poised to move simultaneously on Assad's residence, on Mayor Vankova, Kealy, Judge Greeves and Aaron DeVille. Others were ready to seize Boris and Chatrawalia. All she needed was one tiny bit of evidence to set the whole train in motion. If things got out of hand and she required more unconventional backup, LeeMing waited nearby. Again, she had refused a hidden microphone, leaving the way open for her own choices.

Kal accepted the wine and raised her glass.

"To success," she said.

"To success and… absent friends."

Her back flashed to burning hot. Rein it in, she told herself, wait for your moment.

She raised an eyebrow. "What is it you'd like me to see?"

"You've been smart, much cleverer than you look in fact, though you're no match for me. You should have taken our original offer when you had the chance."

Scott took a stool at the bar and Kal pulled out a chair at the dining table.

"I don't know what you mean."

"Oh, what a wonderful game player you are, it's been so entertaining."

In the quiet, the fire crackled in the grate.

"I know who you are," she said.

"Really?" His eyes glinted. "I doubt it."

There was only one possible explanation and she'd worked it out.

"You are the son of Henderson. And my Grandfather Sunni discovered Henderson senior was a paedophile."

It was the only answer which made sense—the details about her Scott had recounted at the Gala, his emotion towards Alesha, except the emotion he felt towards Alesha wasn't love, rather, Scott had been obsessed with Alesha. It was an obsession so deep it became part of his life. And an obsession like that only came from documenting someone's activities over a long, long stretch of time, never actually meeting them in person—imagining, extrapolating, fantasising.

And why had Scott been obsessed by her mother? Because he had been obsessed by her whole family. He'd been stalking Sunni, Nannie, Alesha, and it was all part of some sick, historical archive he'd been keeping for years. And what fuelled Scott's desire to hunt them? It was because her Grandfather Sunni had informed on Scott's father for abusing children.

Scott's grey eyes were unflinching.

"Your father ran a boarding school in Bengal, and he abused the children. Grandfather Sunni found out. He must have told one of the wealthy Indian families and that's why they sent someone to assassinate Henderson. In those days, it would have been just retribution."

"You're wrong," Scott said, his voice dangerously quiet. "My father was a god."

Scott's reaction confirmed it. Everything clicked into place.

"You tracked my family for generations because my grandfather refused to keep your father's sordid, perverted secret. You killed Sunni Medi as revenge."

"You're delusional."

"It takes a sick mind to send death threats and kill innocent people. You've been tracking my family for years. Did you burn my grandmother too?"

Scott narrowed his eyes. The madness was beginning to show. Kal placed her glass carefully on the table. She was proud of her grandfather, and he had paid the price for his bravery.

"Sunni told one of the wealthy Indian families, didn't he? They sent in the assassin. Henderson senior was your father and you are both paedophiles."

"Kal, have you taken leave of your senses?"

His denials were fuelling her anger. Her rage was close to the surface, trying to break through and her mind flagged red target marks on his body–in the centre of Scott's forehead, over his heart. No. She must keep control. The current crimes were the priority. She must find the location of Amita and save her.

Kal made sure to keep her voice calm. "Where's my mother? Did you kill her too?"

He laughed. "What else are you going to accuse me of? You really shouldn't get above yourself like this."

Who would have thought a girl like her could be so persistent? A few bruises and a scratch or two down the alleyway should have been enough to keep her away. Then again, she was the last of the Medi line and she was sitting right in front of him. He'd been robbed of the satisfaction of looking into Sunni's eyes as he died, but now he had the power to see the end of this one up close. This was an opportunity. He'd always wanted to see a Medi throat slashed. This time around, he could cut her himself and see her head loll just as his father's had done. Scott congratulated himself in bringing Kal this far, in playing her like a stupid fish following bait. This was going to be fun.

"I know about the people you supply–Kealy, Assad, Boris, Vankova and the whole, sick lot of them. I know how it works at ScottBioTec. You think you're above the law only I've news for you, you're not. You supply children to the rich and famous."

Why the hell didn't she shut her little trap.

"Inspired, don't you think? Supply and demand. It's the principle of all good business."

"You mean you've set yourself up as a supplier for stinking rich people who are all paedophiles. Trafficking Indian children from your own goddam hospital. That's not inspired, it's twisted. Sick and perverted."

"Enough!"

Scott slammed his fist on the bar.

"Get up you bitch and lift aside the table."

Kal's back flashed cold.

Scott was pointing at the dining table at which she sat, and at which the two of them had dined. My god, she'd searched the entire house and Scott had a compartment concealed underneath her feet. It was one hundred percent true to his twisted profile.

"Be my guest," Scott snarled, and he indicated for her to get down on her knees.

The exposed stretch of flooring looked flawless.

Uniform squares of wood made up the parquet. The squares were most likely made of oak because they'd worn extremely well, she'd seen that on her first visit. If a seam existed, it had been expertly concealed. Kal swept her palm across the floor. Nothing. Was it possible Scott toyed with her? This time, she didn't think so. She continued searching until she detected the tiniest of imperfections.

"The hidden design is marvellous. I had the cellar built to my specifications when I constructed the house."

Finding no means to lift a trap door, instead, she applied pressure to the seam. A square section of flooring responded with a slight dip, then it swung up with a hiss of hydraulics. A flight of concrete steps led downwards.

She shouted down the stairway. "Mum, are you there? Amita?"

No response.

Scott's lip curled. "Down you go!"

When Kal made no move, he drew a revolver from his pocket. *Good Scott, all the cards are coming onto the table. Very soon, I'll see your whole hand.*

"I said get down there, bitch."

He spat the final word. Since she crouched, the barrel was pointed directly at her head and her muscles contracted, feeling like steel. She could unarm Scott, but first he must reveal the location of Amita.

She went down the steps, facing forward to have the advantage of seeing what she walked into. The air felt warm and dry. The soles of Scott's shoes scraped down the steps behind her.

At the bottom, she stood in what could only be described as a private torture chamber. There was a deep pit measuring around two metres square. The rest of the cramped space was taken up by a bed and video equipment, the same as she'd seen at the suite. And more dreadful than all of it, down in the pit, huddled two forms. One was her mother, and the other was smaller and clothed in red.

A wave of horror washed over Kal. The child was scrunched in a ball. Her mother was slumped in an unnatural position, her face hidden by matted hair. Was Alesha even alive? She went to go down into the pit and Scott waved her away with his gun. His eyes glittered. She could see he was volatile. Right on the edge. One spark would set him off.

"It's not necessary for anyone to descend because Amita's learning to obey orders and she does as she's told. Climb out," Scott ordered.

The child slowly stood. Footholds had been cut in the side of the pit and she put her foot in the first one. Alesha had not stirred.

"You see how easy it is? A click of the fingers brings obedience. That's true mastery. How can that not make you feel like a god?"

On the final word, Scott arched his back, raising his face to heaven.

Now she had Amita, Kal didn't need more. She launched herself at Scott. He reacted quickly, but since he was staring skywards, it wasn't quickly enough. In the confined space, she knocked the weapon from his hand. Scott was strong but he wasn't a fighter. She had a lock on him before he could draw breath. Kal forced him to the ground.

"You evil bastard! You're going down for this. I know you keep a record of each person who goes into that suite in Kolkata. Where is it?"

Scott was obsessive. His record would contain a meticulous index of clients with their victims. All the perversions would be on it, and every single client who believed themselves beyond the reach of justice. All those who believed themselves so important and influential they'd never be exposed. Scott's recordings would bring them down. It was exactly what Spinks needed to bring the bastards to their knees.

Keeping a lock on his neck, she searched his pockets and found a silver hard drive.

"That wasn't so difficult now, was it? This is what I want."

Scott's expression was full of rage. "Your grandfather was vermin. A mere servant."

"Then you are Henderson's son."

"Bravo Kal, bravo. And I'd like you to know killing your grandfather was a great satisfaction, burning your grandmother was also highly amusing."

"And I'll find it highly amusing seeing you humiliated in court and in the worldwide press."

"What a narrow view of life you have–I despise you and everyone like you."

"The feeling's mutual."

"My father made me his apprentice. In his bedroom, he kept a huge mahogany wardrobe. I hid there to watch him enacting his whims on children. It was my initiation, my liberation."

Kal's fingers were inches away from his carotid artery and windpipe. A sustained application of pressure would be sufficient to end him. She was severely tempted.

"Sunni was guilty." Scott's voice racked up. "He had the blood of my father on his hands. I was there the night my father's throat was cut. It was your grandfather who took it on himself to inform others. He is the reason they sent the assassin! How dare he snoop on my father! He was a janitor who cleaned toilets and swept floors! How dare he crawl out from the hole he was born in."

At that moment, Amita's head popped up over the rim of the pit. Scott lunged, grabbing her hair. Amita screamed, her little legs losing purchase on the rungs. If Scott let go she would fall to the bottom of the pit.

"Back off you bitch. Or I'll drop her."

Kal could not reliably reach the child in time. If she continued restricting his airway, Amita would fall. It was a stand-off.

"Back off, that's it, against the wall and use your foot to pass me my gun. Careful now. You wouldn't want me dropping your little friend, would you?"

She kicked it over and Scott dragged Amita out of the pit, depositing her at his feet, where she lay in a heap.

He rubbed his neck. "You can't imagine how delirious I was, the day fate brought your mother to ScottBioTec. A family I had been tracking for generations and then one of them walks into my office? Sublime. My life had moved on and as you've so kindly detailed I had far more lucrative and compelling projects running than punishing the Medis. It was destiny which brought Alesha to me that day. Fate made our bloodlines cross again. It was an opportunity begging for the taking."

Kal was looking straight at her mother. Sarah inviting Alesha to join her research project had been a twist of fate. Perhaps it had been karma after all, just like little Padma believed. And why hadn't Alesha moved? Why hadn't she reacted?

"One false move and I'll blow the girl's brains out. Now pass back the drive."

"Mum? Can you hear me?"

"Shut the fuck up! Alesha belongs to me."

This was a bad situation. She had two people to protect and they were both incapable. Scott could shoot any one of the three of them at any moment. Worse than that, Amita lay on the floor between Kal and Scott. The girl was an obstacle and was at risk in that position. To attack, she would have to jump the gap to put herself between Scott and Amita. The restricted space gave no margin for error. She flexed her knees slightly and a jab of pain ran up her injured leg, causing her knee to buckle.

"You've been very stupid and made a real nuisance of yourself. Nobody can stop us."

Scott picked up the silver hard drive and walked a couple of steps to the corner of the chamber to push it into the computer. Kal watched every move. Now that Scott felt in control, his guard would be down a little. He'd think this was his moment of triumph.

"No one can take this away from me, it's what I live for."

"What have you done to my mother? Please tell me, is she alive?"

She had to know, for her own sanity. And if Alesha was dead, then Kal would not need to try to save her.

"I told you to shut up. Go to the bed. Put on the cuffs. Slowly now, no sudden moves."

He had his gun trained on the child, so Kal did as ordered and limped to the bed. As she picked up the cuffs, she fumbled and they fell with a clatter.

Scott gave a vicious kick to Amita's back. "Get it right, bitch."

Anger and adrenalin made Kal tremble.

"Please can you tell me?" she said, "Is Mum alive?"

Amita lay at Scott's feet. Was it Kal's imagination, or had the girl given a tiny nod of her head? Kal's heart was drumming like thunder. She'd get one shot at this and only one.

"Your knee injury must really be holding you up," Scott said. "Shame you can't use your martial fucking arts. Now put on the damn cuffs."

Click. She placed one cuff around her wrist.

The camera eye on the opposite wall was recording. It seemed Scott intended these to be her final moments. Come on, Scott, come over to me. Leave the child behind you.

"Please don't kill me, I'll do anything you say."

Scott stepped over Amita. "You don't have your mother's allure. She's a Venus, a Cleopatra, you're nothing compared to her."

"You drowned her."

"Oh no, Alesha survived the water treatment several times. I'm afraid I had to set Klaus on her after that and even his methods didn't get a word out of the woman. Such a shame. If only she'd have been prepared to join me. I didn't mean to break her."

"W-what?"

Scott shook his head. "She's a vegetable. Klaus went too far."

Kal marvelled at how calm she felt. Before she realised it wasn't calm, it was numb shock. Alesha had survived only to be broken.

"She's not dead though she might as well be. All that's left is a shell," Scott said.

No, it couldn't be true. He must be lying. Her heart threatened to sever in two. She knew people could die of emotional shock, and that's what it felt like. As if she was dying. Her body slumped like a rag doll.

The hope for her mother's safety had been so fragile. Her mother was a fighter. She always survived, always came back from the wars and the bombings, giving the impression she was immune to ill fate. Charmed. That's what Kal had held on to–her mother's charmed life. But everything has to end sometime, doesn't it?

Click. She fastened the second cuff on her wrist.

Kal looked up to see Amita's dark eyes staring at her. The girl's mouth hung slack with horror.

Scott came closer. He laid his revolver aside, turning her chin to face him.

"Don't worry, it'll be over soon. The gash across your throat will end it all and I shall have my final retribution."

Kal felt her anger gathering. It was black and venomous and full of dark power, just like Khan. She was at last free to be herself. To let everything go as she'd always been afraid to do. To let all the rage pour out.

Scott flicked her hair with his finger.

"I don't condone Klaus' methods. We were forced to step up the interrogation of your mother after Detective Spinks became involved. I gave Klaus the go-ahead the very day Spinks first visited me at my office."

She wanted to tell Amita it would be all right and moved her lips to speak, only nothing came out. *Wait for your moment*, said the voice in her head, and Kal didn't move a muscle.

Scott reached into a drawer and pulled out a surgeon's scalpel. She could see his excitement mounting. Of course, Scott had been too arrogant to imagine she might conceal a weapon. Too assured of his superiority. Too convinced by her meekness. Too bad. One result of David Khan's insistence on secrecy, was her gun training had not figured anywhere amongst Scott's surveillance of her childhood.

A red haze filled Kal's vision. Revulsion. The drive for revenge. A killer instinct. Bright spots danced over Scott's body, highlighting the target points. Part of her became focused and still.

Scott lifted the scalpel. Held it to her neck. When he swallowed, Kal let herself go. Let rage blaze through her like liquid fire. With both hands, she reached between her legs and pulled out her gun.

Scott fumbled for his revolver.

Fury obliterated any shred of reason. The target mark over his heart vied with the one in the middle of his forehead. Blood pounded in her head.

"Bas-tard!" Her own scream was full of hatred.

As her finger squeezed the trigger, she felt the dark part of David Khan rise inside her. She was down to nothing and all that remained was the core of who she was. In the end it was simple–you are who you are. In the space between two heart beats, just as she'd been taught, she blasted one shot.

Chapter Forty-four

Kal pulled Amita into a hug. "You're safe. Did he touch you?"

Amita clung to her. "No, but he scared me. He told me things he wanted to do. He said the big man was coming for me." Amita shuddered.

The big man. Scott meant Boris. "That's not going to happen. It's over."

"She's all right, I mean your mother, she's going to be all right."

Kal realised poor Amita was trying to console her. Trying to make like her mother wasn't a husk.

"Did you kill him?" Amita asked.

Scott lay at the bottom of the pit, his head at an impossible angle to his body. Neck most certainly broken.

"He killed himself and he deserved it."

Her one shot had been a perfect hit, shattering his knee. Scott would have been screaming in agony when Spinks arrived. Too bad for Scott he'd been so close to the edge of the pit and he'd staggered, losing his balance and crashing to his death.

Kal steeled herself and began climbing down the rungs. She'd soon find out how bad it was, soon know if there was anything left to salvage. She bent towards her mother. Wiping strings of hair out of the way, she saw her mother's lips moving. Bending close, she caught the whisper.

"Kal… get me… away from… that sick shit."

Her heart leapt as her mother, not broken, and not at all crazy, stared straight at her.

Chapter Forty-five

Within the space of a few hours, Spinks and his team raided the houses of Kealy, Assad, Mayor Vankova, Judge Greeves and Aaron Deville. The perpetrators were arrested and three children were liberated in London. International teams did the same at the houses of Boris and Chatrawalia.

The evidence captured by Scott on his hard drive was more than enough to charge them. Of course, it didn't take long for the perpetrators to lawyer up with some of the most prestigious names at the bar representing them.

The court cases would be hard fought despite the evidence. However, public opinion was strongly on the side of the children and public pressure would play an important part in securing custodial sentences.

The press ran front-page updates for a long time. And it would prove to be one of Scotland Yard's most high-profile paedophile cases, rocking the upper levels of government and business.

Sarah was promoted to head of the television company, Capital Towers.

In her new role, she spearheaded the setting up of a trust fund, secured by Capital Towers. The trust fund would be used to support any child who had been subjected to abuse and ensure access to resources for their path to recovery. It would also make sure the good work with the street children continued. The hospital was to become an independent charity and Dr Mark, Dr Christina, Sarah and Alesha would lead the new board.

The new charity was going to keep the drop-in clinic for street children and it was renamed after the matron–the Indra Gupta Clinic.

Alesha's physical injuries were severe. Once she was on the mend, she told Kal she had decided to take a sabbatical. Alesha planned to work on the ground in Kolkata, making sure the hospital's transition to charity status went smoothly. She offered Kal the use of apartment 701 while she was away, which made Kal wonder if her mother would ever come back.

Kal had flown over to Kolkata for a few days. The child crime team were in charge of the investigation and they were still gathering evidence, including a full range of forensics. While she was there, she talked to little Padma and explained all about DI Spinks. Kal was careful to let Padma know her help had been invaluable and it was funny how Padma was almost breathless with curiosity about how the prosecutions would be handled. Who knows, thought Kal, perhaps Padma would find her way into law enforcement one day? She introduced Padma and her brother Ashok to Alesha and Alesha wanted to go through the legal proceedings to become their guardian.

Nannie never did remember the part Sunni played in Henderson's downfall, though Kal felt sure her grandfather must have told his wife about it.

Kal found an old photograph of her grandparents, taken soon after they arrived in England. Her grandfather stood by his bicycle and Nannie was next to him.

"Oh yes," Nannie said. "I don't remember when it was taken but I often used to ride on the back of Sunni's bicycle. It caused quite a scandal in Southall."

They laughed and when Kal got home, she hung the photo on the wall of her mother's apartment.

It wasn't until some time later, Kal received a message from Marty's mother. It was two words.

"Come now."

When Marty awoke, it seemed as if moments before she'd been fighting for her life down a London alley. She remembered being alone, and at the end, how scared she had been. With four assailants, the odds were stacked the wrong way.

They'd overwhelmed her, despite her strength and agility which made her so good in the combat room. In the end they beat her down until nothing was left but her will to live. Then, even that had poured out, along with her blood, into the gutter. It was a miracle she'd survived and she'd take that miracle any day. So it was a surprise to wake up and stare at a white ceiling and hear the calm voices of strangers.

Part of Marty recalled her mother's prayers drifting through from far away, and the presence of her mother at her bedside, although she wondered if that was a dream, taken from her childhood and fashioned into the here and now. Anyway, it wasn't long before her mother arrived. Of course, her mother cried, and Kal was on her way.

Kal found Marty's mother sitting by the bedside.

As usual, Marty was surrounded by bleeping and blinking machines, and her eyes were shut.

Mrs King grabbed Kal's hand. "She's speaking. A few words at the beginning and now full sentences."

Tears prickled the back of Kal's eyes and Mrs King passed a box of tissues.

"She remembers the attack and she's asking about you," Mrs King said. 'The doctor told me it's a very good sign. Would you sit with her for a few moments? I've been here for hours."

"Of course, of course," Kal said, though she suspected Marty's mum was allowing her a few precious moments alone on purpose.

When the door closed, Kal planted a kiss on Marty's forehead.

"Is that all I get?" Marty croaked.

"Wh- wh- I mean, how do you feel?"

Marty kept her eyes closed. "Tell me everything," Marty said. "Mum said you found Amita. Spinks arrested people."

So Kal recounted the final events in the sewer and at Scott's house. At the end, Marty opened her eyes.

"You wouldn't believe it Marty, the court cases have been non-stop. Spinks is up to his ears in it and it looks like he will be for months." Kal grabbed at the tissues and blew her nose.

"Not you too. Mum has been crying non-stop."

"You've been comatose for weeks. We thought you might die! And if you didn't, there was a possibility you'd..."

"Be a vegetable? Yeah I heard about it. Jury's out on that one."

Marty coughed. Even to her own ears, it was a weak, horrible cough. The kind you'd expect from a sickly, old person. She heard a small choking sound at the back of her friend's throat.

'For goodness sake, just let it out will you? Of course Mum did, and even my brother did, so you might as well get it over with. A bit of blubbering never hurt anyone.'

"I'm sorry and god, that sounds so inadequate I feel like punching myself in the head. It was my fault you were in that alley. I wish it had been me and not you."

"It's okay, I'm back now, and Kal, I'm sorry, it sounds like your mum went through hell."'

"It will take time but she'll be all right, and you're not the one who should be sorry. Look what I did to *you*."

Marty let her eyelids drift down as she listened to the steady beeping of a monitor.

"I thought you'd be mad at me," Kal said.

Marty took a deep breath. "I *am* mad at you, for thinking you decide what I do. I knew the risks, so you can forget any guilt tripping. You nailed him, that sick bastard. It's all that matters. And you don't realise, but you're the only one who could've done it. *You* realised what was going when we all doubted it. *You* tracked him, *you* manoeuvred yourself into the right place at the right time. You can do things other people can't. All that stuff your father forced into you wasn't a curse because you've got talents and skills other people dream of. Me being in the alley meant you were left free and I don't regret a thing.'

The machines bleeped and Marty rested back on the pillow, short of breath.

The choking sound in Kal's throat was much louder and her friend was grabbing handfuls of tissues.

Marty felt herself phasing out, then remembered there was something else she wanted to say. "Yeah, and with everyone acting so nervous around you, without me to kick your butt, who's there to do it?"

Marty's eyes were firmly closed. Kal smoothed the white sheets and whispered in her friend's ear.

"I found out the truth about my father. I know what kind of dirty man he was. I found out the truth about myself too and you were right, I'm different from him."

Marty smiled. "Proud of… you."

"Sleep tight," Kal whispered. "What would I ever do without you." And, despite the machines and the wires, she put her arm around Marty and held her close.

When Kal left the hospital it felt like the best day ever. She loved life, she loved London, and my god, she loved her friend. Marty was going to recover. She sent a silent thank you up to the skies. It was early evening and Kal decided to take a walk through the park.

Bringing down Scott's network had shown her how all she'd learned from her father could be used for the good. That she didn't need to be frightened of it. She didn't need to hide it away and let it fester, no, why not use her understanding of the criminal mind to bring down criminals? Yes, with DI Spinks as an ally, she had a new purpose in life. And when Marty got better, her secret wish was for Marty to join her.

****

London Noir (Kal and Marty book 2)

A predator who tracks prostitutes. And they've started a new killing spree.

When a woman is murdered in her own bed, Kal suspects the killer is a predator who tracks former prostitutes.

She befriends Sophie, a troubled young woman. Sophie suffers from nightmares and memory loss.
Her mother was murdered when she was a child. Sophie was there and she can't remember a thing about it.

But the deeper Kal digs, the more she unearths disturbing secrets.

Working with Marty and Detective Spinks, she realises they're dealing with a twisted mind, more clever than anyone could imagine.

There's a predator hiding in plain sight, moving ever closer.
And it's time to kill the one who got away…

The creepiest killer you'll meet this year.

Grab your copy today.

Chapter One

Sophie dipped her brush in water and chose sky blue to finish the detail. The colour reminded her of summer days. It also reminded Sophie of her mother, and, as usual, that brought a bitter taste to the back of her mouth. Sophie swallowed. Concentrating to stop the trembling in her fingers, with two strokes, she finished the butterfly wings. The makeup brush clattered onto the dresser. Sophie twisted to see in the mirror and admired the trail of tiny, blue butterflies sweeping over her shoulder.

Her clutch bag was on the bed and she placed inside it the syringe, loaded and ready for its victim. Then she picked up the perfume and pepper spray, the jasmine scent sickly sweet. The spray was a noxious mix, designed to blind the victim and even better, make them writhe in agony. That's why Lady Penny made sure all the girls carried it.

Last, Sophie took the flick knife and touched her finger to the razor-sharp edge. Sugar G trained them – a strike to the eye, to the crease of the groin, or the stomach – all the soft parts of the body. Not all the girls carried a knife, and she was sure of those who did, none of them carried it to commit murder.

Praise for *London Noir*

'A five-star thriller which keeps you guessing until the end'
Jules 1960

'Highly recommended' *Ellie S*

'Had me hooked from the beginning' *SandyJ21*

'An absolutely fantastic read' *S.A.W.*

'The creepiest killer…' *Bloomin' Brilliant Books*

Deadly Motives (Grant and Ruby book 1)

Secrets never stay buried forever…

When a nurse is murdered, Detective David Grant recognises the hallmarks of a serial killer called Travis.

Twenty-five years ago, Grant caught Travis for the murder of five women and the murderer has been incarcerated ever since. The problem is, Travis was at the hospital when the nurse was murdered but he was in the constant custody of two police officers.

Determined to solve the case, Grant recruits a specialist to his team, Ruby Silver, a top criminal profiler. But Ruby is hiding something from her colleagues.

Who is the killer and what is their motive?

Grant and the team must work quickly to solve the case as the body count rises…

Introducing Detective David Grant and Psychologist Ruby Silver.

Chapter One

Nurse Mandy Jones had been trying hard not to do another pregnancy test. She'd been trying so hard, the effort made her ache. This morning she could not bear it any longer. Three weeks was long enough.

That's how it was when you desperately wanted a baby. And after too many disappointments and one terrible miscarriage, they didn't keep any test kits in the house. Her husband had banned them after he came home to find her crying again, a stick showing a negative result abandoned on the bathroom tiles.

She decided to buy one on her way into the hospital. Then not actually use it until she got home in the evening. It would be a difficult promise to keep.

She tossed her blue nurse's uniform onto the bed. She wouldn't tell her husband until she was absolutely sure. Not until she had the positive result in her hand. The idea of it made her giddy.

There was one other thing she had not told him. He didn't know she was a volunteer on the treatment team for the convicted killer, Travis. Definitely he would have objected. But she figured what her husband didn't know wouldn't harm him.

Travis was a multiple murderer. In the past, he'd strangled at least five women. With their own tights. Twenty-five years earlier, the South Coast Killer was hated by the whole country. But it happened well before Mandy's time. She knew the story, yet to her he was simply a sick old man with terminal cancer. A monster, yes, and also in need of treatment. And that was her job.

When they asked for volunteers, her hand went up. It was a mixture of passion for her work, and an understanding of how the senior nurses still remembered the Travis days. They lived through it, and as far as they were concerned, Travis was as dangerous and evil now as he was then. Which meant Mandy, as one of the younger ones, had a chance to help out her colleagues. It was usually the other way around, so this made a nice change.

The closer it got to seeing him, the more wound up she felt. In a few hours she would face him. What would Travis be like? What would she see in his eyes? Would she feel he was a calculating killer? Would his soul be cold? The idea of it made her sweat. Maybe she was too addicted to crime series because it was nerve-wracking and sort of exciting at the same time.

She applied a little of make-up and did a final check in the mirror. On impulse, she swiped up her amethyst necklace. Her sister had given it. For good luck, her sister said, and Mandy knew it was meant as good luck for a baby coming along soon. Wearing jewellery at work wasn't a good idea but she decided to make an exception, for the test. She fastened the clip and slipped the cold, purple tear-drop inside her uniform.

***

Several hours later, nurse Mandy Jones knew she had made a mistake joining the Travis team.

As soon as she entered the supplies room, someone sprang out from behind the shelves. Taking one look at the face in front of her, she flung herself at the door, wrenching at the handle. She screamed and kicked as she was dragged

281

backwards. Her attacker pulled her to the floor. She tried to sink her teeth into the hand held over her mouth.

Though she fought with everything she had, her attacker was stronger. She was punched, and pulled by her hair into the corner. He took off her shoes. Ripped off her tights. The vinyl floor was cold against her bare legs. Something was being put around her neck. She brought up a hand. It was her own tights. They were being wrapped around tighter and tighter. Shutting off her air supply.

She tried to twist. Her fingers tore at the material and at the flesh of her own neck. Staring at the light in the ceiling, her vision started to dapple. Darkness moved in, as she felt the life being strangled out of her.

Time slowed. Everything was going black. Oh God no, these were her last moments. Her life was ebbing away. Soon it would be down to a trickle. And then. Nothing. Her body convulsed.

Her last thought was of the second life inside her. She imagined a tiny being, its heart beating. She'd done her desperate best to fight not only for herself but also for the new life she nurtured. And she would never be able to tell her husband the wonderful news.

Praise for Deadly Motives-

'A truly phenomenal story'

'Superb read. A must for all crime readers.'

'One that will really keep you guessing until the end.'

Killer novel. Five Stars.

Gripping!

A note from Ann Girdharry

First of all, I'd like to say a huge thank you for choosing *Good Girl Bad Girl*.
I hope you enjoyed the first instalment of Kal and Marty's journey.

You can sign up to join my **Reader's Group** to receive occasional news (no spam, I promise!) and I'll drop you a quick note whenever I have a new book out and let you know of any early 'read and review' opportunities.

I usually offer a welcoming gift to new members. You can find details on my website–www.girdharry.com

If you enjoyed *Good Girl Bad Girl*, it would be fantastic if you'd leave a written review, for instance, on Amazon or Goodreads. I always appreciate it when people take the time. Written reviews really help me and they help others discover my stories. Or maybe you can recommend my books to your friends and family…

Thank you for your support, it really is appreciated.
Kind regards,
Ann G

Titles by this author

Good Girl Bad Girl
London Noir
The Beauty Killers

Deadly Motives (previously entitled Killer Motive)
Deadly Secrets